Victoria's Emeralds

For Reg

Victoria's Emeralds

Rose Boucheron

PIATKUS

Copyright © 1996 by Rose Boucheron

First published in Great Britain in 1996 by
Judy Piatkus (Publishers) Ltd of
5 Windmill Street, London W1

The moral right of the author has been asserted

A catalogue record for this book is available from the British Library

ISBN 0-7499-0336-8

Set in 11/12pt Times by
Action Typesetting Ltd, Gloucester
Printed and bound in Great Britain by
Biddles Ltd, Guildford & Kings Lynn

Chapter One

Bal à Versailles – the small glass scent bottle sat on the polished bedside table, its shape undoubtedly feminine with an hourglass waist, the cut glass stopper with the ribbon bow giving the appearance of an elegant French hat. Beside it was a bowl of freesias and narcissus which gave off a delicate perfume.

In the locker on the other side were the usual hospital necessities, the Lucozade bottle, iced water, tissues – although tissues were anathema to Victoria Bellamy for whom snow white lace-edged hankies had always been de rigueur.

Outside the rain fell soft, fine and warm. She could see the blue of the burgeoning plane tree outside the window. Her hands rested lightly on the coverlet. Slender well-kept hands with long almond-shaped nails, her fingers round and tapering. Her rings flashed when they caught the light, heavy ornate rings which sat well on her beautiful hands. Through the door came muffled sounds of activity in the nursing home and she knew that soon her visitors would be arriving. Nurse Liston would let them in when she was ready, and not before.

Victoria sighed gently, trying with difficulty to achieve a position of greater comfort. Having done so she lay back on the soft pillows reflecting over a long life. For she would be seventy-five in June, and could remember many things. Nowadays memories became confused, and what happened long ago was clearer than what had happened yesterday. In fact the longer the memory, the clearer it was. Yesterday, for instance, she had thought of someone she hadn't remembered in sixty years. Josephine Baker, that was her name – the most beautiful creature she had ever seen. It had been in Paris – no, Knocke, in Belgium, at the casino, where her mother was appearing on the same bill – that she had first seen this glorious brown creature. What a figure! Such beauty. And when she appeared on stage ... Victoria could hear the gasp from the audience now as the girl stood there, one breast exposed. It was one of the sexiest things she had ever seen. When they had met her backstage, the magic was still there. Now why had she remembered that?

She could recall the years after the First World War; the young Churchill and the fiery Lloyd George; dresses that swept the floor and hats large and laden with flowers such as her mother always wore, for Mama had been a musical comedy star and always dressed in the height of fashion. She had been so lovely, so pretty, always exquisitely dressed and smelling of perfume.

Victoria glanced at the small bottle to her side. Her favourite scent. She had worn it ever since that wonderful weekend in Paris all those years ago. She suddenly saw the face of the pretty hotel chambermaid. Nowadays, faces would appear out of the past with startling clarity and disappear as quickly, so that almost before she could place them they had gone and she was left wondering who they were.

She could remember being five in Grandmother's garden at Blackheath, wearing the pink silk knitted suit that Auntie Jen had made her. She recalled thinking she must be the prettiest little girl in all the world. What a horror she must have been! On her eighteenth birthday she had stood on the stage of the Duchess Theatre taking wild applause from the crowded auditorium, flowers at her feet. How lucky she had been to have success with her first real West End play. She had never looked back after that – until she had married. For Harry was insistent. After they were wed, there was to be no more acting. Still, she'd had seven glorious years before her marriage, and after he had died in 1965, she had returned to the London stage, and picked up again where she left off.

She remembered wishing never to be older than eighteen, sure it was the perfect age – but it wasn't, the best was yet to come, though you didn't know that. Had no idea that you were on the brink of a new life as a famous actress whose face looked back from a thousand photographs. The other actors, Edith, Gielgud, Olivier, and darling Ralph; the smell of backstage; sticks of Leichner; the crackle of period gowns to be stepped into; the draping of jewel-coloured velvets to your figure; that great deep breath going right down to your diaphragm just before you emerged from the wings to face a live audience; the applause; the admiring crowd waiting at the stage door – there was nothing to beat it for excitement, unless it was the birth of a child.

At twenty-five, on top of the world, in a play at the Garrison Theatre in Woolwich, one free afternoon Victoria had driven her new car to Blackheath on an impulse. She had suddenly thought about Lesley Anderson, whom she had adored when she was at school. His parents lived in one of the Georgian houses on the side of the heath. He was so handsome, with thick fair hair slicked back and a golden skin, so unusual for a Londoner, and he always wore cream silk shirts. She had adored him, then when later on he had married Betty Ralston – that awful girl, plain as a pikestaff, no dress sense – Victoria just couldn't believe it. How could he? Was he still living in the same place? she wondered. It was extremely unlikely, but nevertheless she had an overriding urge to see the place where she grew up.

It was a lovely afternoon as she drove towards Blackheath. Her blood stirred at the sight of old familiar landmarks. At All Saints Church, which still looked the same, down in the village, she parked her car then began to walk, looking in the interesting shops, at the antiques and art galleries and delicious food stores. Blackheath Village had always had such character and it hadn't changed at all.

She made her way over the heath, passing the row of Georgian houses which looked exactly the same. It was as if time had stood still. On that heath as a child she had picked harebells when walking with her father. She breathed in the fresh grassy smell, and walked back towards the Prince of Wales pond. There, too, she had sailed her small boat, remembering the agony of despair in case it didn't come back to her from the middle of the pond which seemed to be miles away.

She was walking down Montpelier Vale when she saw Lesley. There could be no mistaking him, she would know him anywhere. He was walking a dog, a huge Alsatian, and as he drew nearer she found herself blushing a fiery red. He would not have known her, had never known she existed, but she recognised him. Oh, why had she come!

For he was fat. There was a huge paunch under that light shirt, and his hair – almost all of it was gone. She was devastated, it was like finding a slug in a lettuce heart, and she hurried back to the car, and once inside, laughed herself silly.

What a stupid idea of hers it had been! They said you should never go back ... Nowadays, thankfully, she could remember him as he used to be.

There was a gentle knock on the door and her eldest son, Geoffrey, tiptoed in softly so as not to disturb her, followed by his wife, Ruth.

'Ah, there you are.' He bent over and kissed her. 'How are you, Mother?' Ruth laid the bunch of tulips carefully on the bedcover and kissed Victoria's soft, dry cheek.

'I am very well,' she said. Geoffrey was her favourite son, so like his father, dependable as a rock. Ruth was a very worthy woman, she decided, looking at her and wondering why she always wore such dowdy clothes. Not that Victoria held that against her. She had been a good wife and mother, she was an excellent manager – except she wasn't going to manage Victoria if Victoria could help it!

While they told each other how well she looked, Victoria felt a moment's anger. There was nothing wrong with her brain. She was slightly bruised from the fall, which was only to be expected. After all, it had only happened two days ago and they were keeping her under observation for the time being.

'Are they treating you well?' Geoffrey asked, taking one of her hands.

'Very well, dear,' Victoria replied, her magnificent eyes warming. 'The nurses are so kind.'

'That's good,' Ruth said approvingly. Even when she was ill, she thought, her mother-in-law looked beautiful.

She looked up as another knock came on the door. It was the nurse with a tray of tea for the visitors.

'Thank you so much,' Ruth said, busying herself with the tea things.

Geoffrey picked up the sheaf of get well cards and letters, flicking through them.

'How nice to have so many cards.'

'It's lovely to be remembered,' Victoria said.

'Of course they remember you,' he smiled. 'There was a very nice photograph of you in the *Telegraph* with a small caption to the effect that you were well after a minor accident.'

'Yes, I saw it, I expect that's what sparked off the cards. Some of them from strangers, isn't that nice?'

'People have long memories,' Geoffrey said. 'Especially ...'

'Elderly people?' Victoria smiled.

Having poured the tea and handed a cup to Geoffrey, Ruth got busy unwrapping the tulips. 'Well, Mother,' she said, 'you are having a lot of lovely flowers, aren't you?'

Pettishly, Victoria twiddled her rings. Why did Ruth always talk to her as if she were five years old? Did she imagine that with advancing years you became childlike, or mentally deficient? She found Ruth so irritating, but then she found so many things irritating these days. There was not a lot to be said for growing old. A time for reflection, for reading all the books you always meant to read, for tolerance ... that was poppycock! Old age brought its own problems, and if you lost any of your faculties, or had pain, or were unloved – that must be one of the worst – or were alone ... Oh, yes, she still had a lot to be thankful for, she supposed. One day you wake to realise that your youth is gone, for old age is cruel when you think what it does to your physical self. Your beauty fades, but you learn to count each day and wait for its blessings, like the song of the blackbird in spring, the first daffodils, glorious sunsets, the scent of paeonies ... Oh, how that brought back memories! Sitting in a strange garden on a warm day, the scent of paeonies all about her, wartime, a blue sky overhead, the sun in the sky. And a young man in officer's uniform smiling down at her.

Her eyes closed. Geoffrey and Ruth looked at each other then moved quietly over to the window.

'She's dozing again,' Ruth said. 'The doctor says she's strong, she might go on for years.'

Victoria supposed they thought she was asleep. Better to pretend. Come to think of it, it was nice just to lie here and think about the past. There never seemed to be time at home, what with keeping in touch with the children and grandchildren, walking in the park, playing bridge, visiting friends and writing. It had been Vanessa's idea for her to write her life story.

'But isn't everyone writing an autobiography?' Victoria had asked.

'Yes, but not everyone has had such an interesting life as you have,' her daughter had replied.

So she got down to it, but couldn't say it was exactly riveting. The only remarkable thing about it was what you could remember if you concentrated hard enough.

What was that play called? It had been at The Criterion, she could remember that. She could see herself now in that cloche hat, pulled well down over her eyes. What must she have been – twenty or so? That brief apricot georgette dress with the straight bodice and frill, exposing her long slim legs. She had had rather nice legs, in pure silk stockings to match the dress – frocks they used to call them in those days – a flat handbag, a long, long rope of beads. Her hair had been cut close to her head like a cap. And the after show parties – oh, the wonderful parties! The long cigarette holders containing Passing Clouds. Poor dears, today they were warned and threatened with everything from smoking, to food, to – well, even making love.

Victoria wondered what they would think if they knew what she was thinking about. They thought just because you were old you had forgotten about such things, but she could remember ... Even now she felt a slight frisson when she remembered some things and they, her visitors, would have no idea that even at her age the feeling didn't die. It wasn't so overwhelming, so desperate a longing, but it was there.

'Have you heard from Julian?' Geoffrey asked.

'Now, darling, you know what your brother is – he could be anywhere.'

'I tried to get in touch with him, but they said he was out of town.'

'Oh, darling, don't bother him. I shall be home before you know it,' she said.

Charming, thought Ruth. Julian gets away with murder, every time.

'And Vanessa?' Geoffrey asked. 'She telephoned this morning.'

'Yes, I expect she'll call in, but really there's no need for anyone – '

But Geoffrey was scanning through the get well wishes.

'"Your devoted admirer Cecil Aherne." Who's he?'

'I've no idea.' Victoria smiled.

Geoffrey opened a card covered with violets. It was highly scented and he made a face. 'Who's this?'

Victoria smiled. 'It came this morning. I went to school with her. Violet – oh, I can't recall her other name. It explains the card.'

'Violets? Oh, I see. Wonder how she knew?'

'The *Telegraph*,' Ruth and Victoria said at once, and laughed.

'Of course.'

Victoria closed her eyes and lay back again, wondering if the senders realised how warm it made you feel to know you were remembered – and after such a long time. Violet – Violet – Violet Pemberton, that was her name. It was kind of her to write. Victoria had read somewhere that she had married and gone to live in Italy. Ah, well.

Ruth's low voice came from the corner of the room.

'She looks awfully tired, it's probably been too much for her. I think it's time we went.'

'Perhaps you're right.'

Victoria opened her eyes as Ruth bent over her.

'We're going now, Mother.' Oh, how she wished Ruth wouldn't call her Mother!

'Thank you for coming,' she said, managing a weak smile as Geoffrey bent and kissed her.

'Now is there anything you want? Books, sweeties?' His moustache was tickling her cheek. 'Is there any message for Edith?'

'No, thank you, darling, don't worry about me,' she said. 'I'll be fine,' trying to lift herself higher on to the pillows. Ruth was there in a moment.

'There, there.' She plumped the pillows, the scent of lavender wafting from her ample bosom.

'Now, if you're sure . . .'

'Quite sure.'

With a last look from the door they were gone, and she relaxed. She knew what Ruth would be talking about on the way home. What would happen to Mother when she came home? Well, there was nothing for Ruth to worry about. Victoria would be fine. Take up the threads again in her delightful flat in Knightsbridge with dear old Edith to look after her – although, on reflection, Edith was only slightly older than she was, by a month or two. But as strong as a horse. She had been Victoria's first dresser, a girl of her own age who, when Victoria got married, opted to leave the theatre too and look after her. She had been with her all these years. Victoria often wondered what it must be like to live like Edith, a whole life in service to someone else. It was all very well to say what would she have done without Edith, but what of Edith? Didn't she deserve retirement?

The ideal thing would be if they could still live together and get someone in to look after them both. Was that possible today? For to live with Ruth at Jarretts would be impossible, admirable though she was. Victoria loved her freedom too much for that. She thought of the plight of the many friends who had ended up living with their sons or daughters, to be desperately unhappy or put into homes, however expensive. They were often lonely, young yet and with no intention of popping off.

Julian, her other son, she worried about. After leaving school he worked for Blane's, the Fine Art dealers and auctioneers. University was not for him, he'd decided, he wanted to get out there and see what it was all about. And he had. He had a natural gift, a feeling for silver, jewellery and beautiful things. After being with Blane's for fifteen years, he had finally thrown up his job and gone out on his own.

'With all my contacts, Ma,' he had said, 'I'll make it, you'll see.' And she prayed that he would. He certainly might do better now that he and Fiona had divorced. Well, she had been such a bad choice – not right for him at all. Perhaps, thought Victoria, I am one of those awful mothers-in-law who dislike on principle the girls their sons bring home. Not really. She didn't dislike Ruth, only found her irritating because she was so different. Admirable though, she thought, while Fiona was simply a disaster, using one of her daughter's expressions.

She was lucky to have had a good marriage herself. Right through the war until 1965 when Harry died. She had found him, coming downstairs one evening to find out why he was so long coming to bed. He was in his favourite chair, a glass of brandy at his side, an unlit cigar in the bowl.

'Harry, darling!' He had fallen asleep, she'd thought, but there was something odd about him, and when she bent over him, she knew.

Victoria felt a cold tremor run through her after all these years. She wouldn't think about it. Instead she fastened her eyes on the cards, seeing the violets raised on the thick card – she would think about Violet Pemberton. But instead she saw the face of Rex Harrison standing on Denham Station as she had seen him at the beginning of the war. He was about to give up his ticket to the ticket collector just as she was – they must have been on the same train! He turned to look at her and doffed his cap, and one look from those wicked, narrow, clever blue eyes and she was lost.

Once outside the station he asked if he could help her, and when she told him she had an appointment at Denham Studios, offered her a lift in the studio car which had been sent to meet him. She told him that she was an actress and had been offered a part in a film being made by Korda. It was her first ever venture into films and her last. She hadn't liked it. It was nothing like the theatre, nothing at all. But she would never forget meeting Rex Harrison. No one could.

She dozed and woke when the door opened and her daughter Vanessa came in, tiptoeing gently, which was somewhat difficult in her thick-soled boots.

'Mummy!' She carried an armful of daffodils and tulips and freesias. Her hat was askew, she wore no make-up and looked as if she had been hurrying. But she was such a sight for sore eyes that Victoria's heart burst with pride and pleasure at seeing her.

'Oh, darling, you shouldn't have.'

'What do you mean!' Vanessa bent and kissed her mother warmly, holding her tight. 'Oh, perhaps I shouldn't do that?'

'Of course you may.' Victoria's eyes were full of tears. 'Oh, it's wonderful to see you.'

'I didn't get the message until this morning, I was out of

town.' She lowered her eyes. 'I didn't give them my phone number at the office.'

'I thought perhaps you were. Edith tried to ring you.'

'How are you? You look fine. I thought perhaps – '

'I'd be on my last legs?'

'Mummy! I did telephone this morning, twice.'

'Darling, don't worry, you're here now.'

Vanessa sat down by the bedside, taking off her shawl and folding it, then her hat, and shaking out her hair.

'It's warm in here but that's good. It's awfully cold outside.'

'You're well wrapped up, anyway,' said Victoria. The girl looked pale, there were dark rings under her eyes. She had probably been worrying about something.

'I'm fine, you know,' she said to reassure Vanessa. 'It was just a tiny thing. A little warning, the doctor said, that I should take things more easily.'

'Fancy trying to tell you that!' Vanessa said. 'They don't know you as I do.'

'Anyway, apart from the bruising . . .'

Victoria turned back her bedjacket. Her wrist was bruised black and blue. Vanessa stared in horror.

'Mummy!'

'And my knees,' Victoria said proudly, as Vanessa bit her lip. Victoria patted her arm. 'Actually, old people bruise easily. It doesn't mean anything at all.'

Vanessa took comfort from that. 'Who's been in to see you? Geoffrey? Ruth? Julian?'

'Geoffrey and Ruth.'

'That was nice of them.'

'Yes, it was. And I had lots of post – look.'

'Goodness.' Vanessa went round to the other side of the bed and picked up the cards.

'Don't look at them now. Tell me what you've been doing?'

She came back to sit in the chair. 'Well, I'm too old to tell you I stayed with a girlfriend . . .' And Victoria laughed.

'I have a new boyfriend. His name is Jack.'

'Oh!' Victoria's eyes opened wide.

'What's wrong with that?'

'Nothing, darling.' And Victoria tried to keep a straight face. 'Jack? I mean, it's so – well – '

'Basic. That's what he is,' Vanessa said. 'Very down to earth. Ordinary. And nice – really.'

Victoria thought about Gavin Weston and Vanessa's five wasted years. Perhaps that was what her daughter needed, an ordinary man?

'What does he do?'

'He's a lawyer – a solicitor.'

'Goodness,' murmured Victoria. 'That's different. Not your usual type.' Vanessa, in the publishing world, met some very strange characters, but her mother, having been an actress, understood that it took all sorts to make a world.

'Anyway,' Vanessa said, eyeing her mother, seeing the slight flush on her cheeks and the bright eyes, lovely now even without her eye shadow and mascara for Victoria had been brought up in an age when no woman went without make-up, and it would take something like this for her to leave it off. But her lashes were long and thick, even now, her magnolia skin was soft, the hair which used to be jet black was now white, which made her look even more arresting and framed that lovely oval face.

'I haven't come to talk about me. What about you? What did the doctors say?'

'That they will keep me for a few days. I fell over because I was under stress apparently – can't think why myself. They say I must rest and keep on an even keel, as they put it. And after that, I expect I will go home.'

'Great,' Vanessa said. 'Well, Edith is missing you. She's coming in to see you this evening. Bringing things, she said, things you will need.'

'Oh, bless her. Dear Edith.'

'When you do go home, I'll probably take a few days off and stay with you.'

'Oh, but there's no need, darling.'

'Shush. You can't boss me all the time, you know. I have to have a say sometime. Anyway, I've only popped in quickly. I shall come again tomorrow when I'm not quite so rushed. The nurse said I was not to stay long tonight since you've already had some visitors, and Edith is coming later.'

'All right, darling. It's been lovely to see you. And the flowers are beautiful.'

'Shall I put them in water?'

'No, thank you, a nurse will do it.'

Vanessa bent and kissed her. 'Get well, darling, and don't worry about a thing. We're all fine.'

Victoria watched the door close after her. She was such a dear girl, all that a daughter should be. In fact, thinking about it, she was very like her grandmother. Victoria could see traces of Mama in her so often: little mannerisms; the pitch of her voice. It was strange how they came out after all these years. Genes, she thought. That's what everyone was talking about these days ...

Jack? Well, she hoped passionately that it would work out.

She took the scent bottle in her hand and removed the stopper, taking a deep breath to inhale the scent. Then she dabbed a little on to her wrists. There had always been such a pretty label on the bottle. The lady in blue reminded her of Mama, while the girl in pink carrying a bouquet of flowers reminded her of herself when young. Victoria liked to think she'd looked like that.

When she was small, her mother used to sing about the house, moving from one room to another, or in the garden. Old songs, like 'Pale Hands I Loved Beside the Shalimar'. Victoria could hear her now. And another favourite, when she was very small. It must have been after the First World War, a wartime song, but she could hear Mama singing it as clearly as if it were yesterday. It often came into her head:

> *Smile awhile, you kissed me sad adieu,*
> *When the clouds roll by, I'll come to you*
> *So wait and pray, each night for me*
> *Till we meet again ...*

Chapter Two

Geoffrey drove through the heavy traffic and made for the A30 out of London. Ruth sat silently, deep in thought, as he manoeuvred the stop-go procedure which represented driving in most cities. When she deemed they had got through the worst of it, and they were driving through Virginia Water and its deeply wooded area out towards Sunningdale, she stole a glance at him, seeing his concentration on what he was doing. He disliked being talked to when driving. That was one of the many things she had discovered when she married him.

'Well, what did you think of her?'

Geoffrey, who thought Ruth, like most women, often asked questions in not quite the way he would have done, shrugged his shoulders.

'She'll be fine, she's got a strong constitution.'

'You say that, Geoffrey, but you don't know ... After all, it may only be a warning but she *is* seventy-five.'

He laughed. 'Oh, that's nothing these days.'

'Still – '

'What are you worried about?'

'I'm not exactly worried, but I think we should give some thought to the fact that things will not always go on as they are.'

'That applies to everything in life.'

'Geoffrey, don't be difficult, dear. We have to think about it. After all, Edith won't be there for ever, and if anything happened to her, what would become of Mother?'

'We'd have to get someone else in.'

She snorted. 'That's sooner said than done, these days. You

won't find many people who are willing to give up their freedom in order to look after an elderly person.'

He stopped at the traffic lights. 'Look, we'll talk about it when we get home.'

Typical man's attitude, she thought. No thinking ahead, no organisation or preparation for what might happen. Those things were instinctive to a woman. That's why she was as she was. Being a wife, then a mother, organisation ran right through one's life. A man was different. Wait until it happens ... just how would she have got on if she had thought like that?

In any case, what was really at the back of her mind was Jarretts. Her lovely home. Or should she say Victoria's lovely home ... For that was the truth of the matter. Even though Ruth herself had gone to it as a bride and lived there ever since and brought up her daughters there, it wasn't theirs – hers and Geoffrey's. That was the crux of the matter. Victoria would leave Jarretts to the three of them, Geoffrey, Julian and Vanessa. And a fat lot the other two cared about it! They would want the money, though, when it was sold. The house presumably meant nothing to them. They were free to live there had they wanted to for it was large enough to house several families, but they had chosen to opt out.

Ruth loved Jarretts with a passion she had not known she possessed. When she had first seen it, nestling in the Berkshire countryside, its tall chimneys standing out against a blue sky, the plum red bricks and mullioned windows, she had decided then and there that, come what may, she must marry Geoffrey Bellamy. Well, of course she had loved him too. He was handsome, an architect with a practice in Windsor, and came from a family quite unlike hers which was hard-working, practical, ordinary. Her father was a family doctor. It was the sort of family that was worthy and law abiding, one in which nothing untoward ever happened. Babies got born and in due course the elder members passed on. It was all very predictable. No excitement in between, like runaways, or outrageous girls, or adventurous men. Perhaps she should have appreciated that and been grateful, but she hadn't. Not having the courage to break away herself, she envied it in others, so that the sheer difference of Geoffrey's family drew her like a magnet. There was the father, for a start, a self-made man whom she had never met. He had died years before she came on the scene but was somehow still a powerful force. Geoffrey's mother was a glamorous actress on the London stage, having returned to it two years after the death of her husband.

Ruth had often been told the story of Jarretts, its history, and how Harry Bellamy had determined to buy it for the bride whom he adored. 'Bought it with his first million, I daresay,' Julian said. He wished more than anything to emulate his father in this world, so far with little success.

Ruth sometimes wondered how Geoffrey could have fallen in love with her, for she knew herself for what she was – a rather plain little woman. But she had been pretty as a girl, and good at sports, swimming and tennis, where she had met Geoffrey. She sometimes thought it must have been the attraction of opposites. People said men married women like their mothers. They couldn't be more wrong in this case.

She knew in her heart that Victoria had been disappointed at Geoffrey's choice of a wife, and she could understand that. But she was determined to make him a good wife – the very thought of living at Jarretts was enough to inspire her.

The engagement and the wedding brought a kind of luminosity, a beauty, to her face that had not been there before. She was a radiant bride, and knew in her heart that it was not only marrying Geoffrey that had brought that look to her face, but being mistress of Jarretts. Now her face clouded over. Temporarily mistress, she thought. The confrontation had to come one day, and she couldn't bear to face it.

But Victoria had welcomed her, and after they returned from honeymoon, informed her that she was taking up residence in London, in her own flat. She wanted to be nearer to theatreland.

Even Geoffrey had been surprised.

'But, Mother – '

'Darling, it's not good for two generations to live together – and I have had my fill of this house. I have been happy here, and now you must be, and bring up your family as I brought up mine. Your father would have wished it. Julian and Vanessa must make up their own minds. It is their home, too. When I am gone, it will belong to the three of you. It was what your father would have wanted.'

But that had seemed so far ahead. Hardly able to believe in her own good fortune, Ruth moved in and settled down. Each day she told herself she was the luckiest woman in the world.

In due course Julian married and moved away, and Vanessa got a small flat of her own near her office, leaving in residence Ruth and Geoffrey and their two daughters, Sally, who was now at university, and Loveday who at sixteen had only one desire – to be an actress like her grandmother.

The days never hung heavily for Ruth for she was on every committee that existed in the area: Red Cross, RSPCA, RSPCC, the local hospital committee, the Society for Mental Health – everyone knew Mrs Bellamy. She was the one who would get things done. She was the one at the top.

Ruth supposed it was her background which had taught her to be of service to others, it was instinctive with her. The other side of her nature craved the sheer luxury of living at Jarretts – of being able to throw open the gates for charity fairs and galas, fêtes and bring and buy sales.

How could she carry on her good work if they no longer lived here. And they could hardly afford to buy out the other two, for Geoffrey's business was not all that good these days. That was another thing, if Mother had to go into a nursing home, the fees were horrendous. But presumably she had plenty of money? It was not something that had ever been discussed between Ruth and Geoffrey.

When Jarretts came into view she received the same feeling of love and pride she always experienced on entering the high wrought iron gates. The drive flanked by rhododendrons, now in bud, the early pink ones in full spate; the house at the far end of the drive, waiting for them. It was such a friendly place.

Geoffrey dropped her in front of the door before putting the car away in the garage.

Ruth took off her hat and smoothed back her hair, seeing a friendly-looking face in the mirror, unspoiled by make up, with mild blue eyes and sandy lashes. She bit her lips, for they were a little pale, took off her tweed jacket and smoothed down her sweater before going into the kitchen to see if Mrs Manson was there.

'Ah, there you are.'

'How is Mrs Bellamy?' Mrs Manson asked anxiously.

'Very well, considering her age,' Ruth said comfortably. 'She looks wonderful.'

'Well, she's a lovely-looking woman,' Mrs Manson said. 'Oh, I do hope she goes on all right – you never know at her age. I've got the kettle on.'

'Good, we'll have tea in the drawing room.'

'There were a few telephone messages, nothing urgent. I've left them on the telephone pad.'

'Thank you, Mrs Manson.'

Having changed, Geoffrey joined his wife for tea.

They sat in the lovely drawing room overlooking the rose garden. Victoria had furnished this when she was first married and Ruth had not wanted to change a thing. It was a taste that she knew she didn't have herself but admired in other people. Harry Bellamy had insisted that his new bride should spare no expense. She must buy nothing but the best – antiques, beautiful carpets, magnificent mirrors and silken hangings – and it was a time when such things could be bought cheaply, during the war, when people momentarily lost sight of the value of such things.

'That's nice,' Geoffrey said, taking his cup. It was unusual for him to be home at this time of day.

'It was a good drive home, not too much traffic,' Ruth said, deciding to talk of generalities before returning to the question which was uppermost in her mind.

'What time does Loveday get home?'

'About five most days, but today is her music lesson.'

Loveday had just finished her O-levels and had not excelled herself, much to Geoffrey's disappointment. He had always considered her the bright one of the two girls. But Geoffrey, Ruth thought privately, didn't know all the answers. Loveday might be bright, but it was Sally who was clever.

'More tea?' she asked after a while.

'No, thank you, my dear.' He picked up the daily paper, and before he embarked on it, Ruth took her chance.

'Geoffrey, I know you don't like talking about Mother and her future – '

He frowned slightly. Somehow, despite the fact that they had been married for so long, he felt her questions to be slightly intrusive.

But Ruth ploughed on. She had to know just where she stood.

'I am not saying it could happen right now,' she said reasonably, 'but for the future, don't you think we should discuss things? So that we may be prepared for all eventualities?'

'I don't see the point of jumping the gun,' he said mildly. 'Mother is going to get well. She has, I hope, many more years ahead of her.'

'I hope so too,' Ruth said patiently. 'Look, we have never discussed her financial affairs, it's not my business after all.'

'Well, then?'

'But if it affects us – as a family I mean – suppose she needed care and attention? She couldn't go on living alone with Edith.'

'We should have to take steps,' Geoffrey said. 'In the event.'

Ruth took the bull by the horns. 'What I am asking you is, this house – Jarretts? We're lucky to live in it at the moment, but it isn't ours, is it? When she – when anything happens to Mother, it will be left to the three of you, won't it? You, Julian and Vanessa.'

'Of course,' he said. 'Naturally.'

'Well, then.' She thought, it's like pulling teeth to get him to understand. Didn't he care what became of them, the girls and herself?

'So what would we do? Would it have to be sold?'

He took a deep breath. So that was what was worrying her.

'I don't suppose it would come to that. We – I – could buy out the other two if they were willing.'

'Oh! That's what I'm getting at. Suppose they weren't willing or we couldn't afford it?'

'Ah,' he said, with a small smile, 'therein lies the problem. All, of which, my dear Ruth, will have to be decided when the time comes.'

But now, hearing this, she was really concerned.

'I think Mother should come here,' she said. 'To live with us. It *is* her home.'

'She may not want to. She has always been frightfully independent.'

If she lived here, Ruth thought, we would be halfway there. She might leave the house to us entirely and give money to the others as compensation.

'Has she much money?' she asked boldly. 'I mean, for her old age?'

'I really don't know. The accountants deal with all that side of things. I know she is not so well off as she was after Father died. She lost a lot of money in shares and that sort of thing.'

'Well, I've been thinking,' Ruth said. 'You know, it costs a great deal of money to be in a nursing home, and all the while she has a home here . . .'

He knew how she liked to plan, had to have everything cut and dried, why she always booked their holidays a year ahead. She was a born organiser. Left to him, things would drift. Somehow, he always got round to them – in the end.

Ruth took the plunge once more. After all, now that they had embarked on the subject, it was better out in the open.

'Does she still have all that wonderful jewellery?'

He stared at her.

She flushed. 'I'm sorry. It's none of my business, but, well, ever since you told me, I've been fascinated by it.' Also, she didn't add, she wondered to whom Mother would leave the jewellery when she died. As her only grandchildren, surely Sally and Loveday . . .

She wasn't greedy, thought Ruth. Just wanted to know where she stood. It was true that Mother could go on for years, and might well do. Ruth hoped she would, for that way they would still be living at Jarretts. It was just that the fright of her sudden illness had sparked off all sorts of conjectures.

She sighed. 'Well, I'm sure you are right. You know what an old fusspot I am.'

Geoffrey smiled at her, and opened his paper.

She wasn't a greedy woman, he thought. Had never demanded furs and jewellery and clothes, never wanted him to spend money on her, knowing that despite their home and his background there had never been much. Everything she had wanted was tied up in the home, in him and the children. He remembered the wedding anniversary, years ago, when he'd asked her what she would like, and she had answered: a cheap imitation of the diamond ring that Richard Burton had given to Elizabeth Taylor. They were being sold by the thousand then. He had stood, aghast.

'What? Why, you wouldn't wear such a thing!' He didn't add, It's so vulgar.

He saw her blush. 'I would,' she said belligerently.

'It's not nice enough,' he said, 'and I don't like imitations. I tell you what, though, I shall buy you a solitaire diamond ring.'

'No, no,' she said hastily. 'Really, Geoffrey, I wouldn't want it. It's not the same thing.'

He had bought the silly thing, and felt a fool doing so. When he had taken it home, she slipped it on her finger, holding it out to the light where it sat oddly on her small white hand with the short-trimmed nails. She was obviously delighted.

He couldn't make her out. To his knowledge she had never worn it. Although once he had come across her sitting at the dressing table flashing the ring in front of the mirror, the pleasure in her eyes unmistakable.

Women, he had thought then. And still did.

So, Ruth decided, it is in the lap of the gods. And heard the front door slam as Loveday rushed in like a whirlwind.

'Hi – Mother – Daddy. What are you doing home?'

She fled into the kitchen, her school hat on back to front, bent the way she liked it, her thick fair hair tied up in a bun at the back of her head, long grey school sleeves dangling over her wrists, thick black sensible shoes which she loved, at the end of slender legs.

Ruth looked after her. At her age, she had wanted her first pair of high heels, but that wasn't what Loveday wanted. And my hair was pretty and fluffy and fine, she thought. But there it was. She did hope they weren't going to have another argument about drama school.

She must go into the kitchen and see what Mrs Manson had done about the evening meal, for tonight there was a Save the Children Fund meeting in the church hall in the village.

Yes, it would make no difference to their lives if Mother came to live with them, the house was large enough to take them all. And if Edith came too, it would be even better.

It was just a question of organisation.

Chapter Three

Julian Bellamy may have wanted to be like his father but he certainly didn't take after him in looks or in temperament. Where Harry Bellamy had been large, expansive and tough, Julian was slim as a reed, darkly handsome, polite, and had a personality that could charm the birds off the trees.

Harry Bellamy hadn't had an ounce of charm in him, was brusque to the point of rudeness. Like the Northerner he was, he called a spade a spade, was outgoing, and knew what he wanted out of life. Money, a beautiful wife, and a family – in that order. He made it his business to get them all. He'd been a big man, in more ways than one, which was probably why he was attracted to the lovely, ethereal Victoria Mansfield.

Julian knew what he wanted, too, but somehow it had not worked out like that – at least so far. His marriage, for instance, to the delectable Fiona Masters. Everyone had thought how lucky he was to have captured her, that elusive, pampered society beauty, spoiled daughter of Sir Lionel Masters. But their relationship had been a joke from start to finish. Well, not right away perhaps. There had been moments in the beginning when he had thought she might toe the line, but it took him only six months to realise that the idea of conforming to normal married life was the last thing she had in mind. The last thing she was capable of, anyway. Five years it had dragged on – and he wondered now how it had lasted that long. Still, he had seen the light even before she upped and ran off with that polo-playing adventurer Randolph Schofield.

Now all that was in the past, and since then Julian had branched out on his own and was making a good living at it.

With this experience at Blane's and the expertise he had gleaned over the years, he'd had a head start. He had kept up his contacts with Blane's, certain in the knowledge that they trusted in his knowhow, that they would always put to auction or sell anything he came by, knowing it had passed the test of authenticity.

He was about to leave his hotel in Lausanne to see a client when the telephone call came through from Geoffrey telling him that his mother was in hospital. The doctors were being vague about her condition apparently. She had suffered a fall and for a while they had feared that a slight heart attack had caused it, but now they were saying it was just stress.

He adored his mother, and was all for returning to London immediately when Geoffrey forestalled him.

'She's fine, Julian, really. No need for you to rush back, she'll probably go home in a day or two. It was just one of those little scares.'

'I would just as soon – '

'No, stay there until you have finished your business. I'll tell her I located you and that will please her. In fact, I'll give you her telephone number and you can get straight through. I'm sure they will allow her to take calls.'

'Thanks, Geoffrey.'

'Right, here you are. I have it now.'

The men chatted for a few moments until Geoffrey hung up, reassuring his brother that all would be well.

'I shall be flying back tomorrow evening anyway,' Julian said.

'Then that's fine. I'll see you, I expect.'

Julian felt momentarily shattered. He had somehow never expected his mother to be ill. She had always been strong, although hers was a delicate beauty, and being ill or unwell had never been on her agenda. He realised now how lucky they had been. She was quite remarkable. But Geoffrey was probably right. He had one more call to make the next day, to Mrs Salzman, then he would be finished.

Reassured, he made for the lift and went down to the foyer where he left a message that if anyone rang he would be back later that night. Then, hailing a taxi, he drove straight to the Beau Rivage Hotel by the lakeside. There he had an appointment to see Madame Tessier, the widow of a French banker whose jewels were justly world famous. He had discovered that when rich women decided to sell their jewels, they were more inclined to deal privately with someone of repute, rather than put them through one of the big auction houses, where news of the sale might well get out.

With his wide experience, and working for Blane's as their representative, Julian had made many contacts with some of the world's richest women. They trusted him to know the up-to-the-minute value of their possessions. Added to that the special charm he possessed, the confidence he inspired in them, he could hardly fail.

Julian took a deep breath, deciding not to worry about his mother but to concentrate on the business ahead. There must be no sign that he was not concentrating one hundred per cent on the matter in hand, so prickly were clients when it came to their possessions.

He made a handsome figure as he entered the hotel where they knew him well. He was in Switzerland several times a year. It was his favourite place to do business, rating it as he did as not so commercial as Amsterdam, not so cut and thrust as New York, nor as tough as South Africa where he went at least once a year.

'Monsieur Bellamy, – ' the receptionist said, 'Madame Tessier is waiting for you.' He nodded to the diminutive bellboy. 'Will you take Monsieur to Madame Tessier's apartment right away?'

The boy led the way and Julian followed, not unaware of the glances from all directions as, tall, dark and handsome, he strode across the deeply carpeted foyer towards the lift.

Once outside the serviced apartment, the bellboy rang for entry and waited until the maid answered the door.

Even she allowed her dark brown eyes to sparkle brilliantly for a moment, as she allowed Julian in.

He handed her his hat and gloves, which he was never without, and followed her to a pair of great folding doors, heavily ornate with carving and gilding.

She spoke in French. 'Monsieur Bellamy is here, Madame.'

From the deep-seated blue sofa by the marble fireplace, Madame Tessier looked up with a smile.

'*Bonjour*, Monsieur Bellamy,' she said as Julian moved towards her to take her hand and kiss it lightly.

'You are well, Madame?'

'Thankfully, yes,' she answered. 'Do sit down,' indicating a chair opposite. She held out a small key to the maid.

'Bring my jewel box from the safe, will you?'

'*Oui, Madame*'.

'You are looking exceptionally well, Madame.' He smiled charmingly at her.

'Thank you,' she murmured. It was always such a pleasure to see this young man.

Julian took his seat. There was nothing about this life, this sort of setting, that he didn't like. The luxury hotels, the sumptuous apartments, the high living, the elegant women – he loved them all. For it was they who gave him his power and his money – and he had them in the palm of his hand. Not that they realised this. Owning the jewels in the first place, they imagined they reigned supreme. But he knew from the moment they first contacted him that they needed to sell, for one reason or another – usually shortage of money, according to their lights, which were not to be compared with those of mere ordinary mortals.

'Will you have tea later?' Madame Tessier asked.

'That would be lovely,' Julian replied, settling back for what he knew would be the sort of afternoon he liked most: examining and appraising jewels worth a fortune. Nothing pleased him more than to come upon something which he hadn't known existed, but that was rare, for by now he almost knew it all.

After a little more light conversation, Madame Tessier inserted the key and opened the leather case.

'I have made up my mind to sell the emeralds,' she began. He nodded. 'You remember them? My late husband gave them to me on the occasion of our engagement.'

'Yes, of course I do.' And he smiled at her with that special smile that meant he understood how much her husband must have loved and revered her.

'I shall never wear them again, they are much too ornate, and my daughter-in-law has no appreciation for such fine things . . .'

All this meant that she needed money. Like most of these rich elderly women she had lost spectacular sums. No one was safe from the change in the economic climate.

She laid a finger on the emeralds which lay in the open case, sparkling darkly and richly. He had seen them before when she sold her rubies, but these were much more valuable. Colombian emeralds.

'May I?'

He took out the heavy necklace and looked closely through his eyeglass, turning it this way and that before picking up the matching bracelet and earrings. They were really splendid, there was no doubt of that, and cool figures were dancing in his head. A possible sale, plus this, less that, etc, etc ...

'What do you think?'

He had to answer carefully. Returning the jewels to the box, he appeared to be considering deeply.

She didn't pressurize him, but rang the bell at her side for the maid to bring in tea.

When they had both been served, they talked of this and that, of nothing in particular, while into Julian's mind came the thought of those other emeralds which he hadn't seen since he was a child. His mother's fabulous emeralds. What must they be worth now?

He smiled and dabbed at his mouth with a snow white napkin while she waited patiently.

'I would think well over three-quarters of a million,' he said finally.

'Dollars?'

He shook his head and smiled at her.

She was swiftly calculating the commission and costs of the sale.

'Would you have a private buyer in mind?'

'Possibly,' he said without committing himself.

'Then?'

'Then of course it would be less – but you would be certain of it.'

He never pushed a deal, waiting for the owner to make up her own mind.

'Would you advise me to sell at this moment in time? Is it a good time to sell?'

This was different. How could he answer her truthfully?

'My dear Madame Tessier, it rather depends on how keen you are to sell. The market is not what it was. We live in changing times – who can tell what might happen?' He gave her a warm intimate smile, and patted her hand. 'You can rely on me to get the best possible price. They are very fine emeralds,' he said reassuringly, thus establishing an understanding between them that he certainly would not let them go for a song.

'I know I can rely on you,' she said, wishing he would stay longer. He was such a charming man, and she saw so few people these days.

After a few more pleasantries, he stood up and gave her his card.

'I am leaving tomorrow afternoon. If you wish to get in touch with me ...'

'Thank you so much.'

He walked out of the hotel, highly pleased with his efforts. Into the sunshine he saw the snow-capped mountains of the Haute Savoie ranged majestically, the magnificent hotels lending an air of elegance to the scene.

It was a beautiful afternoon. He would walk back to the hotel.

Once in his room, he made a telephone call to New York.

'Mr Wiseman, please, Mr Barney Wiseman.' Julian waited patiently, a small smile on his face.

'Hello, Barney? Julian – Julian Bellamy – hallo there, I think I have found what you were looking for. Yes, superb!' And he laughed. 'Around a million and a quarter, give or take.' He waited.

'Are you interested? Right, be in touch. Bye, now.'

He sat in the bar later, watching people come and go while ostensibly reading his paper. It was important to know just who was doing what and with whom. This evening he was seeing Klara and was quite looking forward to it. He dined alone and afterwards made his way to her apartment overlooking the lake.

Klara was waiting for him, dressed beautifully as always in black, her ebony hair cut short, her fine dark eyes lighting up with pleasure when he came in.

He held her close and kissed her long and hard, while she clung to him, her slight slim figure melting against his.

'Julian, I have missed you.'

'I've missed you too,' he said, looking down into those burning dark eyes. He derived a great deal of pleasure from being in this cool elegant apartment which this very highly paid young woman had bought the year before. Up to then, she had lived with her parents, a hardworking, studious girl who had had no time for boyfriends.

When they'd met two years before she had been introduced to him as a brilliant young executive with a pharmaceutical company, one who would go a long way in her profession. It had been a challenge to charm that cool, distant, attractive young woman. Beneath the calm exterior, he'd suspected, lay a passion that had never been kindled, and as he found later, once unleashed there was no holding her.

The apartment was streamlined and cool with magnificent windows overlooking the lake, its colour scheme black and white with touches of scarlet. The bedroom, with its snow white lacy bed linen and pillows, was sumptuous. A silver ice bucket held the champagne, and two glasses stood ready.

He knew the routine – it was distinctly hers. Champagne, and then she would be waiting for him, undressed and ready, so impatient she was for his lovemaking. In bed she was a wild creature, all the outward inhibitions freed. Sometimes he thought he would never satisfy her. Sometimes he wondered how she lived when he left for London, for he knew she was too fastidious to take another lover. Looking at her, her outward exterior remote, distant, no one would have believed it.

Of late, he had found himself growing a little cool towards her. His quarry finally earthed – and the running had been great fun – the affair had lost some of its charm. He liked to be the hunter, and such complete abandon was to him a little distasteful, but that was after the event. He still found himself looking forward enormously to seeing her again. It was afterwards that the doubts overcame him. One thing worried him. When it came to finishing the affair, she would be the devil of a job to get rid of. He wouldn't think about that now. He would just enjoy himself.

There was a single red lamp glowing when he came back from the bathroom, and this she extinguished, but not before he had seen the sheen of black satin against the snowy lace pillows, while her arms reached up to him and pulled him down. Then he abandoned himself to her. Nothing mattered but being with this sensuous young woman whom most men would have given their eye teeth to have as a mistress.

In the morning he woke, heavy-eyed and exhausted, knowing that Klara would already be up. He could smell the delicious aroma of coffee, and the promise of that was enough to get him out of bed and into the shower. He must be getting old, he thought, for his limbs ached with tiredness. Still, and his lips twitched with the memory, she was quite something.

Klara was waiting for him in the blue and white kitchen looking lovely, clean and shining like a new pin. She wore a beautifully cut suit in pale green, her earrings in place, nails faultless, slim hands holding the coffee pot. She raised dark eyes to greet him.

'Julian.'

'Good morning,' he said, feeling a little sheepish in the face of such cool efficiency.

She poured his coffee. 'Black?'

'Please.'

'Toast?' She indicated the basket of toast and rolls covered with a white napkin.

'Thank you.'

'So what are you doing today?'

Sitting there, looking as cool as a cucumber, he felt she was interrogating him like a very efficient prospective employer.

'I have one more appointment this morning, then I'm flying home this afternoon.'

She buttered her toast, studying him. He looked up, seeing the dark eyes, not burning with passion now but friendly and appraising.

'Could you not stay just one more day?'

'Don't I wish I could!' he answered regretfully, meeting those dark eyes candidly. 'But Friday morning I have an auction in London. Must be there unfortunately. There's nothing I would like more otherwise.' And he stretched out a hand to cover hers.

She raised it to her lips, and kissed it.

'It won't always be like this, will it?'

'Of course not,' he assured her. 'One day there will be no more partings.' And at that precise moment believed it himself.

When she had left for the office, he locked up and let himself out of the apartment. There was a cool breeze coming up from the lake, and he breathed in deeply. Glancing at his watch, he saw that he had an hour or so before going to his next client, and took the chance to visit the exclusive shops where he was always welcome.

Looking at Mrs Salzman's lakeside villa and assessing its value, he was hopeful of finding something really worthwhile there, but was disappointed to find that her jewels were not first class as he had been led to believe; some nice gems, but nothing important. However, he had established yet another contact, another would-be client, and left her well pleased with his visit.

He consoled himself with the fact that you couldn't expect too much luck in one trip, and found himself wanting to catch an earlier plane to London. He was becoming a little anxious about his mother. After all, anything could happen. He should be there.

On the plane he thought about Madame Tessier's emeralds. God, they were fine, some of the finest he had seen – and he stood to make a large commission on them. In a way it was a pity that, yet again, they were going to America, but then almost everything did. The USA or the Middle East. He had more commissions to find emeralds than any other stone, and he thought again of his mother's emeralds, which he had last seen as a small boy. Even then they had mesmerized him. There was something wicked about emeralds. His mother's had winked back at him from the coverlet of the bed where she had laid them.

'There. What do you think of these, eh?' she had asked him. Julian had not been able to reply. He couldn't take his eyes off them. They had a mesmeric quality.

He had never asked her where they came from. He supposed it was his father who'd given them to her. They must be in the bank nowadays. She never spoke of them.

Perhaps he should mention them? Now that she had been ill.

After all, they must be worth a small fortune – and he would be the very person to handle them.

There was a tiny flicker of excitement in the pit of his stomach as the plane landed at Heathrow, and he hadn't thought of Klara once.

Chapter Four

Victoria looked up as Nurse Bilson put her head round the door.

'Your daughter is here, Mrs Bellamy.'

'Oh, yes, show her in, please.'

Vanessa came in, her face wreathed in smiles, carrying an enormous bouquet of roses.

'Darling, how lovely,' Victoria cried. Pink squadgy roses – how she loved them. 'Where did you find them?'

Vanessa bent over and kissed her. 'I put a special order in at the florist's – and how are you today? You look heaps better.'

'I am, I feel wonderful – as if I could get up and walk a mile.'

'Well, you're not going to, Mummy. Not just yet, anyway.'

Vanessa laid the flowers at the foot of the bed. Victoria regarded her daughter. Today she looked more rested, as if she had slept well, although Victoria had always considered that black didn't suit her. Her skirt was ankle-length, of some fine woollen material, and she wore a voluminous white shirt with an open neck and a small black waistcoat over it. Round her neck were long amber beads. If it were not for her colouring, which was fair, she would have looked like a gypsy, Victoria thought.

'Edith came in to see you last night, didn't she?' Vanessa enquired. 'I knew she would have telephoned me had there been a message.'

'Yes, bless her. I feel so guilty lying here doing nothing while she, poor soul, has to keep going. She's not young any more, Vanessa.'

'No, but she's content. There is nothing in the world she enjoys more than looking after you, and she does miss you, you know.'

'I asked the doctor this morning when I would be going home.'

'And?'

'In a few days, hopefully. They wanted to be quite sure I have someone there with me, and of course, I explained about Edith. But when I told Dr Elgin how old she is, he was quite shocked!'

'He doesn't know Edith,' Vanessa laughed.

'Also,' Victoria ventured, 'he suggested it might be a better idea to go down and stay with Geoffrey and Ruth.'

Vanessa turned horrified eyes towards her.

'Oh, Mummy! You wouldn't? You'd die, having Ruth fussing about you all the time.'

'I know, dear,' she said mildly. 'And that's not what I am about to do – although Ruth means well, I know.'

'Of course she does,' Vanessa said hastily. There was no love lost between the two women, not because they disliked each other particularly, but rather because they had no real understanding of each other's temperament.

'Anyway,' Victoria went on, 'Julian is coming in this evening. He gets back from Switzerland today.'

'Oh, that's nice.' But Victoria sensed her thoughts were elsewhere.

They were interrupted by Nurse Bilson bringing in a tray of tea which she put down on the side table. 'Will you pour, Miss Bellamy?'

'Of course, thank you, nurse.'

Nurse Bilson picked up the flowers and smelled them. 'Oh, how lovely! I'll put them in water. How do you think your mother looks today?'

'She looks wonderful,' Vanessa said. Which was true, she thought.

Sipping tea, Victoria studied her daughter when the nurse had gone.

'So tell me what you have been doing with yourself?'

'This morning? Well – I had a pretty grim session with a new author, one of those ladies who suddenly find they have a penchant for writing, and having had success with their first novel, imagine everyone is waiting breathlessly for the next.'

'And are they?'

Vanessa smiled. 'Not usually. It happens sometimes of course.'

Victoria put down her cup. 'You have something on your mind, darling?'

Startled, Vanessa looked at her.

'I can't keep anything from you, can I?'

'I imagine that's why you wanted your own apartment – and had no wish to share mine,' Victoria said drily. 'But, really, I don't wish to pry. Don't tell me anything you'd rather not.'

There was a silence, then Vanessa spoke.

'I had a call from Gavin.'

Victoria frowned impatiently. 'Oh, darling, no!'

'Yes, out of the blue. In fact it came when Jack was with me in the flat – I couldn't have been more surprised. It must be six months since I heard from him.'

'And what did he have to say – Gavin?' Victoria asked. Her voice was cool.

'Wanted to see me. Something has happened apparently. I didn't ask what.'

So she wasn't over him, Victoria thought. That look on her face, part excitement, part despair. It wasn't the look of a woman who had completely recovered from a long, unsatisfactory affair.

'Does Jack know about him?'

'Well – he knows I had a relationship with someone. It's really nothing to do with him.'

'Of course not, darling. So what are you going to do?'

Vanessa looked at her mother with anguished eyes.

'Oh, I'm tempted, Mummy – I can't help it. Curious to know what he wants, curious to know what has happened, yet commonsense tells me it can only lead to more sadness.'

Victoria took her hand. 'Vanessa, think hard before you do anything. When you made that decision last year to finish it all – it took such courage. Don't give in too easily.'

'But what if Suzie has gone – left him?'

Victoria sighed. 'You mean, if that was the case, you would go back to him?'

'Well – '

'What about this Jack? I thought you liked him?'

'Oh, I do. I do. He's so sweet – different altogether from Gavin. Kind, thoughtful, clever.' She looked at her mother and laughed. 'I know you think that's too good to be true!'

'Well, it does sound a bit dull, darling. For you, that is.'

'He makes me behave. He has rules.'

'Oh, dear.'

'It's not like you think. I'm so used to bossing everyone around at the office, having my own way, Jack draws the line – tells me when I'm unfair. He says it's not good for me always to win.'

'That's true.' Victoria nodded. 'Is he much older than you?'

'No, a couple of years.'

'But has he a sense of humour?'

'Oh, Mummy! How could I possibly have a boyfriend with no sense of humour! Of course he has. If he hadn't I wouldn't be the slightest bit interested. It's a sly humour, you know, unexpected – he has a funny slant on things. Not streetwise wit like Gavin's. It's a gentle humour.'

Victoria settled herself back on her pillows.

'Well, it's something you will have to work out for yourself, darling. Only you can do that.'

'I know,' Vanessa said. 'But we've spent far too long on this visit talking about me. Now what about you? How are you really feeling? Weak? Tired? Longing to go home?'

'Yes, I am longing to go home, and no, I don't feel weak or tired. I sleep very well, but I expect it's the pills they give me.'

'I did wonder if perhaps we should get a nurse in once you get home? I suggested it to Edith, but of course she was horrified at the idea. There was nothing a nurse could do that she couldn't! Very up in arms, she was.'

They both laughed.

'I can imagine. Well, they won't let me home until they think I'm ready, so I imagine once there, I shall take it easy for a time. I get up and walk along the corridor, you know, go to the bathroom.'

'Oh, that's great!' Vanessa said, eyes sparkling. There was nothing she wanted more than for things to be as they always were. Victoria's illness had jolted her and the others more than they liked to say. They had never known their mother anything but well.

She glanced at her watch. 'Heavens, I must fly! I'm due back at the office.'

'Have you had lunch?' Victoria asked her sternly.

'Yes, I had a sandwich before I left. You know me, I never eat much at midday.'

You never eat much at any time, Victoria thought, remembering how pernickety Vanessa always was about food. That was why she stayed so slim.

'Be in again, darling,' her daughter said, with a swift kiss.

When she had gone, Victoria closed her eyes. How she prayed for Vanessa to be happy. She was a nice girl, even allowing for the fact that as her mother Victoria might be biased. She was good at her job, inclined to be bossy, a friendly soul, but she always seemed to pick the wrong sort of friends. She was inclined to take people at face value, always believing what they said so that frequently she was hurt. Victoria knew from experience you had to use commonsense sometimes. People were not always what they seemed, sad though that fact may be. And yet to build a carapace around oneself for protection meant losing out on a host of wonderful experiences, good and bad ...

Anyway, that was enough philosophising. Perhaps tomorrow they would tell her when she could go home. She felt ready to die of boredom in here, and had any of her family guessed at it, was already making plans for her future. There was no reason to curl up and die in one's seventies. Good gracious, no! She had no intention of doing so. Actors were famous for going on almost forever. Look at Gielgud! Ninety and still going strong. The other evening she had seen Phyllis Calvert on television. Victoria had once acted on stage with her at the Duchess Theatre. Such a nice girl, and so pretty. Who said there were no parts for elderly women? And what about Wendy Hiller? Now, don't tell Victoria that she wasn't as beautiful as she had ever been. Parts? Of course there were! She still had a few friends in the profession. Mary Ellis ... she was even older. Of course she had been a singer, but even so.

Victoria became quite excited at the thought of what might lie in store for her in this wonderful new future she was planning. Even better, Julian was coming in this evening. Dear Julian – such fun, good-looking enough to be an actor though she was so glad he wasn't. She had never had much time for actors off the stage.

There was a time, when Vanessa was small, when Victoria had thought she might take after her or her grandmother, and want to go on the stage. Victoria had taken her to dancing classes. When the time came for the annual display of young talent, five-year-old Vanessa, the youngest pupil, took one look at the audience and ran off stage. No amount of cajoling could make her go back.

Victoria laughed to herself as she remembered. No, there was nothing actressy about Vanessa. She frowned. Oh, why had that wretched Gavin Weston come back into her life again, just when she was picking up the threads and settling down?

Vanessa got out of the taxi and made her way back to the office. With ten minutes to spare, she sat in the well-laid out adjacent city garden, and gave herself time to think. Her mother was right, she must be sensible about this. But, oh, how difficult it was. She hadn't been strictly truthful with Victoria, either, knowing she had agreed to meet Gavin after she had finished at the office. Now she wished she hadn't done so, but how could she resist seeing him again. Wondering what he would have to say, how he looked after all this time, what had happened to Suzie?

She had met him at a publisher's party five years before and had been drawn to him at once because of his remarkable eyes. Spaniel-like eyes with the longest lashes she had ever seen. His face was boyish, although he was then thirty-one, and he had a head of thick curly dark hair, very slightly thinning in front – which in no way detracted from his charm.

They had just published his first book – a thriller in the style of John le Carre – and everyone had been most impressed with it. He had worked in films, and knew all about scripts, so that writing a novel became almost a natural follow up. The book was full of clever twists and unexpected thrills, surprising in one who looked so pleasantly quiet and friendly. They had liked each other on sight. When Vanessa had taken him to lunch, she found herself talking about herself rather than him. He was that sort of person.

That was the first of several meetings.

She recalled the evening he first told her he was married with a young son. Her heart seemed to stop beating, for she knew already that she was falling in love with him, and couldn't stop herself. She understood his world – the world of books and films – and loved his quick humour, his impressions of people that he met and worked with, his angle on things.

'And your wife?' she had asked. She had smoked in those far off days, and had stubbed out her cigarette and looked up at him, waiting.

He grinned. 'Suzie? She's great. We married young – we were both twenty – and I hadn't a bean. But broke as we were, we were happy living on baked beans and cornflakes until the money came in from my first job. That was ten years ago, and then our son Tom was born.'

'How old is he?' It had been difficult to take the edge out of her voice.

'He's six now.' And Gavin's eyes lit up, showing little golden lights. His eyes were like a tiger's, Vanessa thought, brown and amber and gold.

He was talking again.

'I think one of the reasons we get on is because we are not the slightest bit alike ... We think differently, have opposing views on almost everything, which makes for continued interest, I suppose.'

Vanessa couldn't have felt more bleak. How often had she met the man whose wife didn't understand him, the man who was trying it on, trapped in an unhappy marriage? But this man was different.

It was nipped in the bud, before it was too late.

'I have to go, Gavin,' she had said. 'I've promised to call in to see my mother.'

He stood up at once. 'Oh, sure. I'll give you a lift.'

She had thought about him incessantly. Tried to get him out of her mind. But not hard enough. That summer, he had been alone in London. Suzie, it seemed, was a sun worshipper, and at every available opportunity set off for the south of France, or Greece or Italy – wherever she could find the sun.

'And you?' Vanessa had asked, already hating the beautiful suntanned wife who could walk out on a man like Gavin. She was asking for trouble.

'Me? Hate it,' he had said. 'I get bored stiff lying by a pool all day – not my scene. But I don't mind if Suzie wants to go. Gets her out of London. She's never happier, takes Tom with her.'

They were talking about his latest book, a thriller with a Russian background. As they were then, before glasnost, or perestroika or whatever.

How could golden Suzie bear to leave him? Alone and at the mercy of girls like Vanessa, who would have given her eye teeth to go with him? Well, she *had* gone out with him, but it was on a business basis ...

You would have thought, she told herself bitterly, you would have learned from all that. You knew he loved his wife. Gave into her every whim. Yet still you wanted him. Was it because he belonged to someone else?

She didn't know. She only knew that before Suzie came back from that long sojourn in the sun, and after they had dined one evening, perhaps a mite too well, she had asked him in for coffee – and, well, it had happened. Perhaps he had thought it would be just an interlude, but it went on from there.

She was always there when he wanted her. He was the perfect lover, bought her presents and flowers, took her to dinner. They had much in common, both in the same world, and never talked about Suzie. Then she came home, and that was that ... for a while. Five long summers when Suzie left in June for the sun, with Gavin taking Tom to her in July when the boy finished school, returning after a few days to rejoin Vanessa. Once or twice Suzie went away at other times, early-spring, Easter or darkest November, once at Christmas to Madeira, but then Gavin went with her.

Last summer, their fifth, Vanessa brought up the subject of Suzie.

'I thought we were going to keep her out of it?' Gavin replied, and she saw by his frown that she had annoyed him.

'You mean, you decided to keep Suzie out of it,' she couldn't resist saying.

'I thought you went along with our arrangement?'

'Not entirely,' Vanessa said, wishing by now she hadn't given up smoking. There was nothing she wanted more at this minute than a cigarette.

He came over to her, and tilted her face. 'What's wrong? Something's worrying you.'

How could he be so obtuse?

'Yes, you could say that,' Vanessa replied coldly. 'I feel now that this is an unsatisfactory arrangement. I think Suzie gets away with murder and I'm not sure I want to be a part of this – this – ménage à trois.'

He laughed. 'Ménage à trois! Oh, Van, don't be silly. Don't you want to go on as we are?'

She shook her head miserably, feeling like a child.

He looked down at her, those wonderful eyes reducing her to a jelly.

'Oh, Gavin,' she said as he took her in his arms.

'I don't want you to be unhappy.'

'But I am. Don't you see how it is for me? She has you whenever she wants you ...'

'She's my wife,' he said quietly.

'I see. So that gives her all the rights, does it? What about me?' she asked, and wondered how she could be having this ridiculous conversation.

'I told you from the beginning that we had an odd sort of marriage.'

'You mean, she knows about me?'

'No, of course not.'

'Does Suzie take lovers much the same as you do?' She was unable to stop herself once started.

'She'd better not,' he said darkly. 'If I had any idea that that's what she was up to – '

'You'd what?'

'I don't like to think of it.'

Men! Vanessa thought. And she had played right into his hands. He had the best of both worlds, and it was her fault. She had agreed to it, and now she was upset. If the affair went on, there would be no one to blame but herself, for he was the piper who called the tune.

A few days later, he called her on the telephone. He sounded upset and in a desperate hurry.

'Sorry, I can't make it tonight, I'm off to Heathrow,' he said. 'I'm flying to France – to bring Suzie back.'

'What's happened?' Vanessa asked.

'I'll let you know when I get back – sorry about our date.' And that was that.

A few days later, one lovely September evening, he called round to see her. He kissed her lightly when he came in, and she could see he was not his usual self.

'When did you get back?' she asked, in fear and trembling in case he was putting an end to their affair. She could tell something was wrong.

He stared in front of him. 'Yesterday,' he said, talking almost as if she were not there. 'I drove the whole way across France with young Tom and Suzie in the back, howling her eyes out.'

She couldn't help feeling sorry for him.

'It seems she'd had this man friend. God, Van, I must have been blind. Three years it's been going on – and I trusted her!'

'Can't you begin at the beginning?'

'I got a letter from her, saying she wasn't coming back. She was in love with this man, a widower with two little girls, and was going to stay with him for good.'

'That's when you phoned me – when you got the letter?'

He nodded. 'I don't know why she wasn't expecting me, but she was so surprised to see me. He was, too!' His eyes glinted dangerously. 'I didn't waste any time, found her passport and her purse, grabbed her and Tom and pushed them into the car, and that was that. She screamed and yelled!'

Just like one of his books, Vanessa thought.

'Tom cried, but I went hell for leather and didn't stop until we reached the outskirts of Paris. We had a wash and brush up and a meal.'

He hadn't looked at her once.

'By then she had stopped crying, and she told me that she was going to live in France with Tom for good. Well, I had to put her right on that. She could stay in France but without Tom. Of course, she wouldn't wear that one, so now she's back home, I've got a new nanny for Tom, and we'll see how it goes.'

How lucky the golden girl was, Suzie thought, to arouse

such love in a man that he would do anything to keep her.

'So – ' He looked up, his face tired and drawn. 'So you see – '

She got up, saying nothing, and poured him a stiff whisky.

'Drink this,' she said. 'You need it.'

'Thanks, Van.'

After a while, he looked across at her where she sat sipping wine.

'You do realise, Van?'

'That it's over?' she said. 'Yes, of course.'

He got up, and went to the door. 'I'm sorry.'

She closed the door after him, unable to cry or feel anything.

That had been at the end of last year. Now she got up and walked back to her office. Had she been mad to say she would see him? Was she being made a fool of again? She acted like her own worst enemy.

There was a message for her from Jack when she got back to her room. Would she ring him?

She sat for long moments staring at the telephone. Jack or Gavin? Which one held the answer to her future?

Once back in the office, she telephoned Jack and they arranged that they would meet at the weekend. Whatever happened next, she had to see him.

That evening, when she had finished at the office, she tried to compose herself for the forthcoming meeting with Gavin, making her way down in the lift. When it stopped, she could see him waiting through the plate glass revolving doors.

He hurried forward to greet her.

He looked different – thinner, older – but those wonderful eyes were still the same. They looked down into hers with the same smouldering intensity until she glanced away.

'Vanessa.'

'Hello, Gavin.'

He put his arm around her.

'You look wonderful,' he said, and her heart soared.

Chapter Five

Victoria sat in a chair by the window going through her correspondence. People had been so kind; so many letters and good wishes it did one's heart good to read them. She would reply to some of them, it would be something to do and a change from reading, although the doctor had said, all being well, and if someone was at home to look after her, she could go home at the weekend.

Oh, roll on the day!

She picked up the cards. Cecil Aherne ... heaven knows who he was, and no address. She concentrated hard but the name escaped her. Another one was signed, 'Mary Lassiter – a lifelong fan'. How kind, but no address. There was, however, an address on Violet Pemberton's card – although she wasn't Violet Pemberton now but Violet Santucci, it transpired. The address was written on the back of the card in green ink. Small, quite Continental writing – and an address in Rome.

Victoria concentrated hard, and saw Violet again, a fair-haired girl – they had been at boarding school together, and Violet was always the one on the outside, on the fringes as it were. Never quite making close friends with any of the other girls, and certainly not with Victoria's small côterie who were a sophisticated little lot, each with much the same background. Arty oddballs, most of them, hating sport of any kind, most of them loathing school and only waiting for the opportunity to leave, find a man, and get married. What horrors they had been – and what a trial to the mistresses! Poor Violet, her blue eyes watching them, longing to be a part of their group – they had never paid her the slightest attention unless it was to tell her to get lost. Victoria had known, though, that the girl was lonely. She of all of them had a heart that could be moved, that sensed another's unhappiness, how else could she have been an actress? But in those days, she was far too busy enjoying life ... Poor Violet, she had liked her.

She sighed. It was kind of Violet to write, and at this age there were not many of her contemporaries left. She would write to her this afternoon after lunch. No doubt Edith would not let her lift a hand to do anything when she arrived home. Poor Edith was going to have her work cut out looking after Victoria for the first few days, for they would be bound to insist that she take it easy and rest as much as possible. She couldn't wait to get home!

She leaned back in her chair waiting for Nurse Bilson to bring her a little dry sherry. It was almost lunchtime and she insisted on her customary small indulgence – with the permission of her doctor, of course.

She always loved the first sip, when it burned her tongue and tickled her throat, and left her feeling relaxed and comfortable inside. She believed that a glass of sherry was a real pick-me-up.

Testing her memory, she found she could recall meeting Violet quite by chance once in Fortnum's, where they had lunched together. She had grown into quite a pretty girl, reserved and still a little shy, and had told Victoria of her work for the Red Cross, driving an ambulance, which had impressed her more than somewhat. Good for her, Victoria had thought. At least she is doing something worthwhile which is more than I am.

But that wasn't strictly true. She had entertained the troops at army camps and airfields. They put on plays and concerts and she had even sung at some, like her mother, although she hadn't much of a singing voice. Her mother had still been alive then.

What a time it had been, when she herself was on the crest of a wave – at least at the beginning of the war. Not for her the heartbreak of parting from boyfriends ... Her face clouded over. Except, of course, the one awful thing, but she had promised herself not to think about that, not while she was in here at any rate. It didn't do any good – except she could hardly say it was all water under the bridge. It certainly wasn't that, and for a moment her face looked grim ...

Nurse Bilson appeared with a small glass of dry sherry and a few biscuits on a salver, placing them down beside Victoria with the usual warning to sip it slowly and make it last.

When I get home, Victoria promised herself, the first thing I shall do will be to ask Edith to bring me a whisky – a large one with a splash of soda.

Edith ... how long she had been with her, through thick and thin, and just a girl she had been, almost the same age as Victoria when she had started. Mama had found her, if that was the right word, when she was appearing at Bristol. The stage doorkeeper there, a great fan of Mama's, had said his daughter would give anything to work in the theatre. Not as an actress but something backstage – anything, she just loved the theatre.

So Mama had engaged her to work for Victoria, who was having such a success on the London stage. They had been introduced and taken to each other, and Edith had started her lifelong service to Victoria as dresser and companion. Victoria sometimes wondered how she would ever have managed without her.

Cecil Aherne – it was strange how one's thoughts went off at a tangent. You could be thinking hard about one thing when something quite different intruded. Cecil Aherne – no, she was thinking of someone else. Brian Aherne, that was his name, the British actor who had been married to Joan Fontaine, sister of Olivia de Havilland – or was it the Bennet sisters? No matter, it wasn't her Cecil Aherne.

She sometimes wondered if Mama had engaged Edith to keep her unruly daughter in check. Perhaps she had known about all the things Victoria got up to. By then, Papa was gone, had died suddenly, and after the usual period of grief, Mama had gone back to singing – a Merry Widow in truth, and a beautiful one she was too. There had been no lack of suitors, but although she had had many lovers, she never married again.

I suppose, Victoria thought, I take after Mama in a way, for I loved to be admired and courted, and when I look back, I was really quite naughty. Oh, the men! How they loved me. I was young and beautiful with not a thought in the world but being happy and a success in my chosen profession – what halcyon days they were. Today's young people seemed so set about with problems, wracked with guilt, so conscious of the world's tragedies. And, she thought wryly, when did I ever give heed to anyone else in the world but me? The poor, the starving, the needy? Just a passing thought perhaps, but they were so far away, and the world was so large, and there was no television to put us wise. Not like now.

She glanced down at her right hand, seeing the lovely nails so beautifully manicured and the ring on her little finger, an antique yellow diamond in an eighteenth-century setting. Her first lover had given her that, she had been nineteen, and oh, so anxious to lose her virginity. Now, she could hardly remember his name – yes, Roger something, and he had taken her to Sussex for a weekend where they had stayed at a wonderful hotel with a fourposter bed and beams and a fire in the bedroom. She could see the room now.

It had hurt, she remembered that, then afterwards they had spent an idyllic weekend. They said you never forgot your first lover, and she never had, although his face was vague. There had been many since then, in those early days at least.

Afterwards he had given her the ring, and at first she had not liked the idea. She was generous in her feelings and in giving what was hers, and remembered now that it had felt like being paid. But the ring was so beautiful and he was so courtly and charming, and after all, everyone knew that actresses were showered with gifts by admirers, so she had accepted it, and had kept it all this time. If her husband had disapproved of her wearing it, he had never said. He would have known full well that she would do as she wanted and wear it anyway.

Then with the war came more touring. She had been in Paris when war broke out and came back to find London changed beyond recall. Mama was touring with 'No, No, Nanette', the flat was empty, and Victoria moved in with Edith.

They toured in unlikely places at first, where it was thought that there would be no bombing, but after a while the London theatres opened again, and there was no lack of parts for someone as young and pretty as Victoria. And, what's more, she was a good little actress and capable of pulling in the crowds. She had dreams of becoming a great actress, like Sybil Thorndike in 'St Joan', but now after all these years recognised that she really hadn't had it in her. She could act quite well, and she always looked good on stage. That was half the battle. An actress needs to know what she is best at. Although she had become a much better actress as she grew older, she would never have been an Edith Evans. She knew that now. But I was better looking, she thought smugly, settling for that, and audiences liked me.

She had slept with one or two leading men but had soon discovered that actors were not quite so glamorous as she had thought. There were a few exceptions, of course, the good ones. The others were too wrapped up in themselves and she had quickly tired of them. She had found friends outside the theatre, in society, been fêted and wined and dined, attended parties – she had always been popular.

The early part of the war had been wonderful, at least for her. There was an excitement, an unnatural euphoria everywhere, as though everyone who wasn't actually fighting went about with shining eyes and flushed cheeks. But it was really impatience to find out what was in store, whatever it was, and because they were apprehensive for the future.

'Ah, there we are!' Nurse Bilson usually said this when she entered, and now carried in a tray on which reposed Victoria's light lunch.

She put it on a side table and removed the empty sherry glass, then placed the tray with knife and fork and spoon in front of her patient.

'Dover sole,' she beamed, chin tucked in to her chest, arms akimbo, a satisfied look on her face as though she had personally caught the fish that very morning.

'Mmm, thank you.' Victoria smiled. It certainly looked good. The food here was excellent.

'And a little mousse,' Nurse Bilson said. 'On my recommendation. I told Cook you had a weakness for lemon mousse.'

'How kind,' murmured Victoria, opening the snowy napkin and placing it on her lap.

'And are we all right then?' asked Nurse Bilson. 'The water is iced as you like it.'

'Thank you, yes.'

'Well, I'll let you get on with it,' Nurse Bilson said, closing the door after her.

Her last lunch but one, Victoria thought. One more, and if she went home on Saturday morning, she would have lunch at home.

She ate daintily as she did everything, her fingers holding knife and fork delicately, almost as if she were on stage and had an audience. She ate neatly, and when she had finished, dabbed her mouth with a napkin. Yes, Nurse Bilson was right, the cook here was a treasure. Fifteen minutes later, the nurse came in to collect the tray, looking very pleased when she saw Victoria had eaten everything.

'There's a good girl,' she said, as Victoria winced, and going over to the bed plumped up the pillows ready for her afternoon nap.

'Not just yet, Nurse,' Victoria said, in a tone of voice that would not be argued with. 'I want to write some letters.'

'Can't they wait?' Nurse Bilson frowned. 'You really should get all the rest you can.'

Victoria smiled, showing excellent teeth.

'I'll rest later.'

When the door closed, Victoria closed her eyes then opened them again. Seventy-five ... she had lived more than thirty years longer than Mama. Strange when you thought about it. Luck of the draw, some said. She might have grown old gracefully but she didn't like being old. There was nothing to be said for it, but if that was the way of it, it was up to you to live life to the full. And she would. It had taken this little warning to make her realise she hadn't all the time in the world. She would certainly try to do something in the theatre again for now she felt strong enough to tackle it. Or perhaps television – awful thought. You had – simply *had* – to keep busy. And you must use any gifts you had, otherwise they would shrivel up and die. Who was it who'd said that?

She felt cold suddenly, and drew the cardigan around her shoulders. Oh, what gloomy thoughts! It was not like her. She had everything to live for. A wonderful family, grandchildren, and she hoped more to come. She wished Julian would settle down and marry again. It was what he needed, a wife and family. Like Geoffrey ... As for Vanessa, Victoria prayed that she would not return to her last love – but whatever would be, would be. She mustn't interfere, it did no good, and whatever the children wanted to do, their lives were their own. Think of something else ...

So despite not wanting to, she thought of Philip and Salisbury, the streets packed with troops. She was playing in the theatre there, and on non-matinee afternoons would stroll around the town instead of resting, drinking in the beauty of the buildings and the cathedral, while in the evenings the usual crowd of admirers would wait outside the theatre – soldiers, airmen, fans – waving their autograph books in front of her nose ... That evening, warm at almost eleven at night, everywhere blacked out, by the blue lamp over the stage door she had met the eyes of a man standing at the back of the crowd. Their eyes had locked for what seemed an eternity and Victoria felt as though her whole body was alerted. He smiled, and she looked away and signed autograph books, and when she had finished, he was still there.

They said nothing but stared at each other, knowing that something strange had happened. It might have been for a brief moment or minutes, she didn't know how long. Then he spoke.

'Hallo,' he said, and she smiled. She seemed to get her breath back, and said almost shyly, 'Hallo.'

'I simply had to see you,' he said. 'I hope you don't mind?'

'Of course note, I'm flattered.'

'I didn't think there would be such a crowd. I mean – is it like this every night?'

She smiled. 'Quite often.'

'You must be exhausted?'

'I'm used to it,' she said.

'Would you ...' She waited. 'Would you have supper with me?'

It was so right. There was never any doubt that she would accept. Yet it was something she had never done before, accepted an invitation just like that – at a first meeting, from a total stranger. Yet she was impelled to say: 'Thank you, yes,' and hope that he wouldn't think it was a usual thing with her. He beamed at her, showing excellent white teeth, while his dark eyes shone into hers.

'I say, that's wonderful!' He put out his arm. 'Shall we?'

She wrapped her coat around her and took his arm. It seemed the most natural thing in the world.

'Why not?' she asked, feeling strangely exhilarated.

So had begun the one true love of her life.

They had sat facing each other in the dimly lit dining room, the red lamps glowing, blissfully unaware of their surroundings. He looked so handsome in his dark uniform, and she learned that he was in the Fleet Air Arm. His face was as clear to her now as it had been then. Dark brows, and eyes which were warm and glowing, a strong nose and firmly shaped mouth. His hand had moved across the table to cover hers, and at his touch the nerves sprang to life – it was like an electric shock. She had never felt like this before in her life. It's true, she had thought in wonder. You can fall in love at first sight.

She couldn't remember what they had had to eat, only that he had to be back at the base, and she would be playing Scarborough the following week – it all seemed hopeless. He had seen her back to the small hotel where Edith waited for her, worried as to where she had gone without a word.

He had kissed her, it seemed for an eternity – she couldn't let him go, fearing she might never see him again. But she had.

They met at odd moments whenever possible, grabbing every opportunity, and one weekend he had taken her home to the cottage in Sussex where she met Aunt Anne. Dear Aunt Anne, the only relative he had since his parents were both dead and the estate had long been sold to cover death duties, leaving just the small cottage for him and his aunt to live in.

They had sat in the garden on that lovely afternoon while Anne brought them tea, the scent of late paeonies all around. Even now, the scent could evoke memories so strong she could hardly bear it ...

'Victoria! This really won't do!' She could hear Mama's exasperated voice now. 'You are seeing far too much of this young man.'

But she had spun round in front of Mama, not giving a damn. 'I'm in love,' she said. 'He is the most wonderful man in the world!'

'Yes, and I've heard that before,' Mama said grimly. 'You've only know him five minutes and it's not as if he's ...'

'Anyone special?' Victoria finished, knowing that her mother was ambitious for her. 'But he is, Mama.'

'I just don't want you to get hurt. If anything happened to him – '

A small frown appeared between Victoria's eyes.

'That's just it. We want to make the most of the time that we have.'

The truth was she didn't want to be separated from him for a moment. She thought of him all the time, wanted to be with him, to hear his voice. He was child, father, lover, all in one. She wanted to spend the rest of her life with him.

Mama had shrugged.

'I am thinking of the young man as well as you,' she said. 'It's not fair on him. Actresses have a life apart. They cannot give themselves completely to someone else, there is always a part of them that is private, sacred to their art.'

'Oh, Ma, what high falutin' talk!' Victoria laughed. 'Philip and I love each other, that's all that matters.'

'I can see it's no good talking to you ...'

'Not the slightest good at all,' Victoria said softly.

When they became lovers, she was happier than she had ever been in her life. If he had asked her to give up acting, she would have done so willingly, but he never had. When he asked her to marry him on his next leave, she said yes, joyously and unreservedly, and in the hotel just outside Southampton they had made love wildly and sweetly as the murky waters of the English Channel and the Bay of Biscay hid their dark secrets.

A fortnight later, her world fell apart. Philip and his crew had been brought down by a U-boat, Anne told her later, a U-boat skulking below them as vigilant as a tiger waiting to pounce on its prey. They hadn't stood a chance. When the news came through to Victoria, she sat white-faced, dark eyes huge with horror and disbelief – how could this have happened? It just wasn't possible. But as the days wore on, she had to learn to accept it.

Her mother was surprisingly sympathetic, and Edith was a tower of strength. It was almost as if she felt Victoria's pain herself. But the new play was opening and it had to go on, despite everything, despite the sadness, the loss, and the knowledge that she would never see Philip again.

All of that, together with the suspicion that she might be pregnant in the weeks that followed ...

Oh, what good did it do to go over it, the sadness, the unbearable grief? It was punishing oneself unnecessarily.

Her eyes were smarting from staring unseeing into space. Victoria blew her nose, took a deep breath, and picked up her writing pad and Violet's card. Violet Santucci, with an address in Rome ...

'Dear Violet,' she began – and looked up and recalled another time, just before she left for Canada, hurrying around getting things ready for her departure. They had almost collided in Knightsbridge, and had laughed and excused each other. 'Can't stop!' Victoria had cried, not wishing to talk, especially with the secret knowledge she carried within her. 'See you soon.'

What a hope. By the time she returned and picked up the pieces everything had changed – and she had never seen Violet since that day. What a lot of water had passed under the bridge since then!

Well, get on with it, she told herself, and began again.

'Dear Violet – '

Chapter Six

The drawing room at Jarretts was ready to receive Ruth's guests, and she looked around her with satisfaction. Fresh flowers in all the bowls and vases, cushions plumped, windows shining, the view out over the gardens quite lovely. She took a deep breath and once more tidied the papers on the small writing table, knowing that the ladies of the local Save the Children Fund would be more than impressed. And here they were – two, no, three cars coming down the drive, Molly Foster and Isabel Greenhill, and unless she was mistaken surely that was Lady Glenholm behind? Oh, she couldn't be more pleased.

When Mrs Manson announced her visitors, she went forward graciously to meet them – eight of them – and found them comfortable chairs, and took her place at the table with Sarah Greenhalgh at her side to take notes.

'So pleased to see you, ladies, and not one absentee.' She gave them her friendly smile.

They smiled politely back at her while giving swift glances around the room, noting the exquisite eighteenth-century furniture and heavy drapes, all courtesy of Victoria's taste and Harry Bellamy's money.

'Firstly I would like to tell you that the date we decided upon at the last meeting has now been settled. It is the sixth of July and I hope that will be convenient to all of you?'

There were murmurs among them, and soon the meeting was underway. Ruth was new to this charity, the success of her other fund-raising operations having reached them by word of mouth. They decided between themselves that they had done the right thing in electing her at the last general meeting. By the time Mrs Manson had served coffee you could hardly get a word in edgeways.

With Margaret Greaves on flowers and Lady Glenholm's cakes – everyone knew the pride she took in her cooking – the various stalls and promises of more from friends were being taken note of by Sarah Greenhalgh.

When they left it was to talk warmly outside of further meetings, and with the door closed on them, Ruth was conscious yet again of another effort well received.

It was just what this house needed, to be used for good works and charity. And she was the one to do it. She took after her mother there. As the local doctor's wife, her mother had been the mainstay of the village where they lived.

Mrs Manson cleared away, and Ruth looked around the room, plumping the cushions, something she did quite often.

'How is Mrs Bellamy, then?' Mrs Manson asked.

'She is going home tomorrow.' And there was a slight edge to Ruth's voice.

'Oh, is she?' And Mrs Manson made a face. 'Be all right, will she?'

'Well,' Ruth sighed, 'we shall have to see. I personally don't go along with it – I think she should have come here. After all, it is her home.'

'Oh, that would be nice for her!' There was nothing Mrs Bellamy wouldn't do for others. Not many daughters-in-law were prepared to have their husband's mother living with them.

'We shall have to see. She has her maid, Edith, but she is elderly, poor thing. We shall have to have a family discussion, I can see that.'

Upstairs in her bedroom, Ruth sat and pondered. She strongly disapproved of their allowing Victoria to go home. Home indeed! That large Knightsbridge flat on the third floor. True there was a lift, but for heaven's sake – and it wasn't as if this house wasn't large enough. Of course, it wouldn't be easy, but with Mother in residence, being looked after, even Edith – well, one had to take Edith as well – Jarretts was more likely to stay theirs in future. There seemed to be no other way to deal with it. Certainly Julian couldn't seem to care less, swanning around the world with his jewellery, and as for Vanessa, she had no interest in it at all. And only today Ruth had been reading about elderly folk whose whole personal fortune had been spent on care in nursing homes. She was horrified. Imagine it all going, so that they might have to sell Jarretts eventually – no, she simply couldn't allow that to happen!

She would have another word with Geoffrey when he came in. It really was too bad of him to shelve everything the way he did. One had to plan for emergencies, contingencies – he really was extraordinary. Just suppose Mother had another attack of whatever it was? She could fall, die even, and then you could bet the other two would say: Well, what about my share of Jarretts? She herself didn't want money, she just wanted the house. And of course enough money to keep it going. But with luck Geoffrey could afford it, and at least he was all right at the moment.

'Geoffrey,' she said, when he was seated with his whisky and soda before dinner, 'did you see Mother today?'

'No, I couldn't get up to town, but I telephoned and apparently she is going home tomorrow so I thought if we popped up there in the afternoon ...?'

'Geoffrey, you do realise, don't you, that she really shouldn't be allowed home just yet? Edith is really in no fit state to look after her. Why, she is as old as your Mother – and really it's not fair.'

'Apparently they are going to have a nurse for a couple of weeks, I believe. After all, she is well now, and they think strong enough to go home, so why should we argue? I am delighted it has worked out so well.'

'Yes. Yes, of course, so am I. I just think it's so hard on Edith, and your mother too of course. She wants good nourishing food – and we all know Edith is no great cook. I do feel, Geoffrey, that if she came here – '

He put down his drink and looked at her.

'Ruth, I think you are worrying far too much. She wasn't desperately ill, you know. She had a fall.'

'But why did she fall? It may have been a stroke.'

'I think the doctor would have said.'

'Not necessarily,' Ruth replied with the expression of a doctor's daughter who knows things a layman would not.

'Well, I feel we must just go along with things at the moment.'

She sighed. 'So short-sighted of you, Geoffrey. I must say, I believe in being prepared. We should have a family meeting.'

'I don't think that's necessary at this stage.' And she could tell by his voice that he felt she had gone too far.

'Well,' she said lamely, 'we shall go up and see her tomorrow. See how she is.'

'Yes.' Geoffrey picked up his paper with some relief. 'We'll do that.'

He dropped Ruth off at the flat before going to collect his mother. Victoria turned a radiant face towards him when he entered. Indeed she was already dressed in her outdoor coat, and carrying a warm scarf.

'I saw you arrive from the window,' she beamed. 'Oh, you can't know how wonderful it is to be going home.'

He smiled at her indulgently.

'Was it so awful in here?' he whispered, sensing Nurse Bilson not far away.

'No, not at all – I'm being unreasonable, it's just that one likes one's home.'

'Come along then. Is this yours? Ready?'

She nodded as he picked up the small travelling bag. 'Have you got everything?'

She glanced around the room, and put the scarf around her shoulders.

'That's a good idea, although it's not cold outside. Now we shall take it slowly, there's no need to hurry. Take my arm – '

'Well, we're off then, are we?' Nurse Bilson said, coming into the room. She took one of Victoria's hands. 'It's been a pleasure to look after you. Now take care, and remember what I said – take it easy. Don't hurry.'

'Thank you, nurse, thank you.' And Victoria, head high, left the room on Geoffrey's arm.

She walked slowly and carefully to the waiting car, feeling extraordinarily weak and slightly light-headed in the fresh air. She took a deep breath.

'Oh, how wonderful to be outside!'

'Now make yourself comfortable,' he said, having seated her in the car. 'I was going to bring Edith or Ruth but they thought they would wait for you at the flat.'

'Of course, I'm glad they did.'

Her apartment was full of flowers, they were everywhere: pink carnations, roses and lilies. The scent was almost overpowering, and her eyes filled with tears.

'Sit down, Mother,' Geoffrey said, himself quite overcome by the situation. After all, it could have gone the other way.

'Oh, that's lovely,' Victoria exclaimed when Edith brought a footstool, and looked down at her adoringly.

'Doesn't she look well?' she asked all round.

Ruth kept her opinion to herself, but Geoffrey agreed.

'Yes, she's fine now. A few days and she'll be as right as rain.'

Then the doorbell rang and in came Vanessa – carrying even more flowers.

'Oh, Mummy, I hoped I'd be here to greet you!'

She bent and kissed Victoria. 'But you are, darling.'

'Oh, you look wonderful. As lovely as ever, isn't she?' She turned to the others, sheer delight on her face.

'You spoil me, all of you,' Victoria said, but they could see that she was simply delighted to be home.

There was no point in saying anything at this stage, thought Ruth, but her mind was made up. This flat was most impractical.

'Let's just check the bedroom, shall we?' she asked in her most efficient voice, risking a scowl from Edith who thought she was interfering.

'It's all ready for her, Mrs Bellamy.'

'Yes, I'm sure it is.'

The bedroom was romantic: a froth of lace and cream silk, a flounced French dressing table, hand painted wardrobes, and the wallpaper quite the prettiest Ruth had ever seen. French, too, I expect, she thought. But that's what I'll do. I'll go on a search, and see if I can find something like it. I'll do up the room that no one uses just like it. Her furniture and pictures, her silver photograph frames. Yes, she will be as at home there as she is here. Edith, she thought, can have the room next-door. The boxroom could be made into a bathroom. Oh, yes, it would be something else to get her teeth into, but she would say nothing to Geoffrey yet.

'Yes, the room looks lovely, Edith has done a wonderful job. Very inviting. I suggest you get to bed as soon as you can, Mother.'

Victoria raised inquiring eyebrows.

'Your first day home – be on the safe side.'

'Yes,' she said. 'Well, how about a glass of champagne to welcome me home first?' Her eyes twinkled at them as her heart slowed its excited beat, and she sank back against the soft feather cushions. Oh, it was good to be home.

When Ruth and Geoffrey had gone, the atmosphere was more relaxed. Edith went about her duties, but every so often with a solicitous eye on Victoria, while Vanessa chatted to her mother.

'So now, tell me all your news?' Victoria said. 'You still haven't said what happened when you saw Gavin Weston again – or did you not see him again?'

Vanessa looked down.

'I don't want to talk about it now, Mummy. Let's wait until you've settled in a bit.'

That means she has something to tell me, Victoria decided. She's going back to him, I can feel it. Oh, I can't bear it!

'Very well, darling. If you'd rather not.'

'I don't want to worry you, and I know you do worry – '

'Well, the quickest way to worry me is to tell me you've something to tell me later!' And her brown eyes smiled back at her daughter.

'I shouldn't have said anything.'

'But I asked. Anyway, how's Jack?'

'Jack? Oh, he's fine, I had lunch with him yesterday.'

'You like him, don't you?'

'Yes, he's nice – too nice, perhaps.'

'But you are seeing Gavin . . .' And Vanessa blushed.

'Well, it's no good trying to hide anything from you, is it?'

'Darling, you are as transparent as – as – a polythene bag!'

'There's poetry for you,' teased Vanessa. 'No, you are right. I did meet Gavin, and, well, he's left Suzie – for good. She seems intent on going back to France to be with her lover and his little girls.'

'What about the boy?'

'Tom? Oh, he stays with Gavin. He wouldn't let Suzie take him, anyway.'

'I see. How sad – for the boy, I mean. There is such a bond between mother and son.'

'And daughters?' Vanessa asked.

'Of course, darling, that's special too.'

'What I was thinking was, why don't we – you and I, oh, and Edith, if you'd like her to come – go away for a few days to the Cotswolds, as soon as you feel like it?'

'Oh, that would be wonderful, but are you sure you can spare the time?'

'Yes, I'll work something out. Say in two or three weeks' time, if you feel up to it.'

'I shall look forward to it, that's a lovely idea.'

Edith came in from the kitchen. 'Victoria, you know you will have to go to bed soon. An early night, the first night home.'

Victoria frowned. In truth, she did feel tired, but she wasn't going to admit it.

Vanessa studied Edith. She was small and sturdy, and had been around ever since Vanessa could remember. They had taken her for granted, she was part of the family. Just how did someone make the choice to live for others? She must be happy or she wouldn't have stayed. And she must have been young once, but Vanessa couldn't remember that. In family photographs, she looked young and quite pretty, with a fresh country face, dark curly hair, and she had always kept her slight West Country burr – she had never lost that. Now, an elderly woman, her hair was grey, but her skin was good, and she still had all her own teeth. A lifetime in someone's service – God! Vanessa shivered. It just didn't seem right somehow.

She stayed to the light supper that Edith had prepared and then saw her mother to bed safely before leaving.

'I'm not sure I shall be in tomorrow – I have a few things to do.' She hoped she didn't sound too guilty. Her mother was so perceptive where she was concerned.

'Darling, of course not. You run along and enjoy the rest of your weekend.'

In the taxi taking her to Gavin's apartment, Vanessa sagged with relief. Well, that had broken the ice, and now her mother knew or suspected the truth. All right, so she will think I'm mad, but I just can't help it where Gavin is concerned, thought Vanessa. After all, you can't write five years off just like that ...

It was a good arrangement. She had given up her rented flat

and had moved in with him, to the flat he used all the week near Sloane Square, and weekends would be spent at his home near Haslemere in Surrey. This would be their first weekend and she was looking forward to it with mixed feelings. It would be the first time she had seen Gavin on home ground, the first time she would meet his son.

She would see the fabulous Suzie's home, but suppose the boy didn't like her?

Gavin was waiting for her when she returned, already packed, and they drove down on this fine Saturday evening. She was enchanted at her first sight of the house which nestled on a hillside, an old farm cottage which had been extended and completely modernised. Inside, the housekeeper was waiting for them with Tom at her side. It seemed that the French au pair girl who looked after him had the evening off.

He hugged his father, then turned to Vanessa.

'Hello, Tom.' Vanessa held out her hand. She wasn't used to children. He stared back at her with large dark eyes just like his father's, and Vanessa was filled with sympathy for this little boy caught right in the middle of a broken marriage.

'You can show Vanessa your toys later,' Mrs Benson said, and Gavin took Vanessa on a tour of the house.

So this, she thought, when she had seen all that there was to see, was Suzie's domain. This was once her home. Well, all I can say is, this Frenchman must be quite something for her to give up all this and her husband and child! For she must have spent a fortune on the house. The kitchen was out of this world, and the bathrooms sheer luxury. How could she bear to give it all up? And where do I stand in all this? Vanessa asked herself.

'What do you intend to do?' she had asked Gavin before coming down this weekend.

'What do you mean?' and she knew he was skirting the issue.

'Are you going to divorce her?'

'I suppose so,' he said. 'There's really no alternative.'

'Well, I'm certainly not going to come and live with you unless that's what you have in mind – it's too messy. After all, I want to settle down sometime, have children of my own.'

'I thought for a bit we'd stay as we are.'

'I see,' Vanessa had said flatly. She wasn't unaware that he wanted to see how she got on with Tom.

She couldn't blame him. 'All right, then. Let's give it a whirl, shall we?' she asked brightly. She had always thought she loved him more than he loved her. It was obvious, really. He'd doted on Suzie – did he still? Was he getting over it? Was he? Or would Suzie always come first in his heart?

Well, she had burned her boats now, agreeing to live with him, and after all, it was what she wanted. She had been totally miserable when the relationship finished.

She had told Jack and seen the disappointment and disapproval in his nice brown eyes.

'I know you think I'm a fool.'

'Yes, I do,' he agreed. 'But it's your life.'

'Yes, it is,' she said coldly, and wished she was as sure about everything as he seemed to be. The thing was, she did a damned good job in the office, knew exactly what she was doing, was held in high esteem by the directors and was in line for promotion.

Why then did she make such a mess of her private life?

Washed and changed, she emerged from the bedroom and made her way to the nursery, where she found Tom on the floor surrounded by toy cars and trains.

'Hi, Tom,' she said, sitting down on the floor beside him, 'what's this?' examining a complex piece of Lego and not sure what it was.

'It's a caterpillar tractor,' he said scathingly.

'I can see that,' she said pleasantly. 'I mean, what sort of caterpillar tractor?'

He looked at her with interest, then stared in front of himself for what seemed like minutes.

'You mean, what make?' He looked at her suspiciously.

'Mmmm,' she said, playing for time. 'It looks Canadian to me.'

He pounced on the solution. 'That's it!' he said. 'That's what it is – Canadian!'

She had passed the first hurdle.

Chapter Seven

It was hot in Rome, but the air conditioning in the apartment kept everything cool. By the open window Violet Santucci read Victoria's letter for the third time, her blue eyes alight with pleasure, delighted that her old school friend had bothered to reply to her. She tried to visualise her as she might look now, a woman of her own age, in her seventies, but couldn't imagine it. She could only see a young and vibrant girl, a beauty, with her perfect oval face, that mane of dark hair, the wonderful eyes. But above all she remembered the confidence Victoria exuded, as if she had known even then she was something special.

There was a slight fragrance to the letter. She had no idea what it was, but it reminded her of Victoria. It was difficult to imagine her lying in bed, unwell. Violet had lost track of her after the war, although until then she had kept all the press cuttings about her because they reminded her of home during those long years in Italy after her marriage. She had never returned to England, except for short visits when her parents died; her life had been in Italy, particularly since her daughter Venetia had no desire to live in England, and a life away from Venetia was unthinkable, despite the anxiety she sometimes caused her mother.

Hearing her daughter's key in the lock, Violet's first instinct was to thrust the letter in a drawer, but she was not quick enough. She smiled up at Venetia, never seeing her only child without a sense of wonder that, late in life, she had given birth to such a beautiful creature at a time when she had given up all hope of having a child. Always an admirer of physical beauty, it was as if God himself had taken a hand in making her child perfect, or so she told herself.

Venetia unwound her scarf, and put her package on a chair – Hermès, Violet noted, as it would be, for Venetia never believed in buying anything but the best.

She eased off a very high-heeled shoe and rubbed her silken-clad foot, then looked up with a sigh of relief. 'And who is your letter from? You look quite excited.'

'Well, not excited exactly,' Violet said. 'Still, it's lovely to hear from an old friend.'

'May I?' Venetia held her hand out for the letter, and again Violet felt that slight hesitation in letting her see it, wanting to keep it to herself.

'Of course, darling.'

Venetia took it, then held it to her exquisite straight nose.

'Mmmm – *Bal à Versailles*,' she said, and began to read Victoria's letter as Violet watched for her reaction.

'Oh, this is your actress friend!' she said. 'Is she the one you were at school with?'

'Yes,' Violet said, with some pride.

'I didn't know you kept in touch with her?'

'Well, I haven't really – it was just that I saw in the English *Telegraph* that she had been ill after a heart attack.'

'Victoria Bellamy?' Venetia said thoughtfully.

'Yes, one of our finest actresses before the war – and I believe she has worked since then, after her husband died. She was so beautiful, you can't imagine ...'

Venetia folded the letter thoughtfully, and took off her other shoe. 'Was she in films?'

'No,' Violet said doubtfully. 'I don't think she made films. The stage was her particular forte.'

'Well,' Venetia said, 'it's nice that she answered your letter. I didn't know you had written to her.'

'I saw the newspaper report about her fall. Apparently she injured her leg, something like that, and was in a nursing home, so I thought I'd write for old times' sake.'

'Sweet,' Venetia murmured. She was all for her mother having something to interest her. Life could be very boring for her sometimes, and besides it took some of the pressure off herself.

She removed her jacket, and pulled the blind a little to hide the sun. 'There – is that better? Would you like coffee? A cold drink?'

'Coffee, please. I would have asked Gina to do it, but then I thought I'd wait for you.'

But Venetia had already gone into the kitchen to see to the coffee.

Violet was forty-four when Venetia was born, and now her daughter was thirty and as lovely as ever, despite a failed marriage and many suitors and admirers who seemed never quite to come to anything more. But the divorce certainly wasn't Venetia's fault, Violet told herself. Young Count Tellini was a very spoiled young man, their marriage was doomed from the start.

Violet had brought the girl up single-handed when her husband left her, and had worked in order to give her a good education, sending her to Switzerland and to a finishing school, making sure she received the right invitations from the best families. But Venetia had been expelled from the first finishing school she attended, and only emerged from the full course of the second by the skin of her teeth. Violet put that down to the fact that her father had left them when she was at an impressionable age and spent most of her life making excuses for her daughter's headstrong behaviour.

Venetia came in with a tray of coffee and wafer biscuits.

'And what did you do with yourself today?' asked Violet, eyeing the Hermès package on the chair.

'Oh, I must show you! It's lovely – a silk shirt.' And having put down the tray, Venetia undid the wrapper and held the exquisite shirt against herself.

'Just me, isn't it?'

'Lovely, darling,' Violet said.

Venetia was indeed a picture, with brown eyes which were soft and warm, gentle eyes. Remarkable, Violet thought, since they betrayed nothing of Venetia's temperament, which could be fiery when she was roused. Then they would flash like lightning. All her features were good: the mobile mouth, strong small white teeth, and black glossy hair which she wore smooth and straight, sometimes tying it back or in a chignon – altogether she had a classic look. But it was her voice, low and sexy, her mother supposed it would be called nowadays, which won people over. Husky, vibrant, intimate, but always firm – Venetia knew what she wanted, she had from birth.

She handed her mother the small cup of coffee.

'And you went to the lawyer this morning?' Violet asked.

Venetia frowned. 'Yes, but he is a stupid man. I can see this going on and on with nothing in it for me.'

Oh, Violet thought, it was a sad day when she had married that spoiled young man. She did hope ...

'The Tellini family are determined I won't get a penny out of it – but they are making a mistake,' Venetia said, biting a wafer with her strong even teeth. It wouldn't do for Mama to know that Carlo had caught her in flagrante delicto with that stupid American actor in one of Rome's best hotels. She must have been mad, not to say careless ... It wouldn't have been the first time since her marriage, she had just been unlucky. Unfortunately the Tellini family were as tough as old boots where their son was concerned, especially his mother, and just a little more than a match for Venetia. It was one of the few occasions in her life when she had come up against someone even more resolute than herself.

'Oh, darling, can they do that? Surely not?'

'Mama, you are not to worry, everything will be all right.'

If Venetia had a redeeming feature it was the love she bore her mother. When her father had walked out on them she was fourteen, and all her teenage rebellion took the form of hating her father and protecting her mother. She had an outsize chip on her shoulder, Violet recognised, and just hoped that one day she would meet someone who would smooth it away.

'Tell me more about this friend of yours – Victoria Bellamy? Nice name.'

'She was lovely,' Violet said.

'How come you lost touch with her over the years? I don't recall you mentioning her before.'

'Oh, she wasn't a close friend – we were at school together but I wasn't in her set.'

'Why not?' Venetia said sharply.

'Oh, well, you know.' Venetia did know, knew her mother's shyness, the inferiority complex she suffered from, and her back was up at once.

'I expect you were too clever for them. After all, actresses are not exactly – '

'Now, Venetia, it wasn't like that. They were a sophisticated crowd, you know how they are – and I, well, I was a clergyman's daughter. To me, Victoria and the others seemed so glamorous.'

Venetia felt a surge of affection for her mother. It wasn't her fault she had been born with that temperament – she wasn't a fighter like her daughter.

'Anyway, go on.'

'Well, I envied them, but mostly Victoria. Her mother was a musical comedy star.'

'Oh, well!' And Venetia made a face.

'No, darling, I mean a famous one – a beauty – and Victoria took after her.'

'So?'

'Well, that's it, really. We left school and she went on the stage. I did war work with the Red Cross, she married – I believe, a very wealthy industrialist.'

'Well, she would, wouldn't she?'

Venetia turned bright quizzical eyes to her mother, and Violet laughed.

'I have quite a collection of old press cuttings and photographs of Victoria,' she mused. 'I'm glad I kept them.'

'You have? Where are they?'

'In the little painted chest – the bottom drawer – in my bedroom.'

But Venetia had already gone in her haste to find them. It wasn't every day something happened that was of such interest to her.

When she returned with the folder, she was already thumbing through the contents. 'Wow!'

'Give it to me,' Violet said, for once overriding her daughter. 'It's in chronological order. Here is the first one – me at school, in the sixth form. This is me and that's Victoria and next to her ...'

But Venetia was poring over the photograph, seeing girls in an English school, pre-war young ladies in neat gym slips and white blouses, three rows of them, and it wouldn't have been difficult to pick out the young Victoria without her mother's words – she stood out a mile. And here was Mama, in the background almost, gently fair and quite pretty. But Victoria – hmm, you could see she was going places.

'And this is her in what I imagine must have been her first stage part at The Apollo. I went to see it although I didn't go backstage – oh, she was marvellous! The audience loved her.'

Yes, Venetia could see how they would. Those laughing eyes, a fabulous figure, that smile. You felt she was smiling just for you.

'Here are some more. You'll see the captions. This was the first Noël Coward play she did. He thought she might be another Gertie Lawrence.'

Whoever she was, thought Venetia, she could quite understand why her mother was so captivated.

And then a large photograph of a lovely girl with laughing eyes staring straight into the camera, a long elegant neck, an off the shoulder gown, an unsmiling mouth almost more beautiful in repose. Venetia gave a small sigh for a world long gone.

'In those days, magazines often gave away a large photograph of popular stars,' Violet explained. 'Oh, but this is the best.' It was a page torn from *Country Life* magazine and there she was: 'Miss Victoria Worth, only daughter of Mrs Imogen Worth and the late Mr Robert Worth, of Queen's Gate, London, who is to be married to Mr Harry Bellamy, elder son of Mrs Dorothy Bellamy and the late Mr Charles Bellamy, of Nailstone Hall, Charlcote, Derbyshire.'

But it was the necklace which caught Venetia's eye.

'Oh,' she gasped. 'Emeralds – could they ever be real!'

'Indeed they were,' Violet said, taking out another article from *The Times*. 'Here it is, the priceless emeralds being sold at Sotheby's. They belonged to an Indian Maharajah once and it was Harry Bellamy who bought them for his bride. He paid an astronomical sum for them, as a wedding present.'

They seemed to shine even from the printed page, and Victoria wore them so regally.

'She was given some beautiful jewels,' Violet said. 'Her husband seemed to take a delight in buying her the most expensive gifts.'

'And I don't suppose she minded?' Venetia said crisply. 'Oh, well, is that all?'

'These are just the birth announcements in *The Times* – they had three children, two boys and a girl. I don't know what age they would be now.'

'I wonder if she still has them?' Venetia mused. 'The emeralds, I mean?'

'I expect so. Her husband died – it must have been in the sixties. Of course he was a lot older than she was, but even so, he was still quite young when he died. I remember reading that Victoria had gone back to acting, but I lost touch after that.'

She was immersed in the little file of memorabilia.

'And so she wrote to you?' Venetia said, picking up the letter from Victoria, and reading it through again. 'She does sound rather nice.'

'Oh, she was,' Violet said fervently. 'She was the only one who ever noticed me. Of course, I was a year or so younger than her.'

Venetia leant forward and kissed her cheek.

'Dear Mama,' she said, looking down at her. 'What are we going to do with you, eh? Don't you think it's time you got away for a short break? It will be getting very hot soon and you know you don't like the heat.'

Violet smiled. She didn't say she liked to stay where she was to be near Venetia, that nothing was as important as that. Since Venetia's failed marriage she came to see Violet every day, leaving her own flat on the Via Veneto to visit her mother, although she knew she was in safe hands with Gina living in.

'What's more to the point is what are *you* going to do?' Violet asked gently.

'I'm toying with the idea of doing something, I'm not sure what. It will turn up.'

Venetia knew how difficult it was to live up to the splendour and richness of Roman society. Having been on the fringe of it during her marriage – and no one was more regretful than Venetia that she had wrecked her chances – she had to be very careful. Once you had tasted that life it wasn't easy to give it up, and the Tellinis would make it difficult for her here, she knew that. They could destroy her. It wasn't so much what she had done as the fact that she had been found out, been careless, especially of the Tellini name. She would not be trusted after that.

She had some planning to do.

'What about money, Venetia?' Violet asked. 'You know, I have some – thanks to you – just until your settlement comes through.'

I'll be lucky! Venetia thought grimly. But I mustn't tell Mama about that. Besides I don't want to worry her.

Later that evening, before she returned to her own apartment, Violet found her poring over the cuttings of Victoria Bellamy in her heyday, paying particular attention to the full-page photograph of Victoria wearing her famous emeralds. Yet again she felt that swift stab of apprehension, which she smothered instantly.

A few days later, Venetia's financial problems were solved by the offer of a lump sum from the Tellini family if she would get out of Rome and stay out of their lives, relinquishing all claims on Carlo as his wife.

Before the lawyer, she put on quite an act. The offer was unthinkable, absolutely not, there was no way she would accept that! She stormed out, but he knew, as she knew, that she would accept ultimately, although it wasn't as much as she had hoped. He also knew how impossible the Tellini family could make life for their daughter-in-law if she stayed, and wasn't at all worried about the outcome.

So with minimum loss of dignity on her part the papers were duly drawn up and signed, and with an exit that would have done Victoria Bellamy credit, Venetia left his office, head held high. She had just one month to put her affairs in Rome in order.

She deliberately did nothing for a week, playing it cool as she told herself, and then went to see her mother. She took her the gift of a silk blouse, exquisitely made, and Violet was thrilled.

'Oh, it's lovely!' she cried.

'You can try it on later,' Venetia promised, taking a chair by her mother's side.

Violet put down the letter she was writing to Victoria, and Venetia picked up the open file again and pored over the pictures and cuttings.

'Mama, I've been thinking.' And Violet turned to her, eyes wide. Venetia sounded serious.

'How would you like to go back to live in England?'

Violet was quite shocked. When her heartbeat began to subside, she said slowly, 'Are you serious?'

'Yes, darling, I am. I've thought about it – you must long for England sometimes? I know I've been selfish.'

'Nonsense,' Violet said stoutly. 'You are part Italian, and sometimes I think more Italian than English.'

'Perhaps,' Venetia said. 'But wouldn't you like that? After all, there's not much here for me, I could just as well live in London.'

'But you don't like England,' Violet asserted.

'No, that's not quite true – it's just that I prefer Italy. But I am prepared to give it a try.'

'But I can't allow you to do that – it's too much to ask ... I don't say there haven't been times when I've longed to go back, especially during the hot summers.'

'Well, then?'

'But couldn't we go for a visit? I would be quite happy to do that.'

Venetia demurred. 'What I thought was, if I made a trip to London, say, and looked around, discovered whether or not I liked it, you could follow on later.'

'How long would you be gone?'

'I'm not sure, but think about it, will you? I'm quite prepared to go if you would like to. In fact, I thought I'd go over for a short break anyway, perhaps next week.'

'Yes, you must have a little holiday,' Violet agreed. 'After this dreadful business with the Tellinis. Is it settled yet? Will you divorce?'

'Yes, I am afraid so,' Venetia said solemnly.

'I suppose it's no good suggesting you try again?'

'No, it's impossible,' Venetia said firmly. 'I just couldn't live with him again, Mama.' She turned her head away. 'I would never be able to trust him.' Which was true, she thought.

'I am so sorry, Venetia. You didn't fare any better than I did when it came to marriage. Never mind, you are young, you will meet someone else.'

'I can't think about that now,' she said sadly. 'Well, I must be away. Oh, did you answer your friend's letter? It was so kind of her to write.'

'Yes, I was just writing to her when you came in.'

'You could mention to her that you have a daughter. Tell her I shall be in London. Perhaps I could go to see her? I should like that – and if we did go back, Mama, we would need friends.'

'Yes,' Violet agreed, and bit her lip. 'Yes, I could.' And wondered again why she always had this odd sense of foreboding when Venetia had an idea. She remembered she had not wanted her to read Victoria's letter ...

She pushed away her ungracious thoughts.

'Yes, darling,' she said. 'I will.'

Chapter Eight

Now back in her lovely apartment, Victoria looked around at familiar things. The clock on the mantelpiece with its figure of a shepherdess – she and Harry had bought it together in Church Street in Kensington all those years ago. You forgot what lovely things you had when you were away from them. That vase, with cupids dancing round it and roses – it couldn't be anything else but French. The lace flounces around the bed, the satin eiderdown – a relic of the thirties. It might be over the top, but she loved it. Over the years, the children had given her embroidered pillows and lacy cushions – they knew how much she liked them. And those curtains, drapes they called them nowadays, with the heavy swags and tails, real silk they were, palest blue lined with cream. Possibly threadbare, but what did it matter? She would hate to part with them. Even the Empire bed she slept on with its painted headboard was a collector's piece.

She sat at the dressing table, slim fingers with their long deep pink nails spread before her. Of course, her hands were lined and there were veins where there hadn't been before, and telltale age marks, but a little foundation lotion smoothed over them helped. She was felling especially bright this morning since reading that Joan Fontaine had been brought out of retirement to play a part in a new film. At seventy-five Victoria was two years younger than Joan. And what had age to do with it? If Joan could do it, so could she.

Edith appeared in the doorway with a hot water bottle, snug in its teddy bear cover.

'Come on, Victoria, time for your nap.'

'Edith, dear, there is no need to be quite so rigid. A rest in the afternoon can quite easily be taken in a chair.'

'Not for you it can't. Into bed with you, and try to sleep, that's the best thing. You've only been out of the nursing home five days and already you're arguing with me. Come on, now. You don't want me to call nurse.'

'God, no!' Victoria shuddered. 'Very well. Wait until my nail polish dries ...'

Edith stood by resolutely after putting the hot bottle in the bed.

'No post, Edith?' They exchanged a glance.

'No. No post. And that's the last thing you should be worrying about.'

She looked stern, unbending, and Victoria slipped out of her housecoat, and got into bed.

'Oh, you are good to me, Edith,' she said, a little wearily.

'Where would I be if it hadn't been for you?' Edith asked, smoothing over the coverlet.

'Married perhaps? With a husband and family, grandchildren by now.'

'No, it wasn't to be,' Edith said. 'Don't you fret about that. Now I'm going to pull the curtains, so you can't read.'

In the half light Victoria dabbed a little *Bal à Versailles* behind her ears, and smoothed her hands with almond cream. How fortunate she had been, except of course for Philip, the tragedy of her life. But she had picked up the pieces. Papa would have been dead thirty-eight years ago this week, and Mama – well, twenty something. She had lived long enough to see Victoria married to Harry and had been so pleased. He had been good to Mama when she became ill. And to me, Victoria thought. It wasn't his fault I didn't love him passionately, not as I loved Philip – but I like to think I made him a good wife, and he certainly was proud of me. We raised a lovely family. Her dark eyes clouded over then.

'I can't be pregnant, can I?' She had turned agonised eyes to Edith all those years ago, as if she could supply the answer.

Edith looked at once grim and anxious.

'Well, if you think so, you probably are,' she said. 'You've always been regular.'

'That's what makes me think,' Victoria said, biting her lip.

'And after all,' Edith said mildly, 'you have – well, you know, with Philip.'

'Oh, what rotten luck!' Victoria wailed. 'I was so careful.'

'Easier said than done, I expect,' Edith said. 'Anyhow, if you are, we have to accept it. The Lord works in – '

'Oh, don't give me any of that religious stuff,' Victoria said irritably, beside herself with worry.

'I'm only saying,' Edith said, not to be put off, 'if you are, you are. Now what?'

'My God!' Victoria said, as the full force of it hit her. 'What shall I do? What will Mama say?'

Her dark eyes were almost black with fear.

'You have only two alternatives – and one is not to be thought of,' Edith said briskly.

'Which one? Having it?'

'No, getting rid of it.' And Victoria looked guilty.

'I'd have to, wouldn't I?'

'Over my dead body,' Edith said firmly. 'You could kill yourself. Do you know how dangerous it is? Those backstreet quacks ... septicaemia .... anything could set in. It would be the finish of your looks, your health, everything – '

'But Edith – a baby? A baby? How on earth – oh, this is terrible, dreadful! Isn't there something about gin and a hot bath?'

Edith stood, hands on hips, with such a look of horror and revulsion on her face that Victoria turned away.

'I never thought to hear you talk like that!' Edith said in the coldest voice Victoria had heard her use yet. 'And if that is truly in your mind, then I shall go!'

'Oh, Edith, you wouldn't! I've no one else to turn to.'

'Then face up to it. Go and visit a doctor, see what he says, and we'll work it out from there. And stop frowning, you'll make lines.'

Well, there was no doubt about it, she was about ten weeks pregnant. The strange doctor congratulated her with a beaming smile.

'Husband overseas, I expect?'

'I'm not married,' Victoria replied, feeling guilty. The doctor gave a slight cough at her honesty. Imagine the difference these days!

Fortunately, Mama was touring in 'The Desert Song' – one

of her favourite roles. 'Blue heaven and you and I, the sand kissing a moonlit sky' – Victoria could hear her, singing around the apartment. Oh, if only life were like that now. And Philip gone, she couldn't believe she would never see him again ...

Hopefully she would not begin to show for a long time. Twice she thought of taking something, or going somewhere, but Edith's reaction had more effect than she'd realised. In desperation one day, railing against her maid, Victoria made her way to an address in the Charing Cross Road which had been given to her by a little soubrette in a musical show, but when she found it she got cold feet. Shuddering, she made her way home on top of a bus, hoping that perhaps the jolting and rocking might do the trick. It hadn't.

So she and Edith planned.

Victoria went for an audition with a minor company who were going to tour America and Canada with a series of Noël Coward plays. She had no difficulty getting into the company, but there was some surprise on the part of the producer, who did not give her the usual recognition and admiration. He probably thinks I'm running away from a sinking ship and leaving old England to its fate, so many people are, Victoria thought. Well, in a way, I am. They were to sail in two weeks, three days after Mama returned from her tour.

'Oh, darling!' she cried when she was told. 'You can't mean it – to cross the Atlantic now, of all times? Running away won't help. You'll get over that young man in time, you'll see.'

'It's not Philip, Mama.'

'You're not worried about raids, are you?' her mother asked suspiciously. She was intensely patriotic.

'No, of course not, but there's not much doing here, and it seems a good chance to get some more experience in rep. After all, a lot of them are over there already, Larry and Viv, David and – '

'Yes, but they've been offered big film parts,' Mama said. 'Oh, I am disappointed in you, Victoria. It's a come down, and that's the last thing you need. You've done so well.'

Victoria looked mutinous. 'I just thought it might be interesting – an experience.' But Mama retained her aloofness right up until the day Victoria sailed.

'How long will you be gone?' she asked on the day of departure.

'Oh, six months – it depends,' Victoria said airily. 'America first, Canada afterwards. I'll write, Mama, I promise – and take care.'

Mama dabbed a lacy handkerchief to her lovely eyes. She really was sorry to see her daughter go. 'You too,' she cried. 'Take care!'

With a sigh of relief, and not without shedding some tears herself, Victoria went to join Edith in the cabin they shared.

'That's that, then,' she said. 'I've burned my boats.' She looked down at herself. Almost four months and it was obvious already – at least to her.

'That's a funny thing to say,' Edith said tartly. 'You've got a lot to look forward to.'

There were times on the crossing when Victoria wished with all her heart that she had not embarked on this mad flight. Sick to her stomach with her pregnancy and the rolling of the ship, she spent most of the time in her cabin. Edith was a tower of strength, but it was with sighs of relief that they landed in New York. Most of the other members of the cast had also been seasick. Once on land, Victoria began to feel better. They had digs near the theatre in Times Square, and the company was well received, sometimes winning a standing ovation. It was hard to believe that across the ocean people were undergoing hardship and a war was going on.

For twelve weeks they played to packed houses all over the eastern seaboard, from Washington and New York, to New England and Massachusetts, then the time came to move north. Thanks to the straight and loose dresses of most of Coward's plays, and its being a first baby, Victoria's pregnancy was not too apparent, but by the time they reached Buffalo, it became difficult to hide.

She was entering her eighth month when they arrived in Canada, and after the first fortnight, decided that to save her face, she must leave the company. Just a few more weeks, she told herself, and found a furnished apartment for herself and Edith on the outskirts of Toronto. Calling herself Mrs Caversham, a visitor from England, a young widow who had come to Canada in order that her child could be born in safety, she convinced the local people. She obviously had money, for she had brought her maid, and she was quite accepted into the neighbourhood. Only her passport told the truth, and the general impression was that she was on an extended visit to await the birth of her child. She and Edith decided there was small chance that anyone would recognise her in her present condition. They went nowhere socially and spent long days walking and enjoying some of the most beautiful scenery in the world.

The doctor who had been recommended to her turned out to be not only a medical adviser but a friend. Dr Mallet, a middle-aged Frenchman, spoke perfect English, and from the first Victoria suspected that he didn't believe her story. When a month had gone by and he called on her to see how she was, she told him the truth, grateful to be sharing it with someone other than Edith. From then on he called often and asked her what her plans were, advising her and discussing the future.

'And you are quite sure you don't want to keep the baby?' His kindly expression was searching but sympathetic.

'Quite sure. I've given it a lot of thought and although I decided to go on with the pregnancy, I know now that I must make a new life, without the baby. He, or she, I hope will be adopted here – I couldn't do as much for him at home with a war going on, and my career, and I want to get back and take up my life again. An actress's life is no good for a baby.'

'You may feel differently when the baby arrives,' he warned her.

'Perhaps, but I don't think so. I am prepared for that, but at the moment I know – I feel – I must give the baby up. And that's why I need your help. Could you put me in touch with an adoption society, to do whatever I have to do?'

He regarded her gravely.

'In my position, I know quite a few private families who would give anything to adopt a baby – wives who can't have a child. With your permission, I could arrange it for you. I have someone in mind just now, a nice young couple. It is certain that she is not going to bear a child. You could think about that. But I will do nothing until after the baby is born. Then you can make a decision. You may be surprised how you feel.'

Gerard Philippe was born at two a.m. on an October

morning, weighing six and a half pounds. He had a quiff of black hair. Victoria stared down at him in wonder. Her labour had not been difficult, only six hours, and afterwards she held him to her, tears running down her face. When they took him away, she slept as she hadn't done for months.

When she opened her eyes, eight hours later, Edith was standing by the bedside, holding him, and at first Victoria had difficulty in taking in what had happened. She held out her arms and Edith handed him to her, a red scrap of humanity, bearing a likeness to no one so far as they could see.

Victoria held him for a brief moment, then kissed him, feeling his soft cheek against hers. The nurse came in and took him from her, and Victoria buried her face in the pillows and wept as she had never wept in her life while Edith sat by the bedside, holding back the tears, her hand covering Victoria's.

She never saw him again.

The young couple, called Dupré, collected him at the end of a week, driving away with him, so the doctor said, as if he was the greatest treasure they had ever had.

'They are a couple in their thirties, he has a good job, they can give him a good home. I can give you their address if you like – although I don't recommend it.'

'No,' Victoria said hastily. 'I trust you. It is for the best, isn't it? Best for him?'

'If that's the way you want it,' the doctor said. 'He will want for nothing, and I shall keep an eye on him. You can leave all the legal work to me, the registering of his birth and so on.'

'And you will keep in touch – you promised?' Victoria said. She had never felt so unhappy in her life. Edith mooned around, hardly saying anything. In two weeks they were packed and ready to go home.

Victoria looked down at her now flat figure. 'It's been like a dream – or a nightmare.'

Edith glanced across at her. She'd changed. There was a hard little look around her mouth that hadn't been there before. God knows, Edith thought, what it cost her to do what she has done. But it was for the best, even she knew that. Victoria wasn't the sort of young woman to be saddled with an illegitimate baby.

'I shall never,' Victoria said, 'never come back to Canada again, but I want him to grow up strong and healthy in this wonderful air, with that nice young family, and you must help me, Edith. No hanging around with a long face, I can't bear it.'

'Right,' she said. 'Yes, madam.' And they glanced tearfully at each other before Victoria suddenly flung her arms around Edith and hugged her. 'Oh, what would I have done without you!' she cried. 'You are like a sister to me – more than a sister, a true friend. Now, let's never talk of it again. Back to New York – then home.'

They arrived to a blacked out London, subject to raids day and night, but after Canada it was easier to accept. They were two different worlds.

Mama, who had high hopes of being in Ivor Novello's new show at the Phoenix Theatre, was waiting anxiously for her daughter. She saw a change in Victoria at once. If anything, she was more beautiful, thinner in the face, her eyes appeared larger, more luminous. Something has happened over there, she told herself, but Victoria will tell me when – and if – she wants to.

She kept a low profile and made no enquiries, just watched Victoria pick up the threads again and settle back to a life in wartime London. Theatreland bore no resemblance to what it had been. There had been no shows from Broadway for almost four years, and although Novello himself was still playing at the Adelphi in 'The Dancing Years', the only new prospect was his forthcoming production at the Phoenix.

Victoria embarked on a spree, as Edith called it. Parties, working at the Stage Door Canteen, flirting outrageously ... to have fun was the order of the day. It was as if she was on a social whirl and couldn't stop. If she did, Edith thought grimly, she would collapse with exhaustion.

It was then, when she was at her gayest and most brittle, that she met Harry Bellamy, and it was as if a cinder had sparked off a fire. They were perfect opposites – he, big, tough, hard as nails, a man who knew what he wanted, and Victoria at her most vulnerable.

When they were introduced, Victoria recognised the chemistry between them. He had looked down at her and the expression in his eyes she could read very well. It caused a little shiver to run through her, and she accepted the challenge. He wanted her and in a strange way she needed him. Sex, she thought, purely and simply sex. That was all there was between them. She took a delight in teasing him, looking up at him with eyes that showed the promise of unbelievable delights, and he was like a puppet on a string. As time went by she discovered that she liked him – or perhaps admired was the truer word. Liked the way he went after anything he wanted; his single-minded pursuit of any desire, including herself. And he was rich, and had position. Wasn't that what she wanted?

For all that, she was a little surprised when he asked her to marry him. She took it flippantly, but he looked serious. 'You think I don't mean it?'

She smiled up at him.

'You'd have to give me time to think about it.'

'I must tell you, Victoria,' he said, 'my patience is not limitless.'

She enjoyed those first few days after his proposal. It seemed to give her added strength to know she was desired, craved, by one of the most successful men in the country. True, he had made a great deal of money from the war effort but he had been a great success before that. He was much admired and envied – a man who liked his own way. She wondered what he might be like as a husband, and decided she could deal with him. With her beloved Philip gone, what did it matter?

She had kept him dangling for a week or two when the letter with the Canadian postmark arrived – the first communication she had had apart from a Christmas card from the doctor.

Never so long as she lived would she forget the news that letter contained. That the child she had given birth to nine months before had not been responding to tests, and that there was a possibility he might be retarded. 'I knew you would wish to know,' the good doctor wrote.

Victoria covered her mouth with her hand to prevent a gasp of horror. 'Edith!' she called desperately. 'Edith!'

The doctor had thought she should know, because if this was the case, then it might alter things. The child might require treatment, or a different set of foster parents, and if he required special treatment, Dr Mallet was sure she would be willing to help.

'But they adopted him!' Edith cried. 'Didn't they?'

'But he doesn't become legally theirs until the end of a year,' Victoria said. 'Oh, Edith, why should this happen? We were both healthy people.' And as Edith's eyes met hers, they widened. 'I didn't do anything – take anything – if that crossed your mind.'

'I know you didn't,' Edith said. 'I was thinking how tragic for the little lad. He was so beautiful, there was no way of knowing – '

'Perhaps they are mistaken,' Victoria said hopefully. 'Oh, Edith, I feel I must do something – go and see him – bring him back.'

'You'll do no such thing!' Edith showed astonishing strength of mind. 'He is their child now – and what could you do for him? He is in the best place. What we must do is to be brave and think calmly. And wait to hear again from Dr Mallet.'

Victoria referred to the letter. 'He says these things take time and further tests may be necessary before they are sure.'

'Then let's look on the bright side,' Edith said with a confidence she was far from feeling.

But Victoria was thinking of the proposal. More than ever she needed someone to take charge of her life, to give her security. If she was in for trouble, she would need money and there certainly was not enough to go round as things stood. She lived in her mother's apartment, on which Mama owned a long lease. When she died, Victoria would take it over. Other than that, she had a little money left by her father and whatever she earned as an actress, but you couldn't rely on that to pay the bills – like doctor's bills. She could never let Harry Bellamy know. It must be her secret. But she was good at keeping secrets. There was no way he need ever find out. He would not expect her to be a virgin, but could she keep from him the fact that she had borne a child? It was worth taking a chance on.

She looked exquisite the night she told him she would marry him. In the firelight, over a candlelit dinner in his apartment in Park Lane, overlooking the park, she smiled at him and his heart began to race.

She put out a hand, beringed with the antique yellow diamond and on her little finger an oval emerald set in small diamonds that her father had given her for her twenty-first birthday.

'Yes, Harry,' she said softly. 'I will marry you.'

He was round the table in a second, clasping her to him, feeling her slight body beneath the slippery satin, his heart beating madly, the greatest prize in his arms. She felt her body respond as she slid her arms around his neck and brought his face down to hers.

When he broke away his eyes were dark and smouldering.

'I'll give you the world,' he said thickly.

'I only want you, Harry,' she said, recalling a line from a play.

'There is one thing I forgot to mention,' he said later.

'What is it?' She raised ingenuous eyes to him.

'No more acting,' he said chancing his arm and waiting for a scene.

But she smiled at him, one of her glorious smiles.

'Of course not, darling,' she said demurely.

Chapter Nine

The emeralds were the first gift Harry gave her as an engagement present. She could feel them now as he had fastened them around her neck, standing behind her, eyes glowing down at her, as proud as a peacock at his new possession.

'I won't tell you what I paid for them – but you are worth every penny,' he said, with the self-made man's desire to say how much they cost.

Victoria knew, for it was in all the daily papers for everyone to see. A record figure at auction ... Victoria Worth's engagement gift from her husband to be, and then the photograph in *Country Life*.

She instinctively put a hand to her bare throat, remembering how she felt as they'd sat there, heavy, cold, brilliant. In the mirror they had looked magnificent.

'Come along now, exercise – are we ready?' And Nurse Lindstrom entered, shattering her thoughts. Oh, wretched woman – how Victoria hated anything to do with being ill ... Still, the ogre was due to leave tomorrow. She had already been with them for two weeks.

'Gently does it. Now the right arm – lift, down, and once more. Keep your back straight ...'

Victoria did as she was told, her face expressionless, for the whole of the five minutes, and when they stopped was surprised to see Geoffrey waiting in the hall, carrying a sheaf of roses.

'Thank you, nurse,' Victoria said, dismissing her, and went forward to greet him.

'Geoffrey, darling, how nice to see you.'

'I thought I'd call in on my way to lunch. I'm meeting Julian at one.'

'Oh,' she said. 'Anything special?'

'No, we do this occasionally when he surfaces. As you know he is so seldom free.'

He didn't tell her that it was Julian's suggestion that they meet – he seemed to have something on his mind.

'I know. Well, give him my love. I expect he'll call in sometime.'

He sat down and hitched up his immaculate dark grey trousers. 'So how've you been?'

'Just fine. Nurse was just giving me some remedial exercises.'

'Very good,' he approved. 'You are looking wonderful, and so much better.'

'I know, darling, and I feel so well. I have been sitting here, making plans.'

'What sort of plans?'

'Never you mind. I shall reveal them when I am ready.' And she smiled, a small secret smile.

'How long is she staying – the battleaxe?'

'She's going tomorrow,' Victoria said, delighted at the thought.

'And is Edith coping?'

'Of course she is! You know Edith – she's a tower of strength. What would you like as a pre-lunch drink? Whisky, sherry?'

'A dry Martini if I may – one has to be careful these days, so I caught the train up. It's no hardship and saves all the hassle of driving into town.'

'Of course.' Victoria rang the little bell at her side, and asked Edith for a sherry for herself and a Martini for Geoffrey.

'So aren't you going to tell me what you have planned? Is it to be a well-kept secret?' he asked.

'No, I'm being silly – well, I'll tell you, but don't mention it to the others just yet. They'll try to stop me.'

'Stop you? Doing what?' Edith came in with a tray of drinks and Victoria waited until she had gone.

'Going back to work.' And now he was shocked.

'Mother!' He was going to say 'At your age!' but stopped himself in time. 'Well, if you think that's a good idea – '

'I do. Whether or not I can get work is something else, but lots of people do who are a lot older than I – '

'But you've been out of it so long, and it's quite hard.'

'Darling, I've told you so many times, the hardest part of being an actor is when you are out of work! I can't wait to get the adrenaline going – I might surprise you all!'

She was quite incredible, he thought.

'I shall get in touch with my erstwhile agent, see what he can do for me. Anyway, enough of that. How is everything at Jarretts?'

'Fine.' He was glad to get off the subject. He found it disconcerting, and there was no way he would mention it to Ruth.

'The garden is looking lovely – you must come down with Edith when you feel up to it. Ruth is holding a garden party on Saturday, something to do with deprived children.'

'How nice,' Victoria said. 'Such a worthy cause. It's a good thing there are people like Ruth. If it was left to me – '

'You contribute in other ways.' He smiled at her, and finished his Martini. Stretching his legs, he stood up.

'Well, it's nice to see you looking so well, I must be on my way.' He glanced at his watch. 'I only popped in for a moment.'

'I'm always glad to see you – any time,' Victoria said, reaching up to kiss him. 'Give my love to Julian and the family, and thank you for the roses.'

'I will, Mother, don't worry. I'll see myself out.'

Outside, hailing a cab, he spent the entire short journey thinking of his mother's idea of going back to work, and decided by the time he reached his club that the idea was out of the question, though it did no harm to humour her.

All the same, it was one of the first things he mentioned when he and Julian were seated opposite each other in the pleasant mellow dining room with its leather-covered chairs and rose-coloured lamps.

Julian threw back his head and laughed out loud.

'Isn't she a nutcase! What next? Still, it shows that she must be feeling well.'

Geoffrey took consolation from this. 'Yes, you're right.'

After the soup course, he studied his brother and wondered

what he was up to now. Judging by his tie and his suit, he was doing very well. Good-looking cove, Geoffrey decided, a chap the girls would fall for. They never could resist a handsome face even though commonsense told them other women would feel the same, and they could never be quite sure what he was up to. Dark, aquiline good looks – the phrase came to him from nowhere – but that summed up his brother. He was a slim handsome edition of his father, but there the likeness ended. Much as Julian would have liked to be a successful tycoon, he never would be, although doubtless he earned a good living messing about with his silver and antiques. Something Geoffrey had never been interested in, not in the slightest. He left that side of things to Ruth.

'So what are you up to at the moment?' he asked.

'Got back from Amsterdam last night.'

'Good thing you've got a strong constitution, I couldn't take all that travelling about.'

'No, it's not for everyone. I happen to like it – especially when I pull off a good deal, like I did a couple of weeks ago.'

'Really?' Geoffrey tackled his fillet of beef and helped himself to more horseradish.

'Yes, in consequence of which I decided to ask you to lunch. I've been giving a lot of thought to Mother. I suppose you could say this heart attack, fall, whatever it was, should be a warning to us. Weren't you surprised?'

'Yes, I suppose I was. After all, I never remember her being ill before. But she's fine, honestly.'

'Oh, good.' Julian's long white fingers held his fork delicately as they tackled the salmon cutlet.

'It makes you realise – well – that she is seventy-five. And I suppose ...'

'Yes?' Geoffrey waited.

'Well, if she should be taken ill again, really ill – I mean, what would happen?'

'I'm not sure I follow you,' Geoffrey said, dabbing his mouth with his napkin.

'Well, you know, she could hardly stay in the flat. I suppose she would go down to Jarretts? I mean, the idea of a permanent nursing home – '

'I think you're jumping the gun, old boy,' Geoffrey said,

dealing with the crisp roast potatoes and sitting back to enjoy them.

'Maybe.' Julian munched silently while Geoffrey thought.

Perhaps he ought to be a little more helpful. After all, Ruth had brought up the same topic. Perhaps he had been a little remiss.

'I'm as concerned as you are, Julian, but I don't see any need for us to worry at the moment. After all, she could go on until she's ninety or a hundred. Look at the Queen Mother.'

'Yes, I know. But it made me think of Jarretts.' And now Geoffrey felt a pang of guilt.

'Jarretts – why?'

'Well, it's between the three of us, isn't it?'

'Naturally,' Geoffrey said, 'but look here ...'

Julian suddenly gave him a beaming smile, one that never failed to disarm a client.

'No, I'll tell you what, Geoffrey – I'll tell you what started me off on this tack. Last week I sold a magnificent emerald necklace – you'll never guess what for?' And his dark eyes gleamed.

'No – what?' Geoffrey's face was deadpan.

'Three-quarters of a million,' said Julian.

'Good God!' his brother exclaimed. 'And I suppose your commission on that was quite nice, eh?'

'Exactly,' Julian agreed, 'but it made me think – Mother has a fabulous emerald necklace.' And Geoffrey was reminded anew of Ruth's questions. There were no two ways about it, he just hated personal questions and talk of this sort – and now his brother was at the same thing!

He was so vague and disinterested that Julian felt a little annoyed.

'Well, it's not peanuts, old boy,' he said. 'I mean, where is it? The necklace?'

'In the bank, surely?' Geoffrey said mildly. And not where you can get your hands on it, I hope, he thought.

'I daresay. Still, these things need to be sorted out. I mean –' He hesitated. 'Her will – '

Geoffrey felt suddenly chilled at the thought. 'Look, Julian, let's not talk about this now. We're spoiling a perfectly good lunch.'

And now Julian became obdurate.

'I still think, Geoffrey, we should know where we stand – in the event. I imagine her solicitor has her will, and deals with her personal matters. After all, you don't have anything to do with the financial side, do you?'

'I? No, not at all. She's always conducted her affairs through Casebow – carried on where Father left off, I suppose. And I must say, it's never cropped up.'

'So when she moved out of Jarretts, you and Ruth stayed on. I moved out when I married, and Vanessa left home. That's about it, is it?'

Geoffrey found himself feeling distinctly uncomfortable under close scrutiny from his younger brother.

'Yes, that's the way of it,' he said. 'Well, I suppose in the event we should know a little more than we do – but leave it to me, I'll sort something out.'

'Yes, it might be useful. After all, we don't want to be caught napping, as it were.'

Geoffrey finished his lunch.

'I don't imagine that we need concern ourselves yet awhile. Still you're probably right.' It occurred to him that he'd had the best of the arrangement so far. Living at Jarretts, only paying the bills for gas, heating and electricity – that had been the arrangement.

'Jarretts is still your home, Mother,' they had said.

By the time they had finished dessert and cheese, talk was of other things.

'Who is the lucky lady of the moment?' Geoffrey asked pleasantly. 'Anyone in tow?'

'Not really,' Julian said. 'I quite enjoy being a bachelor again. It's better the second time around.'

'It would be nice if you'd settle down, have a family. I know Mother would be pleased.'

'Yes, I think she would – but a second Mrs Julian Bellamy would have to be someone special. Have you seen Vanessa lately?'

'No, she's up to something. I think she's gone back to that Weston chap. She's keeping a very low profile at the moment, and that's usually when she's doing something that she knows we won't like.'

He motioned the waiter. 'Still, it's her affair, her life,' he said, and smiled warmly.

'Thanks for the lunch, Geoffrey,' said Julian. 'My love to Ruth and the girls – be down to see you soon.'

'That'll be nice,' Geoffrey said, glad lunch was over. With a bit of luck he would be home in an hour.

'More flowers!' Victoria laughed when Julian came in, handing her a spray of white lilies. 'Darling, they're heavenly – the scent!'

'You old spoofer!' he laughed. 'I don't believe you've been ill at all. She's having us on, Edith.'

Edith looked at him fondly. Of the three of them, he was her favourite. She left them to have a chat.

'So tell me what you have been doing?' Victoria said, making herself comfortable in the big wing chair.

'Well, I won't tell you everything.' He gave her a wicked smile.

'Oh, what a pity,' she said. 'I expect you will leave out the most interesting bits.' And she laughed. 'So where have you been?'

He sat down opposite her. 'Let me think. Switzerland, Paris, Amsterdam – '

He was halfway through his travels when the doorbell rang. He looked up and glanced at his watch.

'Edith will get it, I'm not expecting anyone.'

'I'll go,' he said.

'No.' And she put out a hand. 'Now you stay there, I see you far too seldom.' The door opened and Edith put her head inside.

'Someone to see you,' she said, half smiling.

Victoria frowned.

'Who is it?' she mouthed.

'A lady – here's her card.'

Victoria glanced down at it. 'Countess Venetia Tellini – I don't know anyone of that name.'

'Well, she would like to see you,' Edith said patiently, pointing to the address below the name. 'Rome,' she said, looking significantly at her employer.

'Better show her in,' Victoria said, picking up a hand mirror and glancing at her reflection.

'I'd better go,' Julian offered, getting up.

'No, stay. She won't be long, I expect she's from some charity or other.'

They both looked up when Venetia came in, a vision of loveliness. Julian's eyes were riveted on her face, a perfect oval, dark hair pulled back, large lustrous brown eyes, and the loveliest smile he had ever seen.

Victoria stared at her, then held out her hand. 'I am Victoria Bellamy,' she said.

And from that perfect mouth came the most melodious voice either of them had ever heard, low and sweet.

'I am Venetia Tellini. I do hope you don't mind my calling on you like this? I so wanted to meet you.'

'Er – not at all.'

'I am Violet Santucci's daughter.'

This lovely glamorous creature Violet Pemberton's daughter? How was it possible? Julian suddenly came down to earth and held out his hand.

'Julian Bellamy – Victoria's son.'

'How do you do?' The low voice entranced him, and he looked into smiling brown eyes, and took the cool, slim hand she offered him.

'Do sit down. Edith, could we have some tea – or coffee if the countess would prefer?'

'Oh, please, call me Venetia – and tea would be lovely.'

Julian hastily dragged forward a chair and Venetia sat down gracefully, crossing yards of silken-clad leg and knowing exactly how to sit elegantly in a very short skirt. Her suit, Victoria recognised, was of the finest quality. Italian, of course, cream-coloured silk. She seemed quite unaware of the effect she had had on them – probably used to it, Victoria thought drily. Well, what a turn up for the book! as Harry used to say.

'My dear.' She sat back in her chair, now quite recovered from the shock. 'How very nice of you to come. Do you live in London or are you visiting?'

'I am on a visit,' Venetia said. 'Mama often spoke of you, and when she knew I was coming to London, asked me if I would call on you and give you her kind regards.'

'How very kind of you,' Victoria said.

'Not just for Mama, but I had heard so much about you, I had always wanted to meet the famous Victoria Bellamy – you see, your fame spread even to Italy.' And she glanced across at Julian with smiling brown eyes.

He cleared his throat and looked at his mother fondly. 'I'm glad to say she is better now, although as we tell her she must take life quietly.' He saw Victoria's slight frown. 'At least for a few days,' he finished hastily.

'Are you staying in London?' Victoria asked as Edith came in with the tea tray. 'Put it down there, Edith. I'll pour.'

'Yes, at The Dorchester.'

'Is your husband with you?' Victoria asked, pouring the tea into an eggshell thin cup.

Venetia looked at her frankly.

'No – I am divorced, or about to be. I am afraid my marriage was not successful. My husband – ' And she sighed deeply, leaving Julian with a strong desire to kill him, whoever he was, and Victoria to cluck in sympathy.

'My dear, I am so sorry.'

'That is why I came to London. Mama thought I should have a small vacation after the stress of – '

She held her head high, and gave them a small smile.

'But let us not talk about me. Your mother looks wonderful,' she said to Julian, and gave Victoria a look of sheer admiration from those lovely eyes.

'Thank you,' she said. 'I have to admit that I do feel much better. In fact I am quite recovered.'

'I am so glad. Thank you,' as she took the proffered cup of tea. 'No sugar, thank you.' And Julian watched her sip the tea with those luscious lips. That lovely golden tan was the most desirable shade of all and he wondered where she stood in the pecking order of Roman society.

'Is your mother the Violet who sent the get well card?' he asked politely.

'Yes, I believe she did. You were at school together, I think?'

'Yes,' Victoria said, 'at Roedean. We lost touch. Of course the war did that to so many people ...'

Venetia smiled sweetly. That wasn't quite what her mother had said. Still, the son was dishy, which was a bonus, and the old lady herself quite something. She had lost none of her charm.

'How nice that your son is able to call in on you,' she said. 'Do you live in London, too?' She raised ingenuous eyes to him.

'I do when I'm here which isn't often. I travel a lot.'

'I see.'

'I have another son,' Victoria said. 'He is older than Julian, and a daughter, Vanessa – I was hoping she might call in today.'

'What a lovely family,' Venetia smiled, genuinely envious.

By the time she left she felt she knew exactly who was who and who lived where, and had promised to call again. When she got up to leave, Julian did too.

'May I give you a lift? I have my car outside? I have to drive up Park Lane.'

Venetia rose to her feet, as graceful as a gazelle.

'Thank you so much, that is kind of you.'

She took Victoria's hand. 'I am so pleased to have met you, Victoria, may I come again?'

'Please do,' she said warmly.

She was intrigued by this young woman. It was a long time since she had met anyone quite so interesting and she couldn't wait to tell Vanessa about her.

How odd, though, this modern trend of calling everyone by their Christian name. Already she was Victoria to this young woman. How times changed! When she thought back to the protocol of the old days when Mama was alive, leaving calling cards, never addressing an older person without their title – the war changed all that, of course.

But she certainly wasn't going to think about that now. Far better to concentrate on this young woman, and the suit she was wearing – wonderful! The cut – was it Armani or Versace? – at any rate, it was one of the moderns. As distinct from Worth or Schiaparelli as it could be. She took the bottle of *Bal à Versailles* and dabbed it on her wrists. Hmm, it brought back all sorts of memories ...

Chapter Ten

Vanessa Bellamy was packing her weekend case for the journey down to Haslemere. She had got to the stage of looking forward to these weekends, getting out of London and driving down with Gavin to the delightful cottage nestling on a hillside. This one would be a little different, she suspected, because Denise, the French au pair who looked after Tom, would be there, and might feel that Vanessa cramped her style. So far Vanessa had been getting on slowly but surely with Gavin's son.

She wished she knew what Gavin was really thinking sometimes. Was he remembering all the other times when he and Suzie had driven down to the home they had created together? Then she chided herself for fretting over nothing. But she could never quite get over the feeling that she was in another woman's home, a house so redolent of another's personality. Suzie's kitchen and bathrooms, Suzie's taste – it could never be hers. Vanessa just lived in the hope that one day she and Gavin might marry, and then she could change it, have it the way she wanted. And, she thought, have a child of my own. I want that more than anything ...

Gavin glanced at her, and smiled. It was ridiculous, how she felt when he looked at her like that. The way his hair grew, how his skin looked after a shave, the shape of his eyebrows and those long lashes – quite rare in a man – dark eyes, firm jaw and straight nose adding strength – he's like a macho Terence Stamp, she thought.

'Did you see your mother yesterday?' he asked presently.

'No, I didn't. I worked late, and what with one thing and another –'

'How is she getting along?'

'Fairly well, I think. She was fine last weekend, anyway.'

Kind of him to ask, she thought, knowing as he did that her mother had never really taken to him. Polite though she had been on the rare occasions she had met him, Victoria never warmed to him, and being the kind of man he was, Gavin was aware of this.

'I thought I'd stop off and get some wine,' he said, making for a small parade of shops. 'I'm running a bit low, and in case the order hasn't been delivered, I think I should.'

'Shall I come with you?'

'No need.'

She sat in the car outside the shops, her mind on the long-term relationship she hoped to have with him. Vanessa was always asking herself if she was being sensible, or if this was just another flash in the pan as far as Gavin was concerned? She didn't delude herself he felt as deeply for her as he had for Suzie, but she was prepared to settle for the next best thing. There would be nothing she would like more than to be a permanent part of his life.

'That's that, then,' Gavin said, returning from the off licence with a case of wine which he put in the boot.

Vanessa waited until he was settled in the driving seat.

'If we get back to town reasonably early tomorrow, I wonder if you would drop me off at Mother's? I'll get a taxi back to the flat.'

'Yes, sure,' Gavin said, and put out a hand to cover hers, giving her a reassuring smile as they approached the cottage.

Letting himself in, he took the wine into the kitchen, followed by Vanessa. Through the window they saw Mrs Benson in the garden, coming in with a basket of vegetables, and by the light shining through the oven door, it was clear she had dinner cooking.

'Ah, there you are.' She smiled at them, her small sturdy figure enveloped in a garden apron. 'Did you have a good journey down?'

'Yes, thanks,' Gavin answered. 'Where's Tom?'

'He's with Denise at the pool, I expect. I'll go and tell them you're here.'

'No, I'll go,' Gavin said. He turned to Vanessa, saying 'Coming?' and put out a hand.

They walked round to the back of the house to the small blue pool. Tom was playing in a sandpit at the side while Denise sat and watched him. Hearing footsteps, Tom looked up. He got to his feet, ran and threw himself at his father. Gavin picked him up and hugged him.

Denise stood by, half smiling. It turned to a frown when she saw the other arrival.

Vanessa smiled and said, 'Hello, Denise.' She nodded a greeting. Her eyes were so dark they were almost black, her small frame as thin as a reed. She had nut brown skin, and black hair cropped as close to her head as it was possible to be. She wore a navy bikini, espadrilles on her feet.

'Say hello to Vanessa, Tom,' Gavin said to the small boy, who turned and held out his hand formally.

'Hello.'

'Well, let's make ourselves at home,' said his father. 'Are you coming, Tom?'

He took his father's hand, while Denise picked up the towels lying by the side of the pool and followed them.

'Did you swim?' Gavin asked.

'Yes, Denise has been teaching me and I can swim under water.'

'Really?' Gavin turned to ask Denise, who nodded.

'Yes, 'e is doing very well.'

Later Gavin unpacked from the car, while Vanessa took off her jacket and opened her bag, taking from it a small package.

'I hope you like this,' she said, giving it to Tom.

His eyes were dancing as he opened the bag, and withdrew a small yellow bulldozer.

''e 'as one of them,' Denise said.

'It doesn't matter,' said Tom. 'It will go with my collection.'

'So say thank you,' Denise said.

Oh, I'm not doing very well, Vanessa thought. Still, it's early days.

She went upstairs with her overnight bag to the room she shared with Gavin. At the back of the house, it was the main guest room, with pretty mullioned windows, a king-sized bed with blue and white damask bedcovers, and drapes from the ceiling. There were white-painted cupboards and fitments and an ensuite bathroom to match. Snow white towels and lots of blue and white china and a bowl of dried blue cornflowers. The room overlooked the garden and the hill behind. Very designer, Vanessa thought to herself, and why do I feel so bitchy? At least it isn't the main bedroom, the room he shared with Suzie ...

After lunch, she and Gavin took Tom for a walk in the beechwoods, which were lovely at this time of the year. There were squirrels and the sight of a retreating fox's tail, which pleased Tom no end, then back to the house for a swim. The air was fresh and tangy after London, and it was bliss to lie there and do nothing but think.

Tom was allowed to stay up for dinner, a roast prepared by Mrs Benson, after which she went off to spend the evening with her sister who lived in Alfriston.

Vanessa helped to bathe the little boy, who had been tanned by the French sun. He sat in the bath playing with his boats and plastic cups and bottles, anything that would hold water to be poured. Afterwards she tucked him up in bed and read him a story, at which point his thumb went into his mouth, and when the story was over Vanessa tucked him in and kissed him lightly, her throat constricting as she did so. Who knew what thoughts were going on in this little chap's head? Was he missing his mother very much? Being brave? After all, the housekeeper, Denise, herself, even Gavin, nothing made up for a mother's love, and they had been very close. A surge of near hatred rose in her at the thought of Suzie leaving her family behind. What excuse could there possibly be for that? It had to be pure selfishness. Angrily, she went to her room and lay on the bed until she had composed herself, then went downstairs to join Gavin where they listened to music until it was time to go up.

Once in bed, she had no doubts at all. After all, for five years she had shared a bed with Gavin, until they broke up for that year, and although it had not been a continuous thing – she hadn't actually lived with him – still they were as close as two people could be. He made love to her gently, considering her, they had a natural togetherness, but it wasn't passion. Had he been passionate with Suzie? Or was that what Suzie missed? Had she wanted a dynamic man, a man who would dominate her, for Gavin wasn't that kind. He was warm and considerate and kind. Any drama in his life he saved for his books and films. Whatever, Vanessa thought, I love him, I always will, no matter what happens. I just want to make him happy. Be happy. She lay long after he was asleep, thinking in the darkness about him and the little boy who slept next-door.

The next morning was fine and sunny, and Gavin announced at breakfast that he would like a game of golf.
'Would you mind, Vanessa?'
'Of course not,' she assured him. She knew he liked to play when he could, and he hadn't had a game for ages.
'We'll find lots to do, won't we, Tom?'
Denise appeared after breakfast, Sunday being her day for a lie in.
What a serious little thing she was, Vanessa thought. Her dark little face, wide black eyes ... did she ever really smile? This morning she appeared sulky and ate her breakfast in silence, despite Vanessa's efforts to talk.
Having got the message, Vanessa wandered upstairs, leaving Tom in his room surrounded by toys. Alone, she tidied her things, then walked along the narrow corridor. Tom's room, Mrs Benson's room, Denise's room, the spare guest room she shared with Gavin, a family bathroom, and this one.
She opened the door. This must be the main bedroom overlooking the front, a splendid large room which Tom had shown her very briefly when she first came to the house. The walls were panelled in dark wood, and there was a fourposter bed draped in what she imagined must be hundreds of yards of glazed chintz and matching curtains with fringes and tassels – very claustrophobic, she decided. She walked across the room to peek into the bathroom which had been done in the same way, panelled walls and dark towels. She shivered slightly. Feeling guilty, she couldn't resist the temptation to open one of the built-in cupboards and was relieved to find it empty of clothes, but stacked inside with paintings, oils, and they were good, she could see that. Each was signed 'Suzanne Weston'. So Suzie could paint. A fierce stab of jealousy went through her, which she stifled. Not only had the golden Suzie been loved, adored even, had a son and Gavin and a lovely home, but she was talented as well for the paintings were very accomplished. Vanessa bit her lip.

'What are you doing in 'ere?'

She turned to find the accusing eye of Denise on her. After the first wave of guilt, Vanessa stood her ground.

'I beg your pardon?'

Her tone so cool that even Denise realised she had overstepped the mark.

'Can I 'elp you? Was there something you wanted?'

'Not particularly,' Vanessa replied, determined that once and for all she would put things straight with this slip of a girl.

She came towards the door, closing it behind her.

'I was looking at Mrs Weston's paintings. I had been told she painted – they're very good.' The lie came easily.

'She was an artist,' Denise said, almost proudly.

'Yes, obviously,' Vanessa replied. 'Would you like to make some coffee? I'll come downstairs, we'll have it in the kitchen.'

There was a moment's pause, then Denise went downstairs.

The coffee pot stood on the kitchen table, one mug beside it. Vanessa sat down. 'Aren't you going to join me?' Her smile was determinedly pleasant.

Denise shrugged, then got another mug from the dresser. They sat, in silence for a few moments until Vanessa decided to break the ice.

'Have you worked for the family long?'

'Oui – yes, for four years.' It surprised Vanessa. After all, Tom was only just six.

'Oh, quite a long time. Whereabouts do you live in France?'

'Near Nice – a small village, you would not know it. My father 'as a business there. It is a family business.'

She was more relaxed now, talking about her family, and Vanessa listened closely.

'Is that where you met Mrs Weston?'

'Suzie – yes.' And suddenly her whole face was transformed. Her black eyes shone, and she smiled at the memory.

'I was working in a boutique in Nice, in our best hotel, to gain experience, you understand, selling beautiful scarves and belts and handbags – such famous names, such perfumes, for very rich clients. One day Suzie came in with the little boy, and I was very un'appy that day. I 'ad a row with my fiance, and I 'ad been crying, and she was very kind.

'She bought some things, then she asked me if I would like to come au pair to England? Oh, I was so excited. My parents were pleased, for they wished me to learn my English better, and so I come to England.'

Vanessa looked at the sadness in the small dark face.

'You miss her, don't you?'

'I love 'er,' said Denise. 'She was kind to me, and so beautiful, so elegant – it is not the same now she 'as gone.'

'But why – ' Vanessa began. She was about to ask why Denise stayed.

'I promise Suzie. It would break 'er 'eart if I leave Tom. And 'e,' nodding her head, ''e will not let 'er 'ave 'im.'

Realising she was treading on dangerous ground, Vanessa decided to say no more. This whole business became more upsetting the farther into it she got.

'Well, I had better have a peep at Tom. You go, Denise, when you want. He'll be all right with me.'

She hurried to the nursery where she found Tom exactly where she had left him, on the floor with his toys. She sat down and joined him.

'We'll leave early – as soon as Tom is in bed, if you like?' Gavin suggested after their lunch of cold beef and salad.

'Whenever you like.' Vanessa smiled. 'Do you have to get back so early?'

'Well, I know you want to see your mother. And there are one or two things I have to do.'

She hadn't enjoyed this weekend as much as some, Vanessa thought, on the way home. Perhaps because of the conversation with Denise. If she hadn't gone into that bedroom and looked, she might never have learned Suzie was an artist – or heard Denise's story.

'How do you get on with Denise?' Gavin asked suddenly.

'Oh, quite well. She thinks the world of Tom.' And Suzie, she could have said.

'Yes, I've been giving some thought to that.'

'What do you mean?'

'Well, I'm not altogether sure that the present arrangement really works.' And Vanessa's heart leapt. Had he something in mind concerning herself?

'After all, she won't stay forever. I think she's already keen to go back to France, and Tom will be going to boarding school when he is eight.'

'Oh, Gavin, so young!'

He shot her a glance.

'Not really. If he's going, that's the best time for him to go. And I've been considering whether I might get rid of the cottage and move permanently to London.'

'Oh, but you'd miss it, wouldn't you?' she murmured, elated that he would even think about it, breaking all strong ties with Suzie. What else did he have in mind?

But she was not to know the answer for they were caught in a traffic jam approaching Knightsbridge and he hated to talk while he was concentrating on driving.

When they arrived outside her mother's block of flats, Vanessa kissed him briefly and got out.

'I'll see you in a while,' she said. 'I won't be long.'

'Would you like me to pick you up?'

'No, thanks, darling. I'll get a taxi.'

At her ring, Edith unlocked the door and opened it, and Vanessa could hear the sound of low voices and a little laughter.

'Has Mother got visitors?' she asked, surprised.

'Yes,' Edith said shortly.

'Who?' she whispered.

'I don't think you've met her yet,' Edith said a trifle sourly. 'She is Venetia – I beg your pardon – Countess Tellini.'

'Who?' Vanessa stressed, and grinned, before making her way to the drawing room where she tapped on the door and went in.

'Darling!' Victoria cried, delighted to see her. 'Oh, what a lovely surprise! I didn't think I was going to see you this weekend.'

'You nearly didn't.' Vanessa kissed her, staring at the vision of loveliness over her mother's shoulder.

'Oh, of course you haven't met, have you? Venetia, my daughter Vanessa. Vanessa – Venetia Tellini.'

They shook hands, and there was no mistaking the warmth in Venetia's dark eyes or the fabulous scent that emanated from her.

'I am so pleased to meet you, Vanessa.' Her low tones were like music.

'Venetia is the daughter of an old school friend – Violet Santucci,' Victoria explained. Her face was flushed with pleasure, Vanessa noted. Obviously the visitor was good for her. Her eyes were sparkling, and a half smile hovered about her mouth.

'Do sit down, darling,' she said, 'Did you enjoy your weekend?'

'Yes,' Vanessa replied. No point in hiding it now. 'I went down to Haslemere.'

'Oh, lovely,' Victoria said.

'I think perhaps it is time I made a move,' Venetia said prettily, about to get to her feet.

'No, you stay there – I haven't finished hearing what happened next. Besides, we are going to have champagne.'

'What are we celebrating?' Vanessa asked curiously.

'My return to health, darling,' her mother said smugly. 'Can you think of a better reason?'

Vanessa laughed. 'You old spoofer,' she said, taking off her jacket when she hadn't intended to stay long.

What was all this about? She felt she wanted to know more about the beautiful Venetia.

Chapter Eleven

There was a sparkle in Victoria's eyes this morning as she made up her face in front of the mirror. Really, she didn't look too bad – for her age. And today she was going out for the first time, thanks to Venetia. Dear girl. What a lucky day it had been when she'd decided to write to Violet, after all these years.

For Venetia had come into her life like a breath of spring, just when she was most needed, with a glimpse of another world: the world of fashion and smart women and the society pages, Italian and French. No account things, frivolous things, just what one needed when housebound. It was no use Edith looking disapproving. If it was left to her Victoria would probably be taken out in a wheelchair. But she mustn't be unkind. Edith had been a brick. All the way through, she could never have managed without her. But Edith was old – like me, she thought – and you needed youth and laughter around you sometimes. Venetia was certainly amusing, kind, with a gentle humour, and Victoria wondered how old she was. After all, Violet must be seventy something, although apparently she had had Venetia quite late in life. Well, no matter. It was not important.

The startling thing was that this radiant young woman was Violet's daughter. But there, life was full of surprises.

Edith was helping Victoria on with her coat when the doorbell rang, and she went to answer it. She ushered in Venetia, clad in a nutmeg-coloured suit, those excellent legs in simply wonderful tights, around her shoulders a heavenly cream cashmere wrap.

Victoria eased on her gloves and took a last glance in the

mirror as Venetia smiled her approval.

'Oh, you look beautiful!' she cried. 'Doesn't she, Edith?'

'She always looks beautiful,' Edith replied stoutly.

Taking Victoria's arm, Venetia led her to the lift while Edith pushed the button. 'Now you watch your step,' she said. 'And don't let her walk too far ...'

'Of course, Edith,' Venetia said softly. 'I will be very careful with her.' As though she was being given charge of an exquisite piece of old china.

Once outside, they walked slowly towards the park.

'We are not going far,' Venetia said. 'I don't want to tire you out or Edith will have something to say!' And they exchanged conspiratorial glances.

'It's lovely just to be outside the flat. To see people, buses, taxis – oh, it's quite exciting.'

Surprisingly, she already felt a little tired, although she had been full of energy when she started out, but Venetia seemed to know this after a few minutes.

'You are bound to feel tired the first time,' she said understandingly. 'The next time I think we should take a taxi to the park gates. Do you not agree?'

'Lovely idea.' Victoria was enjoying herself, despite the tiredness.

When they arrived home, she put her feet up and Venetia massaged them with strong firm strokes.

'Oh, you have a nice touch,' Victoria said gratefully.

'Thank you. I did a course in Rome on this sort of thing. It comes in quite useful, to know the right exercises when you are feeling tired or recovering from an illness.'

'I am sure your mother finds you a perfect treasure.'

'Well, I don't know about that – but she has had quite a hard time. I do what I can.'

'She must miss you.'

'Yes, I expect, but she has Gina there who is wonderful with her. Is that better?'

'Wonderful,' Victoria said.

Venetia stood up. 'By the way, I shall be leaving The Dorchester at the end of the week.'

'Oh, you are going home!' Victoria sounded quite disappointed.

'Not exactly – I have another two weeks – but, well, it is very expensive. I shall find a smaller hotel, there are many in London.' And she went off to find Edith while Victoria's mind ran in all directions.

'Edith will bring us coffee,' Venetia said on her return, seating herself again.

'I was thinking,' Victoria said tentatively. 'You know, for the rest of your stay you are welcome to the spare room. No one uses it.'

'Oh, but I couldn't!' Venetia remonstrated.

'Why not? It's there, and why on earth should you pay out enormous sums in hotel bills? I would be pleased to have you. You have been such a tonic.'

Venetia's brown eyes were warm when she looked at Victoria.

'How very kind of you.'

'Not at all,' Victoria said, feeling, she had to admit to herself, quite noble. 'It is my pleasure. Come whenever you like.' But Edith made no effort to conceal *her* feelings when Victoria told her later that evening.

'Victoria, it makes more work.'

'Oh, don't be irritable, Edith. In fact it should take some of the work off your shoulders. She is very useful, you must admit.'

'And who is going to cook for her?'

'Oh, Edith, what does she eat? She'll be no bother.'

'You don't think,' Edith said belligerently.

She was jealous, Victoria thought. Hated the idea of anyone new coming into their lives. Well, it couldn't be helped. Venetia was doing Victoria a lot of good. I do get a bit tired of Edith's fussing, she thought mutinously. She makes me feel old sometimes.

'Anyway, you can get the spare room ready. She'll come in a couple of days.'

'How long will she stay?'

'Oh, a week or two at the most, I should think,' Victoria said, with slight misgivings that she was taxing Edith a little too much.

'Come on, Edie, don't sulk. We can both do with a bit of brightening up.'

'You speak for yourself,' Edith muttered with an old

servant's freedom as she disappeared into the kitchen.

By the weekend, Venetia was firmly ensconced in the flat in Knightsbridge, her possessions in the fine walnut wardrobe, the dressing table aclutter with all sorts of pots and jars and perfumes. Her scent invaded the flat.

'Oh, lovely!' Victoria cried, sniffing the air like a greyhound.

'I never saw so many things,' Edith glowered, coming out of the guest room with a duster for it seemed that Venetia's usefulness did not include housework. 'She must spend a fortune on creams and stuff.'

'Well, she's young,' Victoria said. 'Remember all the make-up I used to have on my dressing table?'

'But you were in the theatre,' Edith argued. 'Stage make-up – that's different.'

She'll get used to it, Victoria thought comfortably.

There was no one more pleased than Julian Bellamy to hear that Venetia had moved into his mother's apartment. He had wanted to see her again, had told her so when he took her home to her hotel, and now fate had dropped her into his lap.

'Will you put her on, Edith?' he asked, when he had finished speaking to her on the telephone one night.

Edith crossly did so, and presently Venetia, dark eyes glowing, had taken the telephone and was speaking to him in her delightfully low voice.

'Hallo, Julian.'

'How about coming out for dinner?' he asked. 'Tuesday, Wednesday – you name it.'

'Wednesday?' She had a husky voice that would charm the birds off the trees, he thought.

'Pick you up at seven.'

Venetia was surprised when he called for her in a taxi which waited outside until they were ready.

'I don't keep a car in town,' he said. 'Parking and garage fees, you know the sort of thing. My jalopy is down at Jarretts.'

'Jarretts?' she murmured.

'Our home in the country – Mother's home,' he explained. 'It's in Berkshire. I don't use it all that much unless I am down there, which isn't often.'

'What sort of car do you drive?'

'I have an Aston Martin. It used to be my pride and joy, and worth quite a lot. Of course, times have changed – I don't know what it would fetch now – but I've kept it in good condition.'

'You travel quite a lot then?'

'Yes, here, there and everywhere. Just got back from Switzerland.'

'Your mother says you often go. Is most of your business there?'

'I buy a lot and sell there – jewellery, you know.'

'Oh, yes, Victoria said that's what you did.'

'I'm on my own. Ah, here we are.'

He helped her alight from the taxi and paid the driver. Taking her arm, he led her into The Ritz, where he was pleased to see that she came in for a lot of attention in the nicest possible way. As they walked down the wide entrance foyer to the bar, many eyes were on her. And not to be wondered at her, he thought happily. It was a long time since he had escorted such a lovely companion. In her beige suit with its very short skirt, her gleaming dark hair pulled back into a chignon, she looked like something out of a forties film and yet, simultaneously very much of today.

She chose a dry Martini, which pleased him, and sitting back and crossing her legs, appeared much at home. Surveying him from beneath her long lashes as he studied the menu the waiter had brought him, Venetia waited for him to speak.

'Have you been here before?' he asked.

'Yes, with my husband,' she answered. 'A long time ago – before we were married. We brought Mama to England for a holiday.'

'I was sorry to hear that you are going through a divorce. It's a traumatic business.'

'Yes,' she said sadly. 'I know that now.' Her dark eyes surveyed him. 'You, too?'

'Yes, five years ago.'

She sighed. 'Very sad.'

'It didn't work out,' he said. 'It was quite a relief when it was over.'

'But at first, Julian?' she asked him. She had the faintest accent which only added more charm to her already low-pitched voice.

'Oh, at first, you don't quite believe it's happening to you, and then by the time you've got used to the idea, there has usually been a lot of acrimony on both sides.'

'I think perhaps my experience was more simple,' Venetia said, sipping her Martini. Watching her, Julian wondered how this husband of hers had ever let her go.

'Let us change the subject,' she said, smiling across at him. 'Do you not think your mother is looking well?'

'Absolutely,' he said heartily, 'and I think you have had something to do with it. She has become quite lively again. After all, living with Edith is not exactly exciting.'

'No – but Edith is a very good soul, and kind,' Venetia said. 'She is a real treasure to your mother. How long has she worked for her?'

'Oh, donkey's ages. She started as a dresser with Mother when she was eighteen – in fact, as I understand it, they were both eighteen – and Edith has been with Mother ever since.'

'Goodness,' Venetia murmured. 'Part of the family.'

'Yes, you could say that,' he agreed.

By the time they were called in for dinner, they were both relaxed and chatting like old friends.

'You know, I'm delighted that you are staying with Mother,' Julian told her.

'Thank you.' Venetia speared her salad delicately.

'Tell me more about yourself.' Julian's blue eyes met hers and didn't drop.

'What is there to tell?' Venetia smiled. 'I was born and educated in Rome, went to a Swiss finishing school, took several interesting courses, flowers, cookery, that sort of thing, then met Carlo and married him. Then – pff! It was over.'

Julian felt a little more sure of himself now.

'What went wrong in your marriage – or should I not ask?'

She raised dark eyes to his.

'You may, it no longer matters to me. I am afraid Carlo had an eye for the ladies.'

He could hardly believe it. What more did this Italian bounder want when he had perfection?

'When I discovered . . .' She lowered her eyes. 'When I found out – the first time – I forgave him, but after that, no, no, no!' Her dark eyes flashed fire and her fine nostrils dilated.

'Oh, he begged me to stay, but what kind of life would that have been? I had no idea, and you see, when I married him I had been strictly brought up, and I don't suppose I would have believed it if I had heard. He admitted that he could not help himself, swore that I was the only one he had ever loved, but, well, it was not a life.' Her tragic beauty made him want to take her in his arms, and hold her there forever.

'I'm sorry,' he said simply.

'Thank you. And what about you?'

'Same thing, really. My wife Fiona just liked men, I guess. More than one. I never could have held on to her.'

'So we have something in common,' Venetia said sympathetically.

He smiled across at her. What a lovely, warm person she was. And he thought, for no good reason at the moment, of Klara in her stark white flat. Not that she herself was cold – far from it – but he drew his thoughts away from their last night, picturing instead this girl, this dark-eyed beauty, in her place, and was surprised how hot under the collar he felt.

'Tell me what you do?' Venetia said. 'It sounds so interesting, glamorous even.'

'I don't know about that,' laughed Julian, 'but, yes, I suppose it is in a way. Travelling all over the world in search of wonderful jewels.'

'Goodness,' she breathed. 'Really?'

'Yes, I worked for Blane's but after a while, after Fiona as a matter of fact, decided to take the plunge and go on my own. And by God, it's been worth it.'

'What courage that must have taken.' Admiration was evident in her glowing eyes.

'I wouldn't say that, but I took to it like a duck to water and I've had some good finds. You have some boring times, but there's always the chance of picking up a treasure, as with all antiques.'

'How exciting,' Venetia breathed, hanging on every word.

By the end of the evening they were like old friends, and when the taxi stopped outside his mother's flat, Julian escorted her to the entrance hall.

She reached up and kissed him lightly on the cheek. 'Thank

you, Julian, for a wonderful evening.'

Her perfume filled his nostrils, and he caught her to him, about to kiss her passionately. Deftly she moved out of reach, and looked up at him reproachfully with big brown eyes.

'Julian,' she chided softly.

'I'm sorry,' he found himself saying as she gave him the loveliest smile, and went towards the lift with a wave.

'I say,' he cried out, 'wait!' But she had gone, and he watched the lift doors close behind her.

Damn, he thought. How did that happen? I felt sure she would ...

Venetia closed the outer door of the apartment softly.

'How did you get on? Did you have a nice evening?' Victoria asked. But there was no need. The flush of excitement on Venetia's face told her all.

'We went to The Ritz,' she said, like a child home from her first party.

'Oh, that's always nice.'

'I thought you might have gone to bed,' said Venetia, taking off her jacket.

'No, I knew I wouldn't sleep. I sent Edith off. She was tired out, I thought.'

Venetia stood and looked at her. 'You know, you are right Victoria. I noticed it this morning. She really is tired. After all she's not young.'

Victoria made a face.

'No, like me.'

'Oh, dear Victoria, I didn't mean ...'

'My dear, of course you didn't, but perhaps I ought to think more about her? As you say, she works very hard, and never gets a break.'

After a few moments, Venetia spoke. 'Why don't you give her a little holiday? A few days away in some nice country place or by the sea. Fresh air, long walks.'

'On her own, do you mean?' Victoria looked dubious.

'Well, yes, of course – there would be no point if she had to look after you, would there?' Venetia said gently.

'No, of course not. I see what you mean. Pack her off for a day or two.'

'Why not? Just a few days.'

'Yes,' Victoria said firmly. 'I will. I'll suggest it to her in the morning.'

'I think you will have to be firmer than that,' Venetia said mildly. 'She isn't going to like leaving you.'

'But you are here,' Victoria said. 'Could you cope with me for a bit on your own?'

'Dear Victoria, there is nothing I would like more.' And Venetia's lovely face grew rosy with pleasure at the thought.

'You know, you are a nice child,' said Victoria, pleased. 'Well, I'll think about it and mention it to her in the morning. See what she says.'

'Good. Now may I get you a night cap?'

'Well, if you don't mind. A little hot milk and just a tiny dash of brandy.'

They smiled like old friends.

'Just the thing,' agreed Venetia. 'Now – you hurry off to bed and I'll bring it to you.'

Lying tucked up in bed, the low soft humming of an Italian aria reached Victoria's ears as Venetia busied herself in the kitchen. She closed her eyes the better to enjoy it.

Chapter Twelve

'Who is she?' Ruth whispered to Geoffrey in the kitchen.

'My dear, I don't know. The daughter of an old friend of Mother's apparently. Lives in Italy or something like that.'

'But isn't it strange that we should come and find Edith away and this young woman in her place?'

'I don't think so. Mother will explain.' He saw no reason to tell Ruth that he'd had doubts himself. No need to acerbate the problem.

Ruth carried the bowl of flowers into the drawing room from the kitchen and placed them on the table. 'There – all from Jarretts.'

Geoffrey followed her, his eyes not on the flowers but on the sweet face of the young woman called Venetia.

'Do sit down, darlings,' Victoria said. 'And thank you for the flowers, Ruth. Delphiniums, how lovely. I recall that Jameson used to grow the most wonderful specimens.'

'Yes, the giant ones, but I'm afraid now we're just growing the ordinary ones, but they are lovely, aren't they? Such blues.'

Geoffrey appeared to take charge of the situation. 'Well, Mother, and how have you been?'

'Wonderfully well,' she declared. 'I have this lovely young woman to look after me in Edith's absence.'

'Yes, what happened?' Geoffrey asked. 'She is well, I trust?'

'We – I – thought she looked a little tired,' Victoria said, 'and quite frankly, why wouldn't she be? She has worked like a slave all these years for me, it's the least I can do to send her off for a few days. She's gone to Bournemouth.'

'That was nice of you,' Geoffrey said, unable to take his eyes off Venetia's face, but forcing himself to do so.

'Well, we reasoned it out, Venetia and I, that with her staying as she now is, I could well afford to dispense with Edith for a while. And to be truthful, the change is doing me a power of good.'

'And are you here for a holiday – a visit?' Ruth asked, in her best matronly manner.

'Yes, I am here for about a month, but I have already had two weeks at The Dorchester and was about to change hotels when Victoria suggested I should spend the rest of the time here.'

Victoria? Anyone would think they were old friends! Ruth thought.

'And a good idea, too,' Geoffrey said heartily, causing Ruth to close her eyes briefly. When she opened them they fastened on Venetia.

'And your mother is an old friend of my mother-in-law's?' she asked pointedly. Victoria indeed!

'Yes,' smiled Venetia, showing beautiful white teeth. 'They were at school together.'

'Had you always kept in touch?' Ruth asked. After all, she had never heard of an old school friend before, much less one domiciled in Italy.

'Oh, on and off,' Victoria said airily. She didn't see the need to justify herself to her daughter-in-law.

'Well, that's nice,' Ruth said. She would find out more later. It wouldn't do to ask too many pointed questions, Victoria was likely to get rattled.

She gave them her warm chairman of committee smile.

'And so what have you been doing, Mother? I suppose you haven't been out yet?'

'Oh, indeed I have. Several times. Venetia has taken me for short walks in the park.'

Before Ruth had time to say anything, Venetia gave her a reassuring smile.

'Wrapped up well, and we took it very slowly,' she said in her low charming voice. Geoffrey was captivated. A slight glance across at Ruth and he coughed gently.

'That's excellent progress,' he said.

'You live in Rome, Signora – Madame – er ?' Ruth pressed.

She really couldn't keep these questions bottled up, though she knew she was letting her curiosity show.

'Countess Tellini,' Victoria said, repeating what she had told them when they arrived. 'But I am sure Venetia prefers to be called by her Christian name.'

'Of course,' she said softly. 'Although it may be temporary. I am thinking of returning to England with my Mama who does not enjoy the hot weather. I thought perhaps summer in England and the winters in Italy.'

'Sounds an excellent idea,' Geoffrey agreed.

'And how are the girls?' Victoria asked. 'I have two granddaughters,' she explained to Venetia, 'lovely girls. One of them wants to go on the stage like me. The other is a brainbox, eh, Ruth?'

'They're both clever, Mother,' she said reprovingly, 'and as for Loveday going on the stage ...' She gave a little laugh. 'I don't think so.'

'Perhaps just as well,' Victoria said. 'And how is business, Geoffrey – are you feeling the pinch, like everyone else?'

'Things aren't too bad,' he said. 'Could be better though.'

'Would you all like some tea?' Venetia asked, getting to her feet.

'Lovely idea,' Victoria agreed.

'Oh, let me.'

'No, no – you sit there, Ruth,' Venetia said. 'You must make the most of your visit. I can talk to Victoria any time.'

Ruth recognised that the time for questions was over. Doubts she may still have about Venetia's presence, but for the moment they were best kept to herself.

'Any news of Vanessa? I'm supposed to be lunching with her next week.'

'Not really,' Victoria said. 'She seems busy enough at the office. What she's doing in her private life I really don't know.'

'Oh, I didn't mean to –'

Victoria ignored her. 'Julian came to see me. As a matter of fact, he took Venetia to dine at The Ritz. Wasn't that nice of him?'

She knew she was teasing, knew that Ruth's nose would be put very much out of joint. But she enjoyed needling Ruth, without ever really knowing why.

112

'Yes – very,' she said, while Geoffrey thought that some men, particularly his brother Julian, had all the luck.

Venetia reappeared with the tray of tea things, and laid them down on the centre table, handing out napkins and plates and tiny forks.

'Oh, you've made some more of those delicious little Italian cakes,' cried Victoria.

Venetia smiled.

'You must try them – they are marvellous,' Victoria said as Venetia handed round eggshell thin cups of China tea.

'Mmmm,' Geoffrey said. 'Melt in the mouth.'

'Very good,' Ruth said. 'You must make some for my Mothers and Babies Fête later this month.'

'I should love to – if I am still here.'

'Where did you learn to cook like this?' Ruth asked. They really were good.

'I did a cookery course after my finishing school ended.'

'She's a dab hand at a lot of things,' Victoria said, sipping her tea.

Well, it wasn't the easiest and most relaxed teatime, she thought when they had gone, but it often worked out like that when Ruth came.

The tea things cleared away, Venetia sat on a low chair beside Victoria.

'He is nice, your son,' she said. 'He is like you.'

'Oh, do you think so?' Victoria was pleased.

'Tell me about Jarretts – is that the name? It sounds fascinating.'

Oh, it is,' Victoria said. 'It was my home for so many years.'

How could she explain the wonder of Jarretts? The first time she had seen it rising out of the Berkshire countryside she had fallen in love with it at once. 'For you, my darling,' Harry had said. 'My wedding present to you.'

He had seen it the previous year when he had been playing golf at Wentworth. Learning subsequently that it was up for sale he had asked an agent to take him over it.

He was more than pleased at what he saw although he recognised that he would have to spend a small fortune on it. Grounds extending to three acres, it sat amidst pine trees and birches, rising out of the landscape as if it had always been there, although it transpired it had been built by a Belgian banker some time in the twenties. The rooms were large, with high ceilings and, beautiful parquet floors, just right for the collection of precious Persian rugs in which he had been investing for some time. The windows were long and gracious. and there were many bedrooms and a vast kitchen all of which, with added bathrooms, would make a house fit for a queen. The upper half was timbered, and inside there were many original oak beams said to have come from a Dutch ship which foundered on the English coast in the seventeenth century. Altogether, it was a dramatic house, a romantic house, and all he needed to complete it was the bride.

He bought the property, deciding to keep its name, although no one knew where it had come from, and set to work installing builders and architects to work to his specification. It was almost finished when he met Victoria and from that moment he knew this was the girl he had been waiting for.

Relating this, Victoria was quite carried away with the romance of it all. Venetia listened avidly.

'How simply wonderful!' she cried, dark eyes glowing like coals. 'So romantic. And of course, you fell in love with it too?'

'It would be hard not to.' Victoria said. 'The grounds were beautiful. At first there were overgrown shrubberies and tangled copses. We left some to give a few mysterious hideaways but others were cleared.

'We made a rose garden – an Italian rose garden. You would like that, Venetia – and we planted a lime walk. It's not quite so beautiful now as it was then, you need plenty of gardeners to keep a garden like Jarretts going, but Geoffrey does what he can.'

'So he lives there with Ruth and their daughters?'

'Yes, they love it. In fact, Ruth is quite dotty about Jarretts. I think she loves it even more than I do.'

'You must miss it, though?' Venetia said, wondering just how she could tactfully find out more.

'Well, I like living in London now that I am older, and it *is* still mine.' Venetia felt a renewed surge of interest, waiting for Victoria to go on.

'When Harry died, he left me the house – but I wanted to

move to London. I missed him so, you see. I felt cut off, needed to be with people, and I had some idea of going back to the theatre.'

'And did you?'

'Yes, eventually I did. This was Mama's flat, and she left the lease to me. I have known it since I was a little girl.' She looked around her fondly. 'Yes I have been very lucky.'

'So Geoffrey and Ruth just live in Jarretts? Do they rent it from you?' Venetia wondered if she had gone too far.

'Oh, no, dear. When they married, I moved out and Geoffrey took over.' She saw the slight query in Venetia's eyes.

'So what about the others? Julian and Vanessa – do they live there too?'

'No, dear, they never seemed to be interested. It often happens when you are used to something, you don't appreciate the beauty of it. When Julian married Fiona they had a flat in London, used to go down to Jarretts at first for weekends – after all, it is large enough for all of them. But since he went into business on his own, Julian hardly ever goes down there.'

'And Vanessa?'

'Oh, she has a flat of her own. She moved out soon after she got her first job. She goes down to see Geoffrey and Ruth once in a while.'

How lucky could you be? Venetia thought enviously.

Misinterpreting her expression, Victoria smiled at her.

'You must go down there, my dear, you would love it. We'll go together. Between you and me, Ruth would like me to go back there to live.'

Venetia pondered this swiftly, recognising in Ruth someone like herself who was not above scheming a little to get what she wanted.

'Yes, we'll get Julian to drive us down, he can hire a car. When would you like to go? It's ages since I was there.'

'That rather depends when Julian can manage it, doesn't it?'

'Yes, I'll ring him and see what he can do.'

Venetia's lovely face was alive with enthusiasm.

'Whenever you feel well enough to go – I leave it to you. You mustn't do anything that tires you.'

'Oh, nonsense!' pooh-poohed Victoria. 'That's no problem. I shall look forward to it.'

Venetia took her hand. 'Are you sure there is nothing you want? You have been so good to me.'

'My dear, I love having you here.'

'Then I will go and write to Mama. She will be anxious if she doesn't hear from me.'

She knew she owed Mama a letter – so much had happened so swiftly, and she must allay any worries her mother might have at her prolonged stay. After all, eventually Mama would come to her beloved England, but these things took time to arrange and there was a lot of water to flow under the bridge before that happened . . .

That evening Victoria left a message for Julian to telephone her, and when he rang back the next day, suggested that he drive her and Venetia down to Jarretts for lunch on Sunday.

Julian was only too delighted for an excuse to see Venetia again.

'I'll ring Ruth and suggest it,' he offered.

'No, tell her we are coming,' Victoria said. She could be quite peremptory when she liked.

'Right, Mother.'

Seeing Venetia again on Sunday, Julian's heart leapt. She was a vision in a long dress of light blue voile, carrying a large shady hat. Her luxuriant hair was tied back, her dark eyes shone. He hardly had a moment to absorb the picture she made as he busied himself making Victoria comfortable in the back seat.

'Are you sure you wouldn't like to sit in front with Julian?' Venetia asked.

'No, my dear, I'm perfectly happy in the back – I want you to enjoy the journey.'

Julian was aware of Venetia's perfume which he hadn't yet identified. He was a connoisseur of expensive scent. But the wonderful thing was that she was here at all. He wouldn't have minded where he was taking her. It was enough that she was sitting by his side, she was real and warm, and although a visit to Jarretts was not one of his favourite outings, having Venetia there made all the difference.

On the way out of London, Venetia was thinking something quite different. One of the first things she had in mind was to persuade Julian to move his Aston Martin into town. There seemed to be no point in its lying unused at Jarretts.

Once in Berkshire, they passed through wooded countryside, and sometimes caught sight of a house sitting graciously surrounded by trees, or a glimpse of a blue pool set amongst green manicured lawns. Then they were going down a long drive and at the end Jarretts came into view. Venetia felt a surge of excitement, almost a thrill, as they drew near. No wonder Ruth was keen on Jarretts – it was beautiful, gracious. How wonderful to live there. To own it.

Geoffrey came out of the house to greet them, and she looked at the two brothers standing side by side: Geoffrey stocky and good-looking in a solid English kind of way; then at handsome Julian with those very blue eyes, good bones, fine nose. The face was a little weak perhaps, there was something lacking. But I have enough strength to make up for that, Venetia thought. He will never know what it is to want something so passionately you will allow nothing to stand in the way, but I do. I am like Harry Bellamy, she thought. He knew what he wanted and went after it. I understand that. I understand him.

Geoffrey greeted his mother and helped her out of the car, while Julian held out a hand to Venetia. The touch of her hand, slim and cool, was like an electric shock, more powerful than he had experienced for a very long time. They went into the house, and once inside, it was just as Venetia had imagined. Fine furniture, beautiful rugs, and paintings – all that an English country house should be. Waiting for them was Ruth, in a neat navy and white blouse and skirt. She was quite pretty in a way, thought Venetia, and gave her one of her most dazzling smiles, almost putting Ruth off her stride.

'Oh, it is beautiful,' said Venetia, looking up at the minstrel gallery, the paintings on the walls, and the impressive balustrade.

'Thank you. Yes, it is,' Ruth murmured. She never tired of showing people round Jarretts.

'Quite a lot of upkeep, though,' Venetia said softly. 'But you manage it beautifully. Everywhere sparkles, you must have an excellent housekeeper.'

'Yes, we have.'

'And it is a gift to be able to manage staff,' Venetia said

bestowing on Ruth yet again her wonderful smile. Despite herself Ruth felt she could not have received a greater compliment.

'Would you like to come upstairs to freshen up?' she asked, and led the way up the wide staircase to the landing, where a door stood open to a dressing room.

'What a lovely room!' exclaimed Venetia, sincerely admiring the yellow and white decor.

'Yes, we have changed very little since my mother-in-law lived here. She has such good taste, I really couldn't improve on it.'

Venetia put her gloves on the side table, and looked at herself in the pier glass.

'You know, it would be nice if Victoria could come back here to live – with you to look after her.'

Ruth felt a surge of warmth towards her. Venetia had gained an ally.

'Oh, I'm glad you said that. It's exactly what I want her to do but she won't hear of it.'

'What a pity,' Venetia commiserated as she followed Ruth down the stairs.

Hmmmm, she thought, there were quite a number of hurdles to get over before she finally reached her destination, but there was nothing like ingratiating oneself along the way. It usually paid off.

Both Geoffrey and Julian looked up as she descended the stairs, their thoughts not dissimilar. Venetia could read them like a book.

Her lovely gentle face, the doe-like eyes, the frame of dark hair ... she was like one of the paintings come to life. An early Italian painting, Julian thought, being of a romantic turn of mind. Geoffrey's thoughts were more prosaic.

She was a damn fine-looking girl.

Chapter Thirteen

It seemed strange to conduct a correspondence with a school friend you hadn't heard of in forty years, but truth was stranger than fiction as Victoria well knew and it was time she wrote to Violet Santucci – after all, her daughter was Victoria's house guest, and a very nice one too.

She tried to recall the last time she had actually seen Violet, and came to the guilty conclusion that it was that awful time in Knightsbridge. She remembered her own haste to get away, knowing what she knew and feeling guilty, not wanting to prolong the meeting now that she was about to leave for Canada. Violet's look of surprise, her own regrets afterwards that she had been too brusque – ah, well, she had good reason.

Her mind flew back over the years. The memories came flooding in. It must have been in 1943 she received that letter from Pierre Mallet, the Canadian doctor. It had to be the worst day of her life. She was married in October 1943, and what a wedding it was.

Harry, of course, spared no expense and there was Jarretts waiting for them, newly renovated, the grounds laid out. It was left to Victoria to choose the decor and she was to have just what she wanted. She and Edith had pored over swatches of material for curtains, not easy to obtain in those days, but they had had remarkable luck with antique furniture. People were leaving their homes, even their treasures, to flee to what might be safety. What were possessions when perhaps one's life was at stake? Others more prudently stored fine pieces, but many of them never returned to collect them and the auction rooms were exceptionally busy. A bit ghoulish now when she thought of it, but that's the way it was. Life was cheap in those days.

Jarretts was still not completed when they married. Victoria a radiant bride and Harry just about over the moon. The press were there, and Harry looked so proud, handsome even, although one wouldn't have said he was a handsome man. Victoria wore a traditional white satin gown – heaven knows now where the coupons came from, some donated she was sure – fitted and narrow, showing off her slim figure. It was topped by a most beautiful bridal veil, and her train was ten yards long. Such an indulgence in those hard up days. Her headdress was a coronet of orange blossom – real orange blossom. She could smell the scent now, heady, fresh, yet exotic. She was almost hidden behind her bouquet which was enormous as they were in those days, masses of huge pale pink roses – her favourite – and something blue, she had said. She recalled that the florist had said it was difficult to find blue flowers in autumn, it wasn't like today when flowers reached one from all over the world. At the last moment, they had procured Nigella, or Love in a Mist as it was called. Perhaps that was what it was, she thought. Love in a Mist ...

When she arrived at the church on her Uncle Leonard's arm, she could swear there were tears in Harry's eyes, which he would have died rather than admit.

Then there was her mother, a dream in pale blue and a wonderful hat, lots of stage friends, and Edith looking quite handsome in a cream silk outfit and a rather fetching hat. Victoria remembered looking at her several times, quite surprised.

When Harry slipped the ring on her finger, she remembered the momentary feeling of utter desolation, thinking of Philip. She had swallowed hard – oh, if it had only been – but it had gone in a flash, never to return. From that moment, she had promised herself to make Harry a good wife.

They honeymooned in Scotland, and what a passionate lover Harry was. She recalled now those nights when he couldn't get enough of her, nor she him, come to that. But it was purely physical, the coming together of two bodies, fused like something electrical. After only a year, she recognised that they had nothing in common, hardly anything, except that he adored her as a possession, and she loved to be spoiled. She was an asset to him, to his home, and he was her protector, they admired and quite liked each other. Probably more than most people have in a marriage, she thought wryly.

Of course, she had missed the stage, the theatre, but the children were to fill her life soon. But though everything was going too smoothly there was a price to be paid, of course, and that was in the correspondence that went back and forth across the Atlantic between Pierre Mallet and herself.

She had been married four months when the first of the letters came from him, telling her that further tests had proved that baby Gerard was retarded. He explained carefully what this meant, that she was not to blame herself, it was a freak of nature. But it was almost more than Victoria could bear. Of course, it had always been at the back of her mind – hadn't it been one of the reasons she had decided to marry Harry, so that in the event of her needing money, he would be there?

She had overlooked all that in the excitement of the wedding and restoring Jarretts. How was she ever going to deal with it?

The letters which came were addressed to Edith, supposedly from her brother. The second letter dealt with the problem of the young couple who had adopted the baby. They could not cope, although legally obliged to, and the most they could offer was to have little Gerard put in a home. But there were homes and homes, Dr Mallet stressed. He was sure she would not want the little chap to go into a state-run home. Would she perhaps think about something private? He himself had an interest in such a clinic, and the boy was a high-grade retarded child who deserved special treatment. There were signs that he would benefit by such treatment and tuition. Mallet himself was a great believer in giving every chance to these handicapped children, and it was surprising what results they achieved.

Suspicious, Edith and Victoria faced each other.

'You don't think ...' Victoria suggested. 'I mean ...'

'That he just wants to get money out of you?' Edith never minced her words.

'Well,' Victoria said doubtfully.

'It's on the cards and not impossible,' Edith said, 'but I don't think so. I like to think I am a judge of character, and I would place my trust in him. If he's a villain, I'll eat my wedding hat.'

'Oh, Edith, what a mess!' Victoria had wept, beside herself.

'It's like a nightmare, as if it were someone else – I can't believe now it really happened to me.'

'Well, it did,' Edith said shortly, 'and you have to make up your mind what happens next. Are you prepared for little Gerard to go into a state home? Don't you want him to have the best that money can provide? Could you live the life you live, knowing that you weren't doing all that was possible? Could you tell your husband, have him here?'

'Oh, Edith, don't!' Victoria wept. 'You know I couldn't!'

'Well, then, what next?' she asked. 'You do have a responsibility even though that couple adopted him. Your own conscience should tell you that.'

'Oh, Edith, of course it does! Do you suppose I could have foreseen – that he would be – ' And she wept for the baby son she and Philip had brought into the world.

And then Edith put her arms about her and held her close. 'There, there, my pet. It's wicked, wicked.'

'I must write off straight away,' Victoria said at length, drying her eyes, 'and see that he gets into the best possible place. No money must be spared, that's the least I can do.'

'I am glad to hear it,' Edith said, marching off to the kitchen.

A few days after she wrote to Pierre Mallet, Victoria knew that her suspicions about her own health were right. She was pregnant again, and went through an agony of doubt. Would she have another retarded child? Did it mean that she could not give birth to a normal baby?

Before telling Harry, she made a visit to a private doctor and told him her story. After examining her, and confirming that she was pregnant, he went into great detail about the situation and assured her that there was every chance she would have a perfectly normal child.

Harry had to accept that Victoria's odd depression was due to her pregnancy. Not every woman felt on top of the world, some women had quite a difficult time, Edith told him.

'But she is pleased about the baby?' he pleaded with her.

'Pleased as punch. It's all to do with hormones,' Edith said, having read this somewhere and not having an idea in the world what it meant.

'I see,' Harry said, accepting it. He was like a young man of twenty-five instead of a man approaching forty.

One day, seeing Victoria listlessly gazing out of the window, Edith made a suggestion.

'How would it be if I went over to Canada to check everything?' she asked. Victoria turned wide dark eyes to her.

'Oh, Edith! Would you?'

'Yes, why not? You can say that I am going to see my brother who emigrated before the war – after all, Harry doesn't know that's not true, does he? You have to lie sometimes, Victoria, and we've already got a list as long as your arm behind us.'

'But won't he wonder why you are deserting me while I am pregnant?'

'We'll say my brother is desperately ill – and wants to see me.'

'Oh, Edith! But – '

'Well, either you want me to go or you don't?'

'Of course I do. I feel I shan't rest until I know what exactly is going on.'

'Well, then – we'll stick to that, and you will have to find someone else to look after you while I am gone. How long do you think I shall be away?'

'Goodness knows! I daren't think!'

So they began to plan. Transatlantic travel was impossible in wartime except from neutral countries, so they chose Lisbon as being the most convenient and accessible from which to start the long journey. Edith set out with a mixture of trepidation and excitement. Already Victoria was more relaxed and like her old self. She felt as though a load had been lifted from her mind.

A temporary maid was found to take Edith's place, a girl who was so thrilled with the idea of working for Victoria that she would have done anything for her.

Jarretts was taking shape more and more each day. The gardens were established and the nursery decorated in blue and white, for Harry was sure it would be a boy while Victoria secretly thought she would have a daughter. Bedrooms were fitted out and furnished, which gave Victoria plenty to do, but her mind was all the time on Edith and how she was getting on. When the letter came she tore it open avidly, taking it to her bedroom to devour every word.

> As I thought Dr Mallet is the kindest man, and of course has the baby's interests at heart. Just talking with him would reassure you – everything that can be done is being done. Stay well, and DON'T WORRY.

Victoria burned the letter. But what about little Gerard? Edith didn't mention him. Now Victoria would have to wait until she was home.

She knew on Edith's return, and by her face, that all was well – or as well as it would ever be. Nothing could be said until they were closeted in Victoria's bedroom. There they talked of everything but the trip itself.

'I can't tell you how kind Dr Mallet is,' Edith instantly told Victoria. 'The home, or clinic as he calls it, is lovely, up high in the mountains with clean fresh air, and he has good, caring staff. He took me up to see it. There are eight children there, Gerard is the youngest, and a girl of fifteen the eldest – they hope to have more. He is doing wonderful work, teaching the older ones and looking after the three infants.' And her eyes filled with tears.

'Gerard is beautiful,' she went on. 'A lovely child. And having said that, I will say no more – except that you are not to worry. He is in the best place in the world.' She didn't tell Victoria that watching the doctor at work with his charges, she would have loved to stay and help him. He was that sort of man. But her first duty was to Victoria. She was always Edith's first priority.

So gradually Victoria adapted to her new pregnancy, and when her son Geoffrey was born, a healthy lovely baby, gave thanks to God and from then on vowed that her new family would not be made to suffer for past indiscretions. She would put it all behind her and concentrate on the future.

Two years later, Julian arrived, and looking down at him, Victoria saw he was a miniature Harry. The same nose, eyes, shape of face. But it was Geoffrey to whom Harry gave his love and affection. All through his schooldays he berated Julian – perhaps, Victoria thought, seeing in his second son the weaknesses in himself. And yet in character they were not in the least alike.

Jarretts blossomed, the boys grew, and five years almost to the day after Julian's birth, Vanessa was born. Victoria had waited for this moment, and her eyes filled with tears as she held her. She was not like anyone, least of all her mother.

The years sped by, with Harry becoming more successful, and Victoria's life taken up with voluntary work and her own social calendar. She and Harry were always welcome wherever they went and the years were good to them. Every year, Victoria sent a large sum of money to Dr Mallet, who always acknowledged it, but no words ever passed between them, about baby Gerard. Now, Victoria could hardly remember what he had looked like, or the agony she had gone through when she learned he was not a normal child.

Instead she enjoyed her other three children, knowing that she had done all she could, circumstances permitting, and that little Gerard was in safe hands.

They had just celebrated Geoffrey's twenty-first birthday when Harry died. An aneurism, the doctor said, and they would have had no warning. 'Fifty-seven – it was nothing,' cried Victoria. 'He was still a young man.'

But he had lived hard, worked hard and played hard. There could be no regrets. He had not suffered, and she gave thanks for that. Geoffrey was halfway through his training as an architect, and Julian, not wanting to go to university, had opted for Blane's. Vanessa was still at school.

So Victoria picked up the pieces and made a new life. When Vanessa left school, Victoria moved out of Jarretts and up to town, taking over her mother's old flat which she'd often used when Harry was alive. Geoffrey was to be married the following year, and then he and Ruth would move into Jarretts.

How much of this to tell Violet Santucci? None of it could be of any real interest to her. Victoria would gloss over the passing years and concentrate on the present: her plans, what the family were doing now – and more to the point, how helpful Violet's daughter Venetia had been.

She was busy writing her letter when the postman called for the second time that day, with a letter for Venetia. It had been forwarded on to her and had a Rome postmark.

I hope everything is all right, thought Victoria. She had a

slight feeling of guilt that Venetia was being such a help to her while her mother was alone.

Venetia came in, having been to the hairdressers, looking as lovely as ever.

'Letter for you, my dear.'

'Oh, thank you, Victoria.' She took it to her room opening it feverishly. One never knew what the news from Rome would be.

She almost jumped for joy. She was free! Her divorce had come through and there were no problems. Her dark eyes were dancing to the news. She was free, free! She wondered how Julian would react?

Composing herself, she sprayed on a little perfume, and smoothed down her short skirt, eyeing herself in the mirror. It had to be said that the London hairdressers had no style when it came to hair – the Italians were far better – but she would settle for that. It was a small price to pay for the plans she was making.

'Is all well?' Victoria asked solicitously, seeing the girl's lovely gentle face, the halo of dark hair, the serious set of her soft mouth.

'Yes, thank you, Victoria. My divorce has come through.' She spoke softly, regretfully, and Victoria eyed her sympathetically. She must have felt it more than she showed. She obviously took it seriously. After all, divorce was a sad thing for a young woman to experience.

'My dear, you must be brave. You are a beautiful young woman with your life in front of you. You mustn't regret the past – remember the nice times. After all, everything is for a purpose. I do believe that more and more as I grow older. You will find someone else. No, don't shake your head – you will. Time heals.'

Venetia's eyes filled with tears.

'How kind you are, Victoria,' she said, then blew her nose delicately and smiled bravely.

'That's better!' Victoria said approvingly. 'Now let's have some tea, shall we?'

When Venetia disappeared into the kitchen, Victoria resumed her letter. It was good that she kept in contact with Violet. She hoped perhaps they could meet again. One's contemporaries grew in importance over the passing years. Times changed, and old differences or people one hadn't bothered with emerged again in a new light. Old friends were valuable simply because they had been alive at the same time and so had the same memories as oneself.

When Venetia emerged from the kitchen carrying the tray of tea things, her face was wreathed in smiles.

'There we are – as you say over here.' She placed the tray on the table. 'Have you finished your letter?'

'Yes, dear, I have been writing to your mother,' Victoria said, folding the envelope and sealing it while Venetia felt a moment's apprehension. She would give her eye teeth to know what was in it!

Chapter Fourteen

It was very warm that day in Rome when Violet Santucci folded the letter she had received from Victoria, a frown between her eyes. Opening it again, she re-read the last paragraph:

> So I am delighted to tell you that Venetia has been more than helpful, especially now that my maid Edith is away for a few days – we are both enjoying it hugely and getting to know each other. She is a lovely girl and such good company. You must be proud of her.

Violet bit her lip and wondered what lay behind those words. Venetia certainly had not lost any time getting to know Victoria Bellamy, but then that was like her. 'An eye to the main chance' was the English expression, and loving her daughter as she did, Violet wondered how she could be so disloyal as to think there might be something behind it all. But not for nothing had she been through many harrowing experiences with Venetia. She was wilful, had a temper, liked her own way – but then what daughter didn't?

She consoled herself with this, and awaited a letter from Venetia, which, when it arrived, puzzled her even more.

> I am staying with Victoria at the moment in order to give her maid a break for a few days, and I am really enjoying it. I can quite see what you found so fascinating about her. On Sunday we went down to the family home in the country. It was lovely. And Julian, Victoria's younger son, took me to dinner at The Ritz, which was nice ...

Oh, so that was it! Violet was slightly relieved. A young man behind it all. Well, that was natural enough, and now that Venetia's divorce had come through, there was no reason why she shouldn't be going out with young men. The most important thing was not to worry. Venetia was quite old enough to look after herself.

With Edith due back at the weekend, Venetia was not quite sure of her next move. Thinking it over, she wondered why she had encouraged Ruth's idea that Victoria should go to live at Jarretts and decided that she had done it in order to curry favour. It was as well to have as many people as possible on one's side, and Ruth would not make a good enemy. Meantime, she had certainly made a conquest in Julian, and if, as time went by, she became more enamoured of the family as a whole, who knows? She could do worse than to set her sights on Julian, who was unmarried and obviously attracted to her. But now, after seeing Jarretts, she felt as Ruth must have done.

Still, what were her chances of living there? Not high if you accepted the fact that it belonged to the three children, and Ruth and Geoffrey were already in residence. On the other hand, if she married Julian, she might come into the flat in Knightsbridge, and there was not much wrong with that – and she hadn't even thought about the emeralds yet. As for Jarretts, who knew what might happen? Edith was due back on Saturday, and Venetia could hardly outstay her welcome beyond another week. Unless, unless ... And the thoughts and conjectures went on in her head.

'Venetia, my dear,' Victoria said the next morning, 'before Edith comes back, I would like to get out and visit my agent. My old agent.'

'Agent?' Venetia was genuinely puzzled.

'Yes, my theatrical agent. I still have one, you know.'

'Oh' Venetia was surprised.

'Yes, I am thinking of going back to work. Don't look so shocked, my dear, it's not impossible, you know. I am still capable of playing certain parts.'

'Oh, Victoria, I'm sure you are – but do you really feel up to it?'

'Of course I do. There's nothing like hard work or a challenge, that's how I see it. So if you don't mind, we shall go into the West End this morning. I have already made an appointment for eleven-thirty.'

'Of course, Victoria.' There was no alternative to going along with it, although what Edith or the rest of the family would say, she couldn't imagine.

'I'm doing it while Edith is away because I know what she is, she would only try to stop me.'

'Oh, Victoria, I would know better than to do that!' And they both laughed.

Victoria looked very much the part of an actress of a certain age when she emerged from her bedroom. She glanced in the full-length hall mirror approvingly. In her smart, knee-length black suit, her legs still looked good, slim with nicely turned ankles. She wore a white blouse with a lacy neckline, her face beautifully made up and her dark eyes glowing. And if her make-up *was* slightly over the top, it became her.

She smiled at Venetia, thick lashes encrusted with mascara. Somehow she got away with it. She drew on white doeskin gloves, and picked up a black calf handbag.

'You know,' she said, looking down and patting it, 'Harry gave this to me – oh, twenty or thirty years ago. I can't remember. But look how it wears – as good as new.'

She really was a sight for sore eyes, Venetia decided, and arm in arm they went down in the lift to the waiting taxi.

As they neared Grosvenor Square, Victoria took out her small compact and inspected her face, patting her hair and checking her lipstick.

'Now, dear, when we arrive, you might like to wait in the foyer while I go on up. It's on the sixth floor. Don't worry, there is a lift. And I'll see you when I'm ready.'

'Of course,' Venetia murmured, as the taxi stopped outside an impressive block. Paying the driver, she followed Victoria in as she swept past the doorman. He touched his hat, and gave a smile. 'Good morning, Mrs Bellamy.'

'Good morning, George.' Victoria inclined her head gracefully, then saw that Venetia was seated in one of the sumptuous chairs.

Nodding to her, she disappeared into the lift, leaving Venetia to look around at the opulence of the furnishings. This agent must be a very successful one. She had always imagined they had their offices in back streets up three flights of stairs.

She picked up a copy of *Harpers*, and began to thumb through it.

Opposite the lift, Victoria knocked on a door which was opened almost at once by her old friend, Joe Bernard.

He kissed her lightly on the cheek, taking an elbow and seeing her into his office, which led out of the sitting room.

'Victoria, how nice to see you. You look wonderful, my dear.' And in his eyes was open admiration. 'No need to ask if you are fully restored to health.'

'No, Joe, as you can see.' She placed her handbag on her lap and removed her gloves, smiling across at him. Oh, it was good to be back in familiar surroundings. She could feel a slight rush of adrenaline already at the idea of getting back into the swim of things again. The only thing missing was the smell of greasepaint.

He sat down in a big swivel chair, his sharp eyes seeing everything: her expression, her make-up, her skin colour, her clothes.

'Well,' he began, 'you mentioned the theatre but I don't have to tell you ...'

'Now, Joe, don't start off so dismally. I know things are in the doldrums except for certain shows, but you must know what is on the cards – coming up, as it were – and there surely are lots of parts for older women?'

'Yes, darling, and lots of older women to play them.' He smiled at her ruefully. 'Don't get me wrong, they're not to be compared to you for experience and looks, but, well, you know.'

She sighed. 'You're not called the best in the business for nothing – where else would I go after all these years?' And her smile was warm and lovely.

'You wouldn't consider television?' He saw the drawing together of the brows, swiftly eased away as she looked straight at him.

'I suppose I might,' she said. 'But not with any pleasure.'

'I wonder, darling, if you understand what a long run means?' He saw her swift look of irritation. 'I mean, I know you have had quite a few in the past. God knows, more than your share.' She seemed mollified. 'But do you think you could stand it now, Victoria? Night after night.'

'I know what it means, Joe, but I'm game – I've always been strong.'

'Yes, but you have just had a little setback.'

'Oh, you mean the fall? That was nothing,' she hastily explained it away.

'Oh, was that all? Well, I have made a few enquiries. There is a part coming up next month at the Haymarket – Jessie Maynard is leaving for a break.'

'Oh, is she?' Victoria thought swiftly. Jessie Maynard was about sixty something.

'Do you think I could do it?' she appealed.

'Standing on your head, darling,' he assured her. 'If, that is, you could cope with the same thing night after night? It's a terribly demanding part. If you recall, she has a breakdown. I understand Jessie said it was gruelling.'

'Oh, did she?' There was the slightest note of condescension in Victoria's voice. 'Well,' she said enthusiastically, 'it's good to get your teeth into a part like that. Have you a script?'

'I have,' he said doubtfully, 'but another thing is there are more chances on TV – you're in the public eye, it's hard work but fun to do. A nice bunch of –'

'Not a sit-com!' She looked horrified.

'No, dear, of course not. A new series.'

'What sort of part?' she asked suspiciously.

'The doctor's mother in a medical series for Carlton.'

'Mmm.' She looked doubtful.

Looking at him, she knew what he was thinking. Beggars and ageing actresses can't be choosers. She smiled sweetly.

'Whatever you think, Joe. I'll have a go at anything.'

'How are you on lines?' he asked suddenly.

'You mean remembering them? Well, you know I've always been good. No problem.'

'Not starting to forget?' he suggested. 'You know how it is. I do it myself.'

Yes, she supposed he must be her age.

'No, thank God,' she said fervently. 'If there had been the slightest sign of that, I wouldn't have come.'

'Well, let's hope it stays that way,' he said. 'Look, Victoria, I'll get on to one or two people, and look around. I'll send you a script of the Haymarket thing, that's not settled yet, and anything else that comes in. I'll be in touch. Leave it with me. Of course, there are always voice overs, advertisements ...?'

'Oh, Joe!' she cried. 'How could you? No, I haven't sunk to that yet.'

'It's good work,' he said reprovingly. 'You'd be surprised how much in demand it is.'

'Yes, well, I'm not quite into that,' she said, getting up and putting on her gloves. 'So you will get in touch Joe?'

'As soon as possible,' he said, getting up and leading her to the door. 'Lovely to see you again, Victoria.'

She made an exit like a queen, and when she had gone he mopped his brow. She was good, but the trouble was how many more of them were there out there? She used to have that special bit of magic. Was it still there?

Well, the public always had the answer ultimately. Not even he could foresee their response.

Venetia looked up as Victoria came out of the lift and walked elegantly towards her, holding out her hands in a purely theatrical gesture.

'Oh, there you are, my dear – how good of you to wait. Shall we go?'

They went to lunch – two attractive women who were looked at as they entered the dining room. Some of the women looked at Venetia, her young vibrant beauty, but other, older women looked at Victoria, at her grace and elegance.

'Oh, I know her. That's – er, now what was her name?'

Conscious of the admiring stares, she sat down and removed her gloves.

'I'm going to have exactly what I fancy today,' she said. 'How about you?'

'Whatever you say,' Venetia smiled. You had to hand it to her. But admiration turned to anger as she recalled the last glimpse of her mother, waving, her pretty face already prematurely aged.

Yes, some people had all the luck.

Edith arrived back on Saturday, obviously pleased to be home. She looked well and rested and insisted on taking over again where she had left off.

'Come on, bed for you, Victoria,' she said. 'I'll come and

tuck you in and bring you a hot toddy – and tell you all about Bournemouth.'

Victoria had to admit she felt rather pleased.

When the telephone rang at eight-thirty, it turned out to be Julian, ringing from Amsterdam. He wished to speak to Venetia.

'I should have caught an earlier plane, but I won't get back now until midnight, so what about seeing me tomorrow?'

Venetia was only too pleased.

'That will be very nice,' she said softly.

'We'll drive down somewhere for lunch, the river perhaps, then let's see what the weather is like, shall we? I can't wait to see you again, Venetia.' His voice had sunk to a whisper, and a slight frisson of excitement went through her.

'I've missed you,' she said softly, and his heart leapt.

'Really? Oh, Venetia, just to hear you say that.'

'Sshn,' she said softly, 'I'll see you tomorrow.'

'Pick you up around twelve. By the way, I'll have the car.'

'Yes?'

'I'll get the car hire chap to drop me off at Jarretts on the way back from the airport.'

Even better, she thought.

'Oh, that's lovely, my dear,' Victoria said when she was told the next morning. 'I'm so pleased.' And she looked it.

Edith disappeared into the kitchen.

'I shall be leaving you soon,' Venetia said sadly.

'Oh, my dear, must you?' Victoria looked quite disappointed.

'Yes, Mama will be anxious to know how I have got on.'

Victoria looked puzzled.

'I promised her I would look around for somewhere for us to live. You know she longs to come back to England.'

'Oh, does she?' Victoria said thoughtfully.

'Yes, she loathes the Italian summers – they are so hot – and she has stayed purely on my account. But now that my divorce has come through, and I am free ...'

'You would consider coming to England with her?' Victoria asked.

'Of course, we must never be separated. She has done so much for me.'

'You will come back then?' Victoria asked.

'Yes. I shall go home on Monday and stay for a few days, just to see how things are. I never like to leave her for long.'

'Of course not, my dear.'

'A few days at home, and I shall return.'

'Where would you like to live in England?' Victoria asked.

'London first, I think – Mama is used to a city, she likes to see what is going on. On the other hand, there is the country. Perhaps a cottage somewhere – a little house. We shall see.'

'Well, we must do all we can to help,' Victoria said. She liked to get her teeth into something, and after all, she had no wish to lose sight of this attractive young woman who had been so good to her.

The light blue Aston Martin sat outside the block of flats in the residents' parking allocation. From the third floor where she had been watching, Venetia looked down with approval. The car was in pristine condition, had been looked after very carefully. She had no idea of its age, but thoroughly approved of what she saw. It had style. Top marks, Julian, she thought.

He came up, carrying a bouquet of flowers: delphiniums and roses, larkspur and gypsophila. 'From Ruth and Geoffrey,' he said. 'I stood them in water overnight – hope they're all right.'

Victoria buried her face in them. 'They're lovely,' she said, 'such scent. Venetia will put them in water.'

Venetia met his eyes over the flowers. He thought he had never seen anything quite so lovely as the girl with the soft brown eyes which looked into his so candidly, the gentle smile, the dress of white sprigged with blue flowers.

'Thanks, Venetia,' he said. Two dimples showed in her cheeks as she went off into the kitchen.

'So how are you, Mother?' he asked. 'You look better each time I see you.'

He hitched his immaculate trousers and sat down next to her. It was his intention in the not too distant future to mention her emeralds. He had made up his mind on the plane coming back, having been shown some exquisite emeralds in Amsterdam and told what they were worth. But he must choose the right time. He didn't want to make a blunder and startle her into wondering why he asked. Truth was, he could do with the money. Oh, he was doing well, but he could do with more, and he was making a lot of money for other people. The perks were not enough. It was ridiculous when you considered that there were these priceless gems in the family. Who better to deal with them than him? Besides if – and he wasn't one hundred per cent certain just yet – *if* he were to find a second Mrs Julian Bellamy ... Ah, now that was something else. Come to think of it, that wasn't all his mother had. He remembered a pair of emerald earrings his father had given her, perhaps for their twentieth wedding anniversary – whatever happened to those? He had never seen her wearing them. Oh, yes, after all these years it was a nonsense to keep quiet about them.

'I am just fine, darling,' Victoria said in answer to his question, quite unaware of what was going on in that handsome head. 'But what have you been doing?'

'Looking at diamonds,' he said. 'Beautiful spectacular diamonds.'

She smiled back at him fondly.

Venetia returned with a bowlful of flowers which she placed on a side table so that Victoria could catch the scent.

'Thank you, darling. Would you like coffee?' Victoria asked her son.

'No, thank you, we must be off.' Julian bent low to kiss her.

'Then get along,' Victoria said, watching the pair of them together. What a handsome couple they were. Perhaps, she thought, something may come of it. And couldn't help wishing that it would.

Chapter Fifteen

The drive down to Marlow was pleasant on a lovely day, and Venetia sat back against the soft leather seat, pale blue to match the car, noting with pleasure the luxurious interior, the workmanship that had gone into the making of such a vehicle.

'Will you garage it in London now?' she asked Julian presently.

'Yes, I was lucky enough to find a garage not too far away. It'll cost an arm and a leg, but that's the way it is in London. And free space is worth a fortune.'

'Still, I expect you will be pleased to have it nearby. Public transport is so awful.'

'Don't often use it.' Julian grinned. 'I take taxis everywhere, then it's planes and airports – typical of life today. I'd hate to be a commuter.'

'Perish the thought.' Venetia smiled.

'How do you manage in Rome?' he asked. 'The last time I was there I couldn't see how people managed to get around at all – almost as bad as Athens.'

'You get used to it,' Venetia said. 'I have a small car of my own. We had a Ferrari but of course it belonged to Carlo.'

He shot her a quick glance. 'Is life going to change very much for you now, Venetia? After the divorce, I mean?'

'Yes, of course,' she said swiftly. 'Roman society is different from anywhere else in the world. It is a very closed society, and I have to admit I shall be quite glad to leave it to come to London. Mama will be pleased too.'

'I say, that's great news. I didn't know you were so serious about it.' He sounded enthusiastic.

They were waiting at the lights on Marlow Bridge, just before the entrance to The Compleat Angler.

'Oh, the river! How beautiful – look, there are swans! Oh, what a view – this just has to be England!'

Her dark eyes glowing, she turned to him with a smile that turned his heart over. He took a deep breath.

'Yes, it's lovely, isn't it?' He drove the car into the car park, and when they had got out, walked with her down to the river where he took her hand.

'Pleased you came?' he asked. 'I thought you'd like it.'

'It's quite lovely,' Venetia said, and meant it. An idyllic spot. And who knew what lay in store for her? It was so romantic. Her hopes soared.

They sat drinking iced Martinis before going into lunch, and having given his order, Julian explained some of the history of the hotel to her.

'Mama told me about Marlow,' she said, although nothing Violet said could have prepared her for its beauty. 'I think Italy is lovely, but it's so much grander, older. This place is like a miniature scene, like something you'd find in a fairy tale.'

He smiled. 'Later we'll walk across to the lock. It's quite fascinating to watch the boats go through the gates.'

'Now tell me about you,' he continued. 'Apart from our mothers going to school together, what else do we know about each other?'

She smiled, dimples showing, eyes shining into his.

'There really isn't much to tell. I was educated in Rome, although early on we did come to England quite a bit, but that ceased after my father –'

He looked at her with sympathy. 'I'm sorry.'

'No, he didn't die.' And a cold note crept into her voice. 'He left us. I was fourteen and he left us, Mama and I, for a girl twenty years his junior. She was nineteen and he was forty.'

'That must have been awful for your mother – and for you?'

'It was.' And her voice now was quite hard. 'But my mother is wonderful. She worked and earned enough money to put me through a good school and then a finishing school. I wasn't always the dutiful daughter I should have been, I'm afraid.' And she gave him a rueful smile.

He was sure of it. There was a trace of devilment in those eyes of hers now and again, and you couldn't be quite sure what she would do next, for all her impeccable manners and behaviour. That was what made her so exciting.

'Where did you meet your husband?'

'I was twenty-three when I met him at the Opera House in Rome.' After all, there was no need to tell him of the other little affairs, the worry she had put her Mama through so many times for fear she would do something flagrant, flout Roman society. 'We had been with a party to see *Madame Butterfly*, and I remember we laughed so much because Pinkerton was so small and so fat.' She smiled at the memory. 'We were introduced and, well, that was that.'

'And what about you?' she asked him. 'Fiona, was that her name? How long did it last?'

'Too long,' he said grimly. 'I should have seen the writing on the wall much sooner, but I didn't. I thought I had made the match of the year. Oh, yes, she was lovely, glamorous, rich – lots of boyfriends – but she chose me.' He looked at her ruefully. 'Sometimes I wonder if it was because she thought I would be easy, she would be able to do as she liked and no questions asked. I would feel I was lucky to have got her, as it were.'

'Oh, surely not?'

'Well, for whatever reason, she married me. The first time she was unfaithful, I let it pass. I knew the guy, he was a friend of mine – or had been – but after that, it was just too bloody – sorry – too damn ridiculous. So I decided to make a day of it, and there you are. Mind you,' he smiled, 'I've changed. I wouldn't be so agreeable now.'

No, thought Venetia. She could imagine he could be quite ruthless in his own way. A little like herself, perhaps? Were they birds of a feather?

'I was with Blane's at the time.'

'The fine art people?'

'Yes, I had a good training there, but after Fiona I decided to go it alone. And a damn good thing too.'

Her eyes shone with admiration.

'Well done,' she said. 'Now tell me what it is you do exactly?'

'I advise people on their jewellery – a valuer, in other words – and sometimes buy and sell. It depends what they want. That's where the travelling comes in. I may be in New York one day and Switzerland the next – it depends where the owners of the fine gems are. And of course it is usually women who own them.'

'So you have quite an interesting life,' she teased.

'Yes, you could say that. But I never let pleasure interfere with business. It is too important for that.'

'So you don't deal with industrial diamonds?' she asked him, eyes wide.

'Now what do you know about industrial diamonds?'

'Only what I have read,' she admitted. 'Nothing really.'

'No, that's another field. I deal mainly in set pieces, made up jewellery, necklaces, tiaras, rings, that sort of thing. The occasional antique or piece of fine art – it depends. One often finds that the owner of fine jewellery has something else she wants to have valued or to sell.'

'So, really,' she said, 'you are in a position to make quite a lot of money?'

'Well, yes, it sounds like that, but really it's quite hard work, and a lot of responsibility. You have to know what you are talking about.'

'I'm sure you do,' Venetia agreed. Already she was respecting him more than somewhat.

The waiter came to tell them their lunch was ready and they entered the dining room where a table by the window allowed them to see the river in all its glory, with the ducks and swans nearby and the occasional boat going past.

'I won't forget this in a hurry,' Venetia said, opening her snow white napkin and smiling across at him.

He smiled back. 'I hope there will be many more visits like this, my dear.'

She felt a warm glow run through her. Things might be looking up. She was due for a bit of luck.

'By the way,' he said, after a while, 'I understand from Edith that my mother went to see her old agent – Joe Bernard?'

'Yes, I went with her.'

'What on earth's got into her? At her age.'

'But if she wants to – ' Venetia began.

'Anyway, what happened?'

'I think she is going to read for a part,' Venetia said, eyes twinkling.

He put down his fork. 'You're joking!'

'No. Really. She put in for this part at the – oh, I can't remember where. And as far as I know she probably has it.'

'No one told me,' he said darkly. 'Does Vanessa or Geoffrey know about this?'

Venetia shrugged. 'I really don't know.'

'Well, I'll have to look into it. I thought old Edith was having me on.'

'Not so,' Venetia said equably. 'I can assure you, it is quite true.'

'You know, mother has had a wonderful life,' he said. 'When you look back, she was a fully fledged actress at eighteen – and, as I understand it, the toast of London when she was about twenty-one. Of course, there was a war on then, so who knows what might have happened had there not been? Then she met Pa.'

'What was he like?' Venetia asked.

'Oh, a fantastic man.' There was no doubting Julian's admiration. 'He decided to marry her at their first meeting. Can you imagine? He adored her. Gave her Jarretts to do with as she liked. And not only that, gave her the most wonderful jewellery.' He lowered his voice.

'Between you and me, she has the most incredible emeralds. I've seen them once – oh, years ago, when I was a kid. They were magnificent. Finer than anything I've seen. And yet ...'

She waited. She didn't want to stop the flow of confidences.

'I've never seen her wear them. Once, on that occasion when I saw them, she got them out of a drawer and opened the box and they nestled there on the satin – I can't tell you the effect they had on me. Sparkled isn't the word. They were sheer magnetism. I can see them now, such a green, so beautiful. They had a life of their own.'

They were both silent for a moment.

'Anyway,' he laughed, 'I suppose they are in the bank. She never wears them, or even mentions them.'

Venetia was silent.

'She also had lots of other jewellery – matching earrings for a fact. I remember Pa giving them to her on an anniversary. Beautiful long drops. Then there was a pair of diamond earrings of fabulous quality. Somehow, after Pa died, she never wore much jewellery.'

'Why don't you ask her about them?' Venetia said softly. 'After all, it is only natural, you being in the world of precious stones.'

'Yes, I intend to,' he said. 'They'd fetch a staggering price. And after all, if she's not going to wear them again –'

'She might.'

'I don't think so.'

'I think if I had them I should want to wear them all the time – even in bed.' Her cheeks were rosy, flushed with wine, and he had a mental picture of her sitting up in bed waiting for him, naked except for the emeralds. He felt hot.

'I do believe you would,' he laughed to hide his confusion.

She put down her knife and fork. 'Well, that was an excellent meal, Julian.'

But he was still in a dream world.

'Look,' he said, 'do you have to go home so soon?'

'Yes, I am afraid so – I must see how Mama is, and sort out a few things. But then I shall return and look around seriously for somewhere to live.'

'That's wonderful,' he enthused.

'Now that I know I should quite like to live here,' she added, her dark eyes taking in the scene on the river. He felt his heart leap.

'Can I help in any way – in finding you something? I have quite a few connections. Where would you look?'

'I thought London – an apartment. But I shall have plenty of time when I return.'

'Well, if I can be of any assistance,' he said, as the waiter returned.

'Would you like coffee in the lounge, sir, madam?'

'Please,' Venetia said. One thing about her, she never dithered, Julian thought. Always knew what she wanted. He liked that.

More and more he realised that this girl seemed to fit the bill for remarriage. She was beautiful, with exquisite manners, yet strong – all in all, she was growing on him at an alarming rate.

'Where will you stay when you return? I must know where to find you,' he said.

'I've booked in at The Towers,' she told him. 'All being well, I shall be back next Saturday.'

He couldn't wait for the time to fly. Thank goodness he was off to Holland next week. Driving home, he pulled up outside his mother's apartment and took her in his arms. This time, she made no demur and as his lips met hers, deliciously parted, two warm arms stole round his neck, her fingers caressing him, pointed nails finding their way through the thick curly hair at his nape. His hand reached for the lovely mound of her breast, the warmth of her flesh and the scent of her going to his head. Her mouth tasted sweet and he could feel the tip of her tongue. Just when he felt he must go even farther, she broke away and sat up, eyes shining in the darkness, lips soft and warm.

'Thank you for a lovely day, Julian,' she said softly. 'I must go in, I have to finish packing.'

'Let me come in with you.'

'No, not now.' And leaning across she kissed him on the lips, swiftly, a kiss full of promise – and was opening the car door.

He got out and came round her side and took her in his arms.

'Come back with me,' he said hoarsely. 'Now, come back to the flat. There's plenty of time.'

But Venetia had heard all that before, many times, and knew that to leave him with a promise was by far the best way.

'I wish,' she said wistfully, dark eyes looking up into his. 'But no, we must be sensible. Good night, Julian, dear Julian.' And she laid a hand over his, then ran up the steps, pressed the button for entry and was inside. He saw her go towards the lift. He couldn't wait to see her again.

So far so good, she thought on the plane going to Rome the next morning. And truth to tell, she didn't find Julian unattractive at all. Quite the contrary.

Venetia sat on the balcony in the cool early morning, seeing the scarlet and pink geraniums spilling over balconies, inhaling the scent from the jacaranda tree. What a different scene from the green of England. Yet there was something wonderfully fresh about all that grass, the immaculate green lawns, trees so tall and stately, something gracious about it all.

'So tell me all about it?' Violet said. She had to admit Venetia looked wonderful. Rested, relaxed. Something must have happened to give her this particular glow.

'Well,' she said, pouring coffee for them both, 'your Victoria is something else, of course. She has not been well, I should imagine she had a slight stroke – but then again, perhaps not. But at any rate, she is well now. Not only that, she wants to go back on the stage!'

'No!' Violet sat open-mouthed. 'At her age.' And to think that her own daughter had been staying with Victoria Bellamy! Living there!

'I hope you weren't a nuisance,' she said with a worried frown. 'How did you come to stay there in the first place? I thought you had booked into The Dorchester?'

'I had. I did. But you know it's a bit boring, and after I'd been to see Victoria, we got on like a house on fire and it was she who suggested that I spend some time with them. The flat is large, there is plenty of room, and after all, why not?'

It sounded reasonable enough, Violet thought. Just as long as ...

'And I met the son, Julian. Mama, he really is nice.'

Judging by her expression, Violet thought, he was more than that. Was there something behind all this? Venetia could clam up if you asked too many questions, so she kept quiet.

'He is divorced. Apparently, she was a bit of a handful – like Carlo.' And she found that she was beginning to believe that he really had behaved like a cad.

'Anyway, we went out a few times. Oh, and I stayed there when Edith, Victoria's companion, went away for a few days. So, you see, I earned my keep.'

'And did you find anything for us – me – somewhere to live?'

'I saw quite a few possibilities, Mama,' Venetia lied, 'some suitable, some not. I thought I'd sort it out when I go back. I had to come back to see that you were all right, and besides I couldn't outstay my welcome at Victoria's. I've booked into

The Towers and I'll work from there. Is there any particular part of London you would prefer? After all, it's a big place.' And she smiled warmly at her mother.

'I always liked Kensington,' Violet said slowly. 'We lived there for a while when I was small, before the war. I don't know what it's like now.'

'So what would you think? A small house, an apartment?'

'Whatever. I suppose an apartment. After all, you won't be with me forever,' she said.

'Now, Mama, you don't know that. Of course we will be together. And are you prepared to move permanently to London, take the furniture and everything, or let this and rent furnished?'

Violet frowned. 'Oh, darling, I don't know. It's such a big step, isn't it? You must remember I haven't lived in England since the war, not for any length of time. And it must be suitable for you, since we are going to share. Large enough to take us both. I like space.'

'Leave it with me,' Venetia said.

She spent the next few days shopping, being careful to avoid the little boutiques the Tellini women might patronise. On the fourth day, crossing the Via Veneto, she had a close encounter with a speeding car, having to jump out of the way fairly quickly to avoid being run down. Looking after it, she thought she recognised the back of a Tellini chauffeur, and found she was trembling a little. She wouldn't put it past them. After all, she had been told to get out of Rome ...

Pondering over the move, part of her excited at the thought, the other half almost too nervous to contemplate it, Violet thought the whole venture had a slightly surreal quality about it. But then, she had often been swept along by Venetia's enthusiastic ideas.

She quite liked the idea of going back to England, but she had been away for so long. How would she fit in now? Was it too late to make a fresh start?

After the car episode, Venetia was quite glad to get away. The man sitting next to her on the plane was flatteringly aware of his good fortune. No man could ignore legs like that, that figure, those eyes – and before the plane had left the runway, he knew her name and where she was going.

What a little beauty – and that perfume! He sniffed appreciatively.

'Will you join me?' he asked her, ordering champagne.

Her great dark eyes were full of merriment.

'I am celebrating a very successful business deal.'

'Why not?' Venetia said, and met his blue eyes over the glass.

She had always believed in making the best of things. By the time they had lunched and reached London, they were like old friends.

He handed her a card. 'I am often in London – usually staying at The Savoy,' he said. 'Do ring me if you are free.'

She glanced down at the card. Stephen Manderwood, Managing Director of Manderwood Oil etc, etc. New York, Texas, Rio de Janeiro. She looked up at him, and smiled.

'How can I reach you?' he asked.

'I'm not sure where I shall be,' she replied. 'If I have time, I'll be in touch.'

That was the whole point of going first class, she told herself. Aim for the top, nothing less would do.

He watched the slim legs disappear out of sight and sighed.

It was the luck of the draw.

Chapter Sixteen

Five o'clock on a Friday afternoon and Vanessa was finishing for the day. Papers put away, the desk cleared, her weekend bag packed and stowed in the boot of her car. But first she must call on her mother, there would be plenty of time before setting out for Haslemere, and perhaps, only perhaps, she would broach the news of her marriage to Gavin – when his divorce became final.

She had thought it over carefully, wondering whether to tell Victoria after the event, but decided against it. Upset though Victoria would be, and Vanessa knew this was true, she would prefer to know rather than be told later.

It was quiet when she buzzed the door of the flat, and Edith came out to greet her.

'Vanessa, how nice, your mother will be pleased to see you.'

'Is she asleep?'

'No, no, writing letters, I think.'

Through the open door, she saw Victoria in the drawing room, as elegant as ever in a navy blue suit and gold chain belt, scrupulously made up, her hair immaculate. Vanessa was conscious of her own deficiencies. It just didn't seem to be in her nature to be so smart. She did, though, tweak at her sweater and pull down her long skirt, rubbing one boot against the calf of her leg to take off the dust marks. Glancing in the mirror, she saw a pleasant-looking young woman, her face devoid of make-up, hair cut just anyhow. But her eyes were nice.

She tapped on the door.

'Vanessa darling, how lovely.' Mother and daughter kissed.

If Victoria was thrown by her daughter's appearance, she made no sign. She was used to it by now and expected nothing else. Sometimes she dressed her mentally, and saw how wonderful Vanessa could look – but these days it was a waste of time talking about it. Vanessa was Vanessa. She would never change now.

Her bright eyes looked up at her daughter.

'Are you on your way home?'

'Yes, darling. Then we are going down to Sussex for the weekend.' She saw her mother's frown and the way her eyes darkened.

'Oh, how nice. How is Gavin? Well?'

'Yes, he's fine.' And Vanessa jumped in. She made a business of dragging a chair whilst talking at the same time. 'We are going to get married, Mama, as soon as his divorce comes through.' By the time the sentence was out she was seated in the chair and facing her mother, eyes wide and a little apprehensive.

There was a brief silence before Victoria spoke.

'Well, darling, that's nice. If that's what you want.'

'Mummy, you know it is. I shall be the happiest person in the world.'

The old endearment crept out. Victoria wanted to hug her, to reassure her, but she couldn't. She had such misgivings about their future together.

'Then I wish you all the luck in the world, darling.'

'Thank you, Mummy.' And Vanessa's eyes filled with tears. 'I've known him such a long time,' she said, as if wishing to explain the situation.

'Darling, you don't have to make excuses – you love him, I know that, and my only wish is to see you happy. You will understand that when you have a daughter of your own.'

'At this rate, I never will,' Vanessa said ruefully.

'Oh, yes, you will – there's plenty of time. You are a baby yet.'

Vanessa relaxed.

'Well, how have you been? I brought you some chocs,' handing her a gift-wrapped pink parcel.

'How lovely. Thank you, darling.' Victoria placed them by the side of her on a table.

'And I gather that Venetia has gone?' Vanessa looked pleased.

'Yes, and I miss her – she kept me young,' Victoria said.

Vanessa felt a swift stab of jealousy.

'You haven't known her five minutes,' she commented almost tartly.

'No, but she came in like a breath of fresh air. Anyhow, she is coming back next week.'

'Coming back?'

'Yes. Not here, darling. She will be staying at The Towers but she – '

'Why is she coming back?'

'She is looking for somewhere for her mother and herself to live.'

'Her mother? But doesn't she live in Rome?'

'Yes, that's the whole point, darling. Violet is not awfully well, and hates the hot summers in Italy. Apparently she longs for England. I think I can understand that. And now that Venetia's divorce has come through – '

'I didn't know she was divorced?'

'It's quite recent, I believe.'

'What went wrong?'

'Apparently she had quite a time with him chasing other women.'

'Hmm.' And Vanessa's lip curled despite herself. 'Well, that's nice,' she said of nothing at all. 'Anyway, you are feeling better, are you?'

'Yes. And there's something I want to tell you. I have been to see Joe Bernard.'

'Your agent?'

Victoria nodded.

'What for?'

'I want to get back to work.'

Vanessa's mouth was open. 'You're joking!'

'Indeed I am not. Why shouldn't I?' her mother said haughtily

'It's so exhausting – would you be up to it?' But she knew that when her mother had a fixed idea nothing would budge her.

'Of course I am up to it. Just because I ... anyway, I've

been offered Jessie Maynard's part at the Haymarket. I went to read for it yesterday and they were over the moon about having me take over.'

Vanessa could hardly believe it.

'Well! Good luck to you,' she said for want of something better.

'If you are going to suggest I'm too old, I shall hit you!'

Vanessa had to laugh. 'Too old! You? I should say not. Darling, I'm delighted, but a bit concerned. You can understand that, can't you?'

Victoria patted her hand. 'Of course I can. I should feel exactly the same. But I tell you, Vanessa, I'd rather die in harness, than sit here all day being careful of myself. There's a lot of life in me yet, you'll see.'

Vanessa got up and hugged her. 'Of course there is,' she laughed. 'Well, you won't mind if I hurry along, will you? Gavin will be waiting.'

It was on the tip of Victoria's tongue to ask where Suzie was, but she thought better of it. It was none of her business. Better keep out of it.

Vanessa kissed her mother and waved from the door.

Driving back to Gavin's flat, she pondered over her mother's news. It was a great achievement to secure a part at her age. How had she done it? The producer must have a soft spot for her. And perhaps she was still a draw, even if most young people had never heard of her. Vanessa sighed. Well, good luck to her.

Gavin was waiting and moved her bag into his car. 'How was your mother?'

'Just fine. And you'll never believe it, Gavin, she's going back to the stage.'

His expression showed his disbelief.

'Really? Good for her.'

'Unless I'm very much mistaken she is taking over from Jessie Maynard at the Haymarket. Of course, it's not a long part, but still.'

'She'll do it,' Gavin said. 'Once an actress ...'

'Yes, I suppose you're right. She's amazing though, isn't she?'

Once settled in the car, he drove out of London and waited until the roads had cleared a little.

'We are lucky with the weather this summer,' Vanessa said. 'Another beautiful day.'

'Yes, but I hate to disillusion you, rain is forecast.' And he turned to her briefly with his quirky smile. Those eyes, Vanessa thought. Little Tom's are exactly the same. They stopped for tea on the way down, then resumed the drive.

'Yes, I've come to the conclusion that it's a good idea to get rid of the cottage,' he said. 'Get a larger flat in town, big enough to take us and Tom and the nanny.'

'Denise?'

'No, I don't think so. Did you tell your mother about us, Van?'

'Yes, I did.'

'What did she say?'

'Not a lot. Wished us luck.'

'She's never liked me, has she?'

Vanessa flushed. 'Oh, I wouldn't say that.'

'No, I can tell. Perhaps she didn't dislike me personally so much as what I stood for. A married man.'

'Yes, I think that's it. Still, it won't be long now. Why don't you think Denise will come?'

'I have an idea she is anxious to get back to France, and I won't be sorry. I told Mrs Benson on the phone during the week what I had in mind. She rang about something or other and the subject came up. I gather she wouldn't be sorry to move on. She wants to retire to live with her widowed sister in Alfriston.'

'You'll miss it, though, Gavin – coming down here, that lovely house.'

'Nothing is for ever,' he said succinctly, and the subject was dropped.

As they drove down the lane to the house on the hill, they could see Mrs Benson in the front drive. She appeared agitated and waved to them.

Gavin parked the car and got out.

'Mrs Benson, what is it?'

'Tom – he hasn't been home from school. Denise went to collect him and they haven't been back.'

'Good God!' Gavin said, looking at his watch. 'Stay by the phone, I'll get down to the school.'

In silence he drove the short journey to the school, which

appeared closed down and empty, but he rang the bell at the side of the house until someone came. The caretaker answered his ring.

'Mr Weston, isn't it?'

'My son Tom, he hasn't been home.'

'Oh, dear. Your girl collected him – Denise, isn't it? I'll get my wife.'

She came hurrying out. 'Is something wrong, Mr Weston?'

'Tom – have you seen him? He didn't return home.'

'Denise collected him at the usual time. I know because I saw her take his hand. We always make sure of that.'

'Did you see the car?' Denise usually drove an old Peugeot.

'Yes, being Friday I watched them go down the path, and they turned and waved.' She frowned. 'Come to think of it, there was another car there, one I haven't seen before, a pale blue one, rather smart looking.' And looking at Gavin's face, Vanessa saw how white he had gone.

'What is it?'

'Suzie has a pale blue car, a BMW. Or she did when she went to France.'

'Oh, Gavin, you don't think ...'

'No, of course not,' he said swiftly. 'Still, where did they go? There are no shops on the way.'

'Perhaps she took him for a walk?'

'That isn't like her. She knows I'm coming down to see Tom. All right, thanks. Would you please ring me if you hear anything?'

They hurried back to the car.

'Let's get back to the house,' he said. 'I should have checked to see if the car was there. If it is, it means either Denise walked to the school or she was given a lift.' He looked grim.

It was a nightmare journey back to the house, each of them sure that they would not find Tom there. Each of them scared that something awful had happened, that his mother had kidnapped him.

'You don't think Suzie – ' Vanessa began.

'I wouldn't put it past her,' Gavin said bitterly. He glanced at his watch. 'An hour since he left school. They've had ample time to get home by now.'

Mrs Benson stood in the doorway, and shook her head.

'No, nothing,' she said. 'No calls, nothing.'

'Did Denise take the car?' Gavin asked, walking towards the garage.

'I don't know, I didn't see her go.' But Gavin lifted the door of the garage and there was the dark blue Peugeot.

His face was grim. 'I'm going to the police station.' He turned to Vanessa. 'Want to come?'

He was brusque now, all warmth gone, treating her like a stranger.

'Yes, of course,' she said, and waited for him to get back in the car.

It was a short drive to the station. After telling the story, and having the particulars taken, it was obvious they knew nothing but would put available men on to it at once. Had Gavin had any idea where they could have gone? Was it possible that the girl was taking the boy to France? Were they making for the ferry crossing? Did he think – was it likely – could they have a description of his wife and the pale blue car? And all the time the situation seemed to grow worse.

It was six-thirty when the telephone call came.

The pale blue car, a BMW, had been found just outside Newhaven Dock. It had been making for the ferry, and had been involved in a slight accident. There were two women inside and a small boy. No one was hurt.

Gavin was as white as a sheet, and Vanessa thought she would never forget the look on his face.

'Are they all right?' he asked hoarsely.

'Yes, sir, no one hurt. A bit shaken, but otherwise all right. The car's a bit of a mess – lucky to get away with it, the other driver seems to have been at fault – but any rate, sir, there it is. They're in a hotel nearby – The Cricketer's Arms. I suggest you might like to get down there as quick as you can.'

Gavin put down the phone and turned to Vanessa.

'Thank God, he's safe ... I shall drive down there straight away. Perhaps you would like to stay here?'

'I want to come with you,' she said.

'You're sure?' he asked dubiously. He obviously wanted to avoid a confrontation between the two women.

'I'm sure,' Vanessa said. She had never been more certain of anything in her life.

She surprised herself by the strength of her feelings. Whatever the outcome, she was determined to see it through. If indeed Suzie had taken Tom, it was a criminal action, and heaven knew what was going on in Gavin's mind. She stole a look at him, seeing the jaw flexing, his teeth clenched, his hands rigid on the wheel.

Poor Gavin, he didn't deserve this. At one point she opened her mouth to speak, but saw that he wouldn't have heard her anyway, he was so wrapped up in his thoughts and his concentration on the road. She might as well not have been there.

But I am, she thought stubbornly. Let's get to the bottom of this, once and for all.

The road was fast and presently they left the countryside behind them, and the lights of Newhaven shone in the distance. As they drove towards the dock area, they saw the brilliantly lit Cricketer's Arms. On the parking lot was a pale blue BMW with its side stoved in, and on the pub forecourt, a police car. Gavin pulled alongside.

Whether he wanted her to or not, Vanessa got out and followed him.

Inside the atmosphere was typical. Thick smoke and a brown-varnished ceiling and walls – it looked as if it hadn't been cleaned for years. There were a few regulars by the bar, and a policeman in uniform standing by the entrance to the restaurant.

Gavin went up to him.

'Weston,' he said tersely. 'I've come about my son and my wife – the blue BMW outside.'

'Ah, good evening, sir.' He glanced at Vanessa. 'Will you come this way, sir? Miss?'

He led them to a small ante-room obviously set aside for the purpose. Inside was a policeman and a woman constable, but of more interest to Vanessa was the sight of Suzie, the golden girl, sitting holding Tom's hand. Denise sat beside her with a small satisfied smile on her face.

Vanessa's first shocked reaction on seeing Suzie was: Why, she isn't even pretty! For Suzie was small and plain with no make-up. She was very tanned, wore jeans and a checked shirt, and her hair was dragged back into a pony tail. She was so unlike Vanessa's preconceived idea of her, that she was almost shocked.

As they went in, Tom broke away from his mother. 'Daddy, Daddy!' He leapt at his father who picked him up and held him tight. 'Are you all right, son?' The boy hugged him.

Gavin put Tom down. 'I'm the boy's father,' he said to the constable, and turned to Vanessa. 'This is Miss Bellamy.'

'Yes, sir.' And the policeman took out his notebook. 'Is this the boy who was reported missing at four-twenty-nine this afternoon?'

'That's right,' Gavin said shortly.

'And you had collected him from school, miss?' the policeman asked Suzie. But she was staring at Vanessa. It was impossible for Vanessa to tell exactly what was going through her mind, but she was evidently as astonished at what she saw as Vanessa had been.

What was going through her mind? Vanessa wondered.

The constable repeated his question and Suzie turned back to him.

'Oh, I'm sorry, yes. I collected him – '

The policewoman came over and took Tom by the hand.

'As I understand it, miss, you were about to take the boy without his father's permission.'

Suzie bit her lip, and looked nervous. She threw Gavin an anxious glance.

'I am not pressing charges,' he said firmly, and Vanessa heard Suzie's soft intake of breath, her sigh of relief. 'It has all been a misunderstanding.'

Vanessa's eyebrows lifted. So Suzie was to get away with it!

The constable closed his book. 'We don't like to interfere in domestic affairs, sir, but there is the matter of the car accident. I understand Mrs Weston has given all the particulars to my colleague.'

'What are you going to do about the damaged BMW?' the policewoman asked.

'The garage is going to pick it up as soon as possible,' Suzie said. 'I shall stay here until they arrive.'

The policewoman took Tom's hand. 'Shall I take him downstairs for some lemonade and crisps?' she asked. 'It might be a good idea. I expect you'll want to sort things out.'

'Thanks,' Gavin said gratefully. 'Denise, you go too, please.'

He, Suzie and Vanessa were left standing until, like a game of charades, they came to life.

'This is Vanessa – Vanessa Bellamy,' Gavin said. 'Suzie.'

And, thought Vanessa afterwards, we actually shook hands. Somewhat limply.

He glanced at Suzie, and at the look on his face Vanessa's heart stopped. He and Suzie stared at each other for what seemed like minutes until Gavin spoke.

'I think we all need a stiff drink,' he said, white-faced, and the two women followed him down to the bar.

So that was the truth of it, Vanessa thought. He was still in love with her. There was no mistaking that look. He had never looked at her like that. What Suzie was thinking she had no idea.

In truth, Suzie was stunned. Just seeing the other woman face to face, was something she had never contemplated. So this was the girl who would take charge of her son, the woman who would live in her house, take over her home – her husband. It was different, seeing her. For so long she had been an unknown quantity. But now, face to face ... She was pretty. She had an air about her. She was young and trendy, in that long skirt and little boots, and she had a kind of dignity – oh, she was nothing like Suzie herself, and nothing like she had imagined. She had known about her, known all along. After all, who could blame Gavin? He was an attractive man, you couldn't expect him – if only she hadn't had that car crash she might have been away by now – on the other hand, it had been madness to think she would get away with it.

Vanessa found it difficult to analyse her feelings. Anger, sorrow, grief and disappointment were all there, mixed with a love for this man that was hopeless. Even if Suzie went back to France, even if he allowed her to take Tom, even if Tom stayed, whatever the outcome Gavin was in love with Suzie – always would be. Vanessa would always be second best. She had thought it would suffice, but knew now that it wouldn't. Always he would be thinking of Suzie. She would always come between them. And Suzie, what of her? She was willing to put a lot at stake for her son, even to the point of kidnapping him. Would she come back? Would she give up her lover in France?

What, Suzie thought, about Yves? And the two darling little girls, motherless. They needed her, and she loved Yves – but Tom needed her too, and you couldn't tell her that Gavin's love for her was dead – finished – over.

Vanessa felt drained as she realised that suddenly she didn't care. She wanted no part in this couple's affairs. She was an outsider. It was between them, and them alone. She had come on the scene to help Gavin come to terms with a vanished wife. She had wasted precious years – and for what? Surely this wasn't the answer, playing second fiddle, married to a man who loved someone else? Surely there must be more to life and the future than that?

The two women sat side by side as Gavin ordered drinks at the bar. Even his back view was attractive. Tall, dark haired, broad-shouldered. They both looked away.

'Well – ' Vanessa began, as Suzie got to her feet.

They both spoke together. 'Excuse me, I'll be back.' And Suzie made for the ladies' room.

Gavin looked shocked at Suzie's absence when he returned to the table with the drinks.

'Don't worry,' Vanessa said, a trifle maliciously. 'She's only gone to the Ladies' Room. She'll be back.' And taking her drink, took a long gulp.

There was no mistaking his expression when Suzie returned. He must love her very much, Vanessa thought. How could I have been so dumb? Mummy always said I was.

Suzie picked up her drink and spoke directly to Gavin.

'I'm sorry, Gavin, I shouldn't have – '

He took a deep breath. 'No, you shouldn't have.' He looked grim and it was then that Vanessa made up her mind.

'Will you excuse me?' she said, and ostensibly made her own way to the Ladies' Room. There, she wrote a note to Gavin, telling him she had gone back to London – she would be in touch about her bag. She asked the barman to be sure to give it to Mr Weston, and pointed him out. Then she asked at the desk for the telephone number of a car hire service who would be willing to drive her back to London.

Then, going into the public bar, thick as it was with smoke and locals playing darts, she ordered a double whisky. On the way back, she wept alcoholic tears which streamed down her face. She would stay with her mother until she found somewhere else. She had lived in a fool's paradise. Commonsense told her it was better to make the break now than later.

It was late when she arrived in Knightsbridge. Victoria was

asleep, but Vanessa left a note for Edith: 'Staying overnight – see you in the morning, Vanessa.' She crept into the bed in the spare room where she lay awake for hours mulling things over until morning came, when she finally slept, exhausted.

Chapter Seventeen

Vanessa woke late on Saturday morning with a blinding headache, uncertain as to where she was until the events of the last twenty-four hours crowded back into her mind. She felt lost, drained of all sensation, yet with the benefit of hindsight, what else could she have done? In the cold light of day, she was sure she had done the right thing, but that wasn't to say she hadn't been left feeling devastated, the rosy picture she had painted of life with Gavin and Tom gone forever.

She crawled out of bed, reeling slightly from the after effects of the whisky, and glanced at herself in the mirror, turning away quickly. God, what a mess!

She hurried into the bathroom and cleaned her teeth and showered, feeling just fractionally better afterwards. Then, in the old cotton dressing gown that still hung behind the door as it had when she was living at home, she made her way to the kitchen.

'Morning, Edith,' she said, going over to put the coffee on.

Edith knew better than to enquire what Vanessa was doing there. If she wanted to talk she would.

'Nice morning,' she said. 'Nice morning for a walk. You look as if some fresh air would do you a power of good.'

'I might do that,' Vanessa said without much enthusiasm as the events of the night before passed through her mind and the knowledge that she had made an irreversible decision flooded through her.

Well, she had decided, and in the cold light of day, could only hope she had done the right thing.

'I'll do that,' Edith said, taking the coffee pot from her.

'Oh, thanks, Edith.' Even the coffee pot seemed to weigh a ton.

Edith shot her a swift glance.

'Is Mother awake?' Vanessa asked.

'You know your mother – she wakes early. She's probably reading the paper in bed.'

'Does she know I'm here?' Vanessa asked.

'Of course she does,' Edith said. 'She'll see you after you've had some breakfast.' But Vanessa made a face.

'How much do you know about your mother going to see her agent and all this acting business?' Edith asked suddenly. 'You could have knocked me down with a feather when she told me – I never heard of such a thing!'

Vanessa gave a small smile. 'It was an impulse thing – except that once she's made up her mind, she always carries things through.'

'I don't know, after all this time. I suppose she'll let me in on the secret when she's ready.'

'Yes.' Vanessa bit into a piece of toast. Food tasted horrible this morning, and she put the uneaten bit down.

'You should have something more substantial,' said Edith, 'like a boiled egg.'

'Oh, no thanks, Edith. I'm not in the least bit hungry.'

'Well, as you like. Of course, you know who put her up to it, don't you?' she asked grimly.

'Who?' Vanessa asked, knowing the answer.

'Miss Bossy Boots. You know, Venetia thing.'

'Oh, I shouldn't think so,' Vanessa said. 'It's not easy to tempt Mother unless the idea is already there.'

'No, but even so,' Edith said, stomping out again.

After finishing her coffee, Vanessa walked into her mother's bedroom where she found Victoria sitting up reading the daily paper.

'Oh, there you are,' she said, as though she had been expecting her. She folded the newspaper and caught sight of Vanessa's face. 'Oh, darling, I'm sorry.'

Vanessa flung herself on to the bed. 'I'm so miserable,' she said. 'Wretchedly, horribly miserable. I want to die.'

Victoria put an arm over her shoulder. 'Of course you do, darling – and if you want to talk about it, I'm here. But I expect you'll feel more like it later on. Now – what shall we do today? Shopping? Let's go and buy something!'

Vanessa lifted her head and groaned.

'At the moment I can't think of anything worse,' she said. 'I never want to see clothes – or anything – ever again!'

Victoria laughed. 'Well, go and have another strong black coffee, you look as if you can do with it, and I'll think of something.'

After Vanessa had gone, Victoria bit her lip. Oh, that dratted man! She could see way back how the wind was blowing. Poor Vanessa, she was so gullible, and always getting hurt. Victoria couldn't bear to think of it.

Vanessa, however, made up her mind. After dressing, she announced her intention of going to Gavin's flat and picking up her belongings. 'There will be no one there, so it will be a good opportunity.'

'And presumably you have your own key?' her mother said.

'Yes, so I expect I'll be gone most of the morning. It is all right if I stay here until I can find somewhere, isn't it?'

'Vanessa dear, this is your home for as long as you want it,' Victoria said. 'You must feel free to do exactly as you wish.'

'Bless you,' she cried, and a little later Victoria heard the front door close and knew she had gone.

Well, that was that, and certainly from her point of view, she hoped Vanessa had seen the last of that wretched man.

She got out of bed and went into the bathroom where she bathed and dressed ready to go out.

'Edith, are you coming with me? I'm going round to Harvey Nicks.'

'Do you want me?' she asked.

'Yes, it's a nice morning. What are you doing?'

'Turning out the linen cupboard – it's a mess,' Edith said.

'What, on a Saturday? No, that won't do. Put your hat on and we'll go. We must take advantage of the weather.'

It was a short walk, and there were plenty of people about.

'Not a good idea to come on a Saturday,' Victoria said. 'Still, I particularly want to buy something for Vanessa. I saw it the other day – a dream of a dress – blue and very short. I can just see her in it.'

'But will she?' Edith asked doubtfully.

'What?' Victoria said.

'See herself in it.'

'I can't help that. It will look lovely on her – it's about time she took a bit more trouble over herself. She has a nice figure, and good legs. I get tired of seeing her in those long draggy dark grey things, and those horrible boots.'

'I shouldn't wonder if her feet have grown so large she'll never get into the shoes you're thinking about,' Edith said gloomily.

'Oh, Edith, cheer up!' Victoria cried, 'I'm going to buy the dress anyway, and if she doesn't like it she can take it back. Let's just hope it's still there.'

An hour and a half later, emerging with the dress and having had coffee in the restaurant, they walked out into Knightsbridge to see, head above the clouds, Julian.

He saw them at the same time.

'Ma! What are you doing here? Ah, been shopping, I see,' observing the carrier she was holding. 'I say, what have you been up to?'

'Buying a pressie for Vanessa,' she said.

'Lord, did I forget – is it her birthday?'

'No, don't worry, It's in aid of something rather special.'

'I see.'

'And where are you off to?'

'Harrods, with something similar in mind. Venetia gets back from Rome about lunchtime today.'

Victoria looked genuinely pleased. 'Oh, that's nice. Give her my love. Do send her round or bring her.'

'I will,' he promised. 'See you later.'

He wondered what his mother's reaction would be if she knew just what he had in mind. For he was quite certain now he was going to ask Venetia to marry him. He had thought about it carefully while she was away and quite made up his mind.

Venetia stood in the lift in the hotel, while three pairs of male eyes eyed her up and down. The air around her was heavenly with scent, and she looked like a dream. That lovely face and dark hair, the long legs, the beautiful suit. She was noticeable at a time when good-looking girls with super legs were quite common – but this one had something else. Charisma, a touch of magic, presence ... whatever it was, she had it.

Venetia didn't see them, she was thinking of the telephone message that Mr Julian Bellamy was waiting for her in the reception area. She took a deep breath, smiled, and led the trio behind her out into the foyer.

There he was – tall, good-looking, as presentable as she remembered him. She wondered if he had come to a decision yet, for when he'd left her she was in no doubt that he was nerving himself up to say something.

He kissed her briefly on each cheek, and stood back to look at her.

'You haven't changed a bit.'

'After a few days?' She smiled.

'I was terrified I had imagined you,' he said with a grin. 'But here you are.' And he threaded his arm through hers. 'Shall we?' They walked to the bar.

Side by side on the comfortable sofa, they waited as the waiter poured two flutes of champagne and replaced the bottle in the ice bucket.

'To us,' he said, raising his glass.

'Are we celebrating something?' Venetia asked, eyes dancing and dimples showing.

'I hope so. I trust you have no engagements for this afternoon? I thought we might go for a drive.'

'First, how is your mother?' she asked, looking very concerned.

'I left her not half an hour ago. She is well, in fact has been shopping, so you see, all is normal.'

'I'm so glad,' Venetia said, her swift glance taking in his immaculate appearance. He always looked elegant whatever he wore.

'And how was Rome? And your mama? Well, I hope?'

'Yes, reasonably.'

'And can you wait until Monday to start looking around for somewhere to live?' he teased.

'Oh, I think so.' Venetia smiled.

'Good, because as soon as we have lunched, I think we should wend our way – '

'Where are we going?'

'– down to Jarretts for tea. I know how much you enjoyed it last time we visited, and I thought it would be – appropriate.'

Venetia looked at him quizzically. 'Appropriate?'

'For what I have in mind,' he said, and held her hand for a moment.

Well she would be a fool if she didn't know what *that* meant, Venetia decided, and played along with it right through lunch, talking of this and that, and Rome and London, while all the time secretly rejoicing.

Just as Ruth felt each time she saw it, so did Venetia as they drove through the wide high gates of Jarretts, and the drive stretched out before them, mature trees dotted here and there beside it. As they drew up to the house, she felt again that strong desire to own it, for it to be hers, hers and Julian's, and found herself resenting Ruth and Geoffrey's possession.

When they came out to greet the visitors, however, she smiled prettily, and again Ruth thought how lovely she was. By the look on their faces, too, she was in no doubt that a romance was blossoming.

'How nice to see you!' she cried, holding out both hands to take Venetia's in her grasp. 'You have a lovely day for it. And the girls are home too, and longing to meet you, Venetia.'

Graciously she followed Ruth into the house, her heels clacking over the stone-flagged hall, the sun throwing myriads of colours through the stained glass window on the landing. Everywhere was quiet luxury. In the drawing room the two girls sat: Loveday so like her grandmother to look at, and Sally a smaller edition of her mother, serious-eyed, quite different.

'This is Venetia,' Ruth said. 'I've told them so much about you.'

Loveday's eyes were glowing, Venetia was just the sort of person she admired, while Sally, more introspective and slower to judge, smiled politely.

'Venetia comes from Rome,' Ruth announced. 'She has just returned from visiting her mother. She is well, I hope?' Her concern was clear.

'Yes, and looking forward to making the trip over here, so I have to get busy trying to find somewhere to live.'

'Oh, it is quite decided then?'

'Yes, we talked of it before I came, and both feel it is time we made a move.'

'Well, I wish you luck,' Ruth said. 'If I can help in any way, please let me know.'

'How kind,' Venetia murmured.

'Perhaps Julian and Venetia would like to take a turn around the garden?' Geoffrey suggested. 'The roses are just going over, but everything else is in full spate.'

Julian took Venetia's arm and led her out across the paved terrace, down the three wide steps on to the lawn, surrounded by shrubs and trees, flowerbeds full of roses, then out into a small orchard with trees laden with apples and pears. Through a wooden gate in a brick wall, and then they were in a cool shady copse.

'This was always my favourite part of the garden,' he said, leading her towards a huge chestnut tree whose branches almost touched the ground. 'I used to come and play here as a child. It was my very own world – no one else ever came here.'

'It's beautiful,' Venetia said softly, for it was. A little bit of heaven, she thought, and felt for the first time a surge of affection for Julian, imagining him as a small boy, sitting here under the tree or playing alone.

'That's why,' he said, drawing her to him, 'I wanted us to be here when I asked you to marry me.' And he held her close. 'Will you, Venetia? Will you marry me?'

She affected shock. 'Julian! We hardly know each other.'

'I think we do,' he said, and she caught a glimpse of the determination which went to make up the many facets of this man.

'I don't have any doubts – do you?' he asked, blue eyes looking down into her dark ones.

'Well,' she prevaricated, not wishing to appear too eager. 'You know nothing about me. Or I you, come to that.'

'You've met my family,' he said. 'My mother adores you, but no more than I. If I am prepared to take a chance ...'

'Dear Julian,' she murmured, lowering her eyes.

He lifted her chin and looked into her eyes, but Venetia had had much experience of this sort of thing.

'Will you? Please?'

She smiled at him, which he took for a yes. He kissed her, long and passionately, almost sweeping her off her feet with his intensity, but there was always a little bit of Venetia that stayed on the ground.

'Julian – '

'My darling.' He traced the outline of her face with his fingers, and closed her eyes with kisses, finally searching for her warm mouth again. And this time, she submitted until, his senses reeling, he was swept away by the overwhelming sensuousness of her, knowing that at this point they must go on – or stop abruptly.

Breathing heavily, he released her.

'Venetia,' he began hoarsely, but she smiled, her lovely eyes dark with promise.

'And you will?'

'Yes, darling,' she said, 'I will.' He swept her into his arms again, and she could feel him hard against her, and deep inside felt a tremendous surge of triumph that she had achieved what she had set out to do.

She broke away. 'Julian, we had better go in. They will be wondering.'

He smoothed her hair, and put an arm around her. 'You are the most beautiful woman I have ever seen,' he said. 'I love you, Venetia. Do you love me?'

'Madly,' she said, snuggling into him, and they walked back to the house.

Ruth let go of the curtain where she had been watching. 'Well,' she said, 'I do believe ...'

'Ruth,' Geoffrey admonished.

'Well, it's romantic,' she said. 'And I'll bet you a pound to a penny he asked her to marry him.' But Geoffrey shook his head. The ways of women were a mystery to him.

They came in hand in hand, both smiling and looking delighted.

'You are the first to know,' Julian said proudly. 'Venetia has agreed to marry me.'

'Oh, wonderful!' Ruth cried, and kissed her warmly.

'Congratulations, Julian.'

'Thanks, Geoffrey. I expect everyone will think this is the quickest romance they have ever experienced. But, well, we know what we're about, don't we, my darling?'

I hope I do, Venetia thought. 'Of course, Julian.'

'I suppose champagne is the order of the day.'

'No, let's have tea – it's more suitable for a lovely afternoon,' Ruth said. 'It's almost ready. There'll be plenty of time for champagne later.'

'What do you think your mother will say, Venetia?' she asked, as she poured tea into the paper thin cups.

'She will be surprised to say the least, but I know she only wants me to be happy – like any mother.'

'Of course,' Ruth said understandingly. 'Well, I expect you will want to get back and tell your mother the good news, Julian. I have the feeling she won't be that surprised.' And she smiled meaningfully.

After the young couple had left, Geoffrey stood with his back to the fire, his favourite position whether there was a fire or not, and was silent for such a long time that Ruth looked up from her paper. The girls had gone to their rooms.

'I don't know whether it has struck you, Ruth,' he said.

It was so unusual for Geoffrey to begin a conversation that she stared at him.

'What?'

'Well, we could have a complication or two here,' he said. 'Er – I wonder where the young couple will live?'

'Live?' Ruth repeated. 'In London, I suppose. Is that a problem?'

'No, perhaps not. But suppose they have it in their minds to come to Jarretts, eh?'

Ruth frowned. 'Come to Jarretts? How can they? We live here.'

'Yes, my dear, but it is not ours. They have as much right to it as we have.' And Ruth paled.

'You don't mean – they wouldn't – '

'Well, it gives room for thought, my dear. We've been lucky up to now but that doesn't mean that we shall go on being so. In the event of Mother's demise – '

'You see!' Ruth cried. 'That's exactly what I meant! We simply have to know where we stand.' She thought for a moment. 'No, I can't see there being problems. She doesn't look the sort of young woman who would want to live in the country.'

But Geoffrey thought otherwise. He had caught a look on Venetia's face which he had tried hard to fathom. It had been gone in a flash, but had left him wondering. Just suppose they did want to live at Jarretts – what then? Suppose Venetia was as dotty about Jarretts as Ruth was? It wasn't impossible. Then the cat would be among the pigeons.

He was getting old, he decided, constantly aware of possibilities that were not pleasant.

'I'll be in the study, my dear,' he said.

'Yes, Geoffrey,' she replied, and bit her lip.

On the way back to London Venetia was thinking hard. So far so good – but where exactly did she stand now? With Ruth and Geoffrey living at Jarretts, what chance did she stand of its ever belonging to her – or rather Julian and her? Was there any way in which she could be sure of that? Perhaps if she went to stay with Victoria again she could gradually ... what? There must be a way. After all, Ruth and Geoffrey had had a good run and it just wasn't fair that one of the three children should have it all to themselves. She must think hard about it, plan. She usually got her own way in the end.

'Here we are!' Julian announced as they pulled up outside Victoria's apartment. 'I can't wait to tell Mother the news.'

Victoria looked up when they came in and put down her magazine.

'Venetia, my dear, you're back. How nice to see you again.'

Venetia went over and kissed her. 'You are looking so well.'

Suddenly the drawing-room door opened and in walked Vanessa.

'Oh! Hi, Julian – Venetia,' her voice growing perceptably cooler.

'Vanessa,' Julian said, going over and kissing her. 'Nice surprise.'

'Yes, she'll be staying with me for a while.' And Victoria looked at her fondly while Venetia smiled warmly, hiding the disappointment she felt.

'Well – ,' Julian took Venetia's hand '– we have some news for you, Mother. Venetia has agreed to become my wife.'

'Your wife!' Vanessa said, shocked beyond belief.

'Oh, wonderful!' Victoria said, going over and kissing him. 'Congratulations, my dear.' And then she kissed Venetia, finding her cheeks cool and soft.

'Golly – you've only known each other five minutes!' said Vanessa.

Julian grinned. 'Sisterly love,' he said to Venetia.

Vanessa went over and kissed her swiftly, but both girls knew how much warmth there was in the exchange.

'I hope you'll be very happy,' Vanessa said politely. 'Well, I must go and unpack a few things.'

When she had gone, Julian raised his eyebrows in his mother's direction, but Victoria shook her head. 'Not now, darling,' she said. 'She's a bit upset.'

Julian nodded. 'Oh, I see. Well – this calls for a drink, eh?'

Victoria looked at them both. Vanessa was right, it had been a bit swift – but, well, that's how it was sometimes. She did pray they would be happy.

Chapter Eighteen

That week started off like any other, but it would be a week she would long remember, Edith thought grimly. On Monday it was raining, the sky overcast and leaden, showing no signs of clearing.

Edith had got out of bed on the wrong side, and went about her duties in a somewhat resentful frame of mind. There was no doubt Victoria had not thought what it would mean to Edith to go back into the theatre. Her task, as Victoria's dresser, was arduous, long, and, she felt, unrewarding.

All very well for her, Edith grumbled to herself as the remembrance of what it all meant came back to her. Out late, hours closeted in their small stuffy dressing room – that's if Victoria had one to herself, she thought gloomily. Then the rushing around, then another long sit – just time to get used to what you were doing before you were rushing around again. And, what's more, Victoria was in every act.

Well, she would make no attempt to continue with her chair seats. She had had it in mind for a long time to embroider the eight dining chairs with tapestry seats as a gift for Victoria, and so far was halfway through one. She had long ago realised that she would never live long enough to finish the eight. And what for, anyway?

No, she had better take up knitting again, it lent itself more easily to being put down and picked up and she could do with a couple of sweaters. Oh, but she did wish Victoria was not so headstrong. Even at her age. What was the point of going back to the theatre? She was just being difficult.

By mid-morning, though, the mood had worn off and she

was about her duties again, her usual cheerful self. After all, if that's what Victoria wanted, bless her, then so be it.

Victoria had gone shoppiing on her own. She had lots of things to buy, and around her hung an air of repressed excitement. She had booked matinee seats for Wednesday, so that they could see the show – and Edith looked forward to that. 'Not,' Victoria said, 'that I could learn anything from Jessie Thing. She and I are not in the same ball game.'

Funny, Edith thought, how someone as kind as Victoria, with such humility usually, could be so sure of herself. She had never had any doubts at all about her acting ability.

Vanessa telephoned to say that she was calling in to Harrods on the way home. Would Edith like her to get anything – some chicken, perhaps, or fish?

'Dover soles would be nice if you can get them, but don't put yourself out.'

'Will do,' Vanessa said.

Edith was smiling when she put down the phone. Vanessa always brought a warm glow to her heart, and it was lovely to have her living back at home. Edith had adored her ever since she was a baby, although Julian was her favourite. And that's another thing, she thought darkly. That minx Venetia Whats-it – nothing would convince her that she wasn't trouble! Edith felt she could see through that wonderful smile and low, musical voice. She didn't blame Julian for falling for her – any man would – but it was all a mite too quick. Nothing good came of rushing things.

And Vanessa? Now what had all that been about? For sure, she had broken up with her young man, that had been patently obvious, but she had said nothing to either Victoria or herself. Well, she would when she was ready. And besides he wasn't the man for her. She had been living in cloud cuckooland.

Love! thought Edith with resignation. The troubles it caused. Like religion. She was fortunate that she had never known what it was like to fall in love. Funny really. Only Victoria had stirred her heart – to work for her and serve her, that was all she'd ever wanted. And the family. Of course, there had been a time, long long ago, when if she had stayed in Canada ... she had often thought about him, that wonderful Canadian doctor, but it was all water under the bridge. He had been so much older than her at the time. She was a natural born spinster.

Vanessa was meeting Jack for lunch, and wondered how he would react to the fact that she had broken up with Gavin Weston for good. For this time, she assured herself, it is. I'm not over it yet, but I will be, given time. It's early days.

Seeing her coming towards him in the City restaurant where they occasionally lunched, Jack felt again that thrill he always experienced at the sight of her. If only ... but there it was. They were friends and he had to settle for that.

The way she walked, head held high, her expression, she seemed so sure of herself, and the way she dressed, so out of the way even these days. Slightly eccentric was what she was. Perhaps that was what he liked?

'Hello, Jack,' she said with a smile, pulling out a chair. 'Been waiting long?'

Loving her as he did, he saw a change in her and couldn't put a finger on it. There was no excitement there, her eyes were empty. His heart leapt. Was it possible?

'No, just got here,' he lied. 'Did you have a nice weekend?'

'No, not particularly,' she replied, reading the menu. 'Did you?'

'Played golf,' he said. 'My sister came to tea, brought the children. Not much else.'

'Jack,' she said, smiling at him, 'you should find youself a nice girl. There are a lot of them about.'

'You know my feelings on that score.'

The pert little waitress came up and took their order, her bottom almost visible beneath the minuscule black skirt, wonderful legs going on forever in their black velvet finish tights.

'Well?' Jack said, dying to hear an explanation of the failed weekend.

'I'll start at the end,' Vanessa said. 'It's over, Jack. Finished.' And his heart took a sickening leap, only to settle down again and thump like mad.

'Really?' he said weakly, then rallied. 'I'm not going to say I'm sorry.'

'I don't expect you to. Nothing like being honest.'

His grey eyes looked into hers.

'Want to talk about it?'

'Not really, it wouldn't do any good. We went down to Sussex – and, to cut a long story short, Suzie came back.'

'My God!' Jack said through clenched teeth. 'You mean – '

'I mean I left them to it. It's quite a long story actually, to do with a kidnapped child.' Then, seeing his look of disbelief, 'No, not quite as bad as that, but an attempt – and suddenly, Jack, something came over me, and I thought: To hell with all this – to hell with Suzie. So I came home, moved my things out of the flat and here I am.'

'Where are you staying?'

'Gone back to Mother for the time being.'

He was so happy he wanted to jump for joy. Not only because now he might stand a chance with her, but because she had ditched that swine Gavin – Gavin who had had her heart for all that time, and then was prepared to give it up. Oh, he had had it coming to him for a long time. He had used Vanessa, knowing how much she loved him.

'I suppose you want to say, I told you so?' Vanessa said.

'No, although I am pleased. I mean, I'm sorry because you are obviously upset at this point, but I never thought it was on.'

'Well, you wouldn't, would you? I don't mean that unkindly, Jack.'

'You know my feelings where you are concerned.' he said. 'I just thought you were throwing yourself away.'

'I love him, Jack,' she said quietly, and suddenly her eyes filled with tears.

Fortunately, the waitress chose that moment to serve them, and pulling herself together, Vanessa gave him a bright false smile.

'I am my own worst enemy,' she said.

'You can say that again. Look, why don't we go out to dinner this evening. It might take your mind off things.'

'Thanks, Jack, but I'm dining at home, and for a while I'd like to lie low as it were. I still have to get used to the idea that the future is not going to be as I thought. It will be quite different now, a future without Gavin.'

'Didn't you do the walking out?' Jack asked. 'I mean, you had a choice, didn't you?'

'Yes, I needn't have done, but I suddenly saw how futile the whole thing was – particularly when Suzie turned up.'

'Oh, you saw her?'

'Oh, yes, I saw her.' And Vanessa's face was grim. 'The awful thing was, Jack, she's nothing like I imagined. Gorgeous, beautiful, sexy ... well, she may be that, I suppose, but she looked so ordinary. It made it all so much worse somehow. But when I saw Gavin's face, the way he looked at her, the penny dropped. And that was that.'

She put down her fork and pushed the plate away. 'I'm not very good company.'

She looked across at his kind, sympathetic face, the candid grey eyes, the horn-rimmed glasses. He was such a nice man. Why couldn't she love him?

'Tell me about your sister,' she said. 'And the children.'

Relieved, he smiled across at her. 'Edward is my godson, he's seven – '

And nothing more was said about Vanessa's failed affair.

Back at the office, she got into her stride again, though from time to time she half-expected the telephone to ring and Gavin's voice to come on the line.

At the end of the day, she knew she had irrevocably burned her boats, and felt to her astonishment that she could finally accept it.

'Oh, they're nice,' Edith said, when she unwrapped the fish. 'Lemon soles.'

'I asked for Dover soles.'

'These are the small ones, lemon soles,' Edith said, 'and just enough for us. I shall grill them in butter.'

'What are you going to grill in butter?' Victoria asked entering the kitchen.

'Soles,' Edith said. 'Vanessa brought them from Harrods.'

'Oh, I could have done that,' Victoria said. 'Well, perhaps not, I was busy shopping for other things.' She looked at her daughter. 'You look much better. How did you get on today?'

'Very well. I lunched with Jack.'

'Jack? Oh, the solicitor. I remember you mentioned him before.' And she looked at Vanessa hopefully.

'No, nothing like that,' she said. 'He's just a friend.'

'Of course, darling,' Victoria said. 'I think,' she went on, 'that Julian and Venetia are calling in later this evening. I believe he is off to New York tomorrow.'

'Lucky him,' Vanessa said.

'Well, you could go. Why don't you take a few days off?'

'I will,' Vanessa said vaguely. 'I will, I'll give it some thought.' But where to go, she thought, where to go that would interest me?

Oh, she couldn't help hoping that it had all worked out all right, that they were all together again, Suzie, Gavin and little Tom. She hoped she hadn't made the sacrifice for nothing. Deep down, it was her liking for the child that had prompted her actions – he was so small, and so likeable, it was only right that children should be with their proper parents. What a pity it so often didn't work out that way.

'You're a romantic,' Jack had said. 'That's your trouble.'

'Can't help what I am,' Vanessa had replied.

It was true. She wasn't going to change now.

When Julian and Venetia arrived, Venetia looking as wonderful as anyone on the Italian catwalks, she was sporting an engagement ring. Proud as a peacock, she held it out for them to see.

'Oh, it's lovely!' Vanessa said. 'Antique, isn't it?'

Venetia nodded.

'She chose it out of four I treasure. I've been holding on to them in case one day I should meet a lucky recipient, and she chose my favourite.' Also the most valuable, he refrained from saying.

It was an emerald, surrounded by tiny diamonds, and sat well on Venetia's slim finger.

'Lovely, darling,' Victoria said. 'You're off to New York tomorrow, then?'

'Yes – and Venetia is coming with me.' Julian looked at her adoringly.

'Can you spare the time from looking for somewhere to live?' Vanessa asked. The words sprang from her impulsively. She had no idea why she was so catty towards Venetia. Somehow she just put her back up. Jealousy, I suppose, she thought moodily.

'Oh, yes, there is no hurry now,' Venetia said. 'In any case, we are only going for three or four days, right, Julian?'

'Yes, I've got some wonderful – at least I hope wonderful – things to see out on Long Island. Belonging to the Deschamps.'

'Oh, friends of the Kennedys,' Victoria said.

'Yes, the grandmother is selling some things and I have to give my verdict, I'm delighted to say.'

'Quite an honour,' Victoria said proudly.

'Oh, yes, Ma, I've come quite a way since Blane's,' laughed Julian.

At the back of his mind all the time was the desire to see his mother's emeralds. It had been burning inside him now for so long, and he knew one day he was going to broach the subject. Each time he put it off, he felt more nervous. It was ridiculous, really. Such a perfectly normal request to make, of something he had seen when a young boy. Why couldn't he ask about them? But the words stuck in his throat somehow.

'Yes,' Venetia was saying, 'I have an aunt in New York, my father's sister – she left Italy to settle there when I was very small but I remember her.' Her low melodious voice was a pleasure to listen to. You felt you wanted her to go on talking.

'And do you keep in touch?' Victoria asked.

'Yes, the odd letter, Christmas time, birthdays. That sort of thing.'

'That's nice,' Victoria said.

'Well, I hear you got the part you wanted?' Julian commented. 'You really are quite something, Ma.'

'You were going to say "at your age",' she said. 'Well, perhaps I am, but I'm looking forward to it, enormously. To be back on the boards again ... oh, you can't know the excitement it generates. The adrenaline flows and there you are, the audience poised, waiting for your words.' She shivered delightfully.

'It must have been wonderful,' Venetia ventured. 'You had such success when you were so young – I know, Mama told me.'

'Of course, I don't suppose there are stage door johnnies around these days?' Julian ventured.

'Not at my age, darling,' Victoria laughed.

'And did they shower you with flowers and gifts?' Venetia asked.

'Victoria's eyes sparkled. 'Yes, it was wonderful!'

Julian saw his chance.

'Yes, she had some lovely jewellery given her, although the most wonderful thing I remember are the emeralds – the ones that Pa gave you.' He saw the look that came over Victoria's face.

'You never wear them, do you?' he asked. Once embarked, it was difficult to stop.

'These days? Of course not,' she said sharply.

'But you still have them?' he asked, and saw her back stiffen. 'Yes,' she said softly.

'Oh, I'd love to see them,' Venetia murmured.

Victoria turned suddenly as though making a decision. 'Then you shall,' she said politely. 'Edith!'

She put her head round the door. 'Did you want me?'

'Yes, dear,' and their eyes held, 'Julian and Venetia would like to see the emeralds. Would you get them for me?'

'The emeralds?' Edith repeated. 'But they're – '

'You know where they are hidden,' Victoria said. 'Take your time, dear, there's no hurry.'

Edith softly closed the door after her.

Victoria smiled at them, and Julian took a deep breath. This excitement was mounting – the excitement of a dealer on the brink of a discovery.

'I suppose they should really be in a bank, Ma,' he said. 'I hope you've got them well insured. Still, you've kept them all these years.'

'Yes, I've kept them all these years,' she said.

Presently Edith returned, with a white pillowcase, which Victoria took from her. 'Thank you, Edith.'

From the pillowcase she withdrew a large flat box, ornate enough itself, and slowly unlatched the tiny clasp and lifted the lid.

Julian heard Venetia's soft voice as she breathed: 'Oh!'

On a bed of blue satin the green jewels shone under the electric light, brilliant, their setting magnificent. Julian put out a finger and lifted one of the pendants. His face was as white as a sheet.

Victoria closed the lid, and returned the box to the pillowcase. 'There, Edith, you may put them back where they belong.'

Her wide dark eyes fastened themselves on Julian's pale face.

'Well?' she countered.

He managed a smile, but all he could say was, 'Thanks, Mother.'

'Well, we must go,' he said, getting to his feet. 'We have an early start tomorrow.'

'Of course, dear. Now take care – and have a good trip.' She kissed Venetia fondly.

It wasn't until they were driving home that Julian spoke through stiff dry lips.

'They're fakes,' he said, and heard the sibilant intake of Venetia's breath.

'Fakes?' she repeated harshly. The voice didn't sound like hers.

'Excellently done but fakes,' he said. 'A copy of the original.'

'Julian!'

But there was no more to be had from him on the subject that night. Grim-faced, he drove in silence back to her hotel and left her at the entrance.

'Pick you up at nine,' he said, kissing her briefly, and drove off into the night.

Chapter Nineteen

There was a smile on Edith's face as she put away the cutlery, hearing Victoria in full spate going over her lines. It was like old times. She could imagine the emotion and the passion Victoria was putting into them, necessarily so since Edith had read the script through with her only the previous evening and knew what a demanding part it was. Oh, well, no good worrying about it – if that's what Victoria wanted to do, bless her heart, so be it.

She crossed to the table and picked up the envelope addressed to Victoria from Rome. The scent of violets ... such an evocative perfume and one which Violet Santucci obviously still used to this day. A bit overpowering for Edith's taste. Still, it was a nice old-fashioned scent, even if you wouldn't use it yourself.

Her face darkened as she thought of Venetia, for try as she would, she couldn't like her. There was something – but she couldn't put her finger on it. Well, she was alone in her estimation of the young woman for Victoria had fallen for her hook, line and sinker, and usually she was a good judge of character. Mind, she wasn't as young as she was, they neither of them were. And as for Julian, he was quite besotted with her.

She filled the coffee machine and turned it on, Victoria would only ever drink ground coffee, and after adding the merest touch of cream, placed a cup on a tray with two plain biscuits and Violet's letter. Tapping on the door, she went in.

Victoria, head thrown back, eyes closed, the dark lashes on her cheeks like twin fans, was quite lost to the world. She's probably unaware I've come in, thought Edith drily. Once she's away, that's that. But Victoria opened her eyes. 'Oh, lovely,' she said, eyeing the coffee. 'I can do with some. And what's that, a letter?'

Edith handed it to her, and waited while Victoria opened it neatly and devoured the contents. Once or twice a slight frown crossed her face, or the glimmer of a smile – then she put down the letter.

'Thank you, Edith,' she said, obviously immersed in thought. She sipped some coffee and picked up the letter again.

'Listen, Edith, it's from Violet Santucci – Venetia's mother.'

My dear Victoria.

What excitement! I am delighted to learn of our young people's engagement – what a SURPRISE! So sudden. And of course I shall send them my very best wishes. To think that after all these years we shall become related, as it were! I am very proud, and although I have never met Julian, he sounds a fine young man. At any rate, Venetia seems to think so, and she is quite a discerning young woman!

As a parent yourself, you will understand my concern for her, having already had one failed marriage. It was a good marriage – there was no one more disappointed than I when it came to an end. He was such a nice young man, and his family were so kind to her. It was quite a relief to me when she made such a marriage, more than I could hope for, not being of the very well-connected and wealthy set which form an important part of Roman society.

Imagine my disappointment when I learned the truth about him. She is a beautiful girl. Although I am her mother I can say so proudly, and it was such a joy for me to have her so late in life. I expect I spoiled her, and she always had so many admirers. Now she is to become Mrs Julian Bellamy – I can hardly believe it! Quite the nicest thing is that I shall see you again after all these years, something I never thought possible. Julian has kindly sent me the money for the air ticket, so you must let me know when it is convenient for me to come to see you. I am quite excited! I do hope your health continues to improve, dear Victoria, and I look forward to seeing you again before long. Please let me know when I may come.

Your affectionate friend,
Violet

Victoria looked up to find Edith's eyes on her, and they held their gaze for a time as neither of them spoke. Edith finally looked away. 'Well,' she said.

Victoria sipped her coffee slowly and twirled her finger round the base of the cup.

'The odd thing is that I got the impression they had money and were quite well off. I wonder where I got that idea? If Julian has sent the air fare it must be because Venetia has told him they are not so well-to-do – not that it matters.'

She nibbled at a biscuit. 'Well, no matter.'

Could it be, Edith wondered, that she is wavering a little? Something in that letter has disturbed her. It could be the broken marriage ...

'I would have thought Venetia would have been settled quite comfortably, seeing it was his fault the marriage broke up. I would have thought she would have done very well out of it – the wronged wife.'

If I sit here long enough, Edith thought, she will come out with what is worrying her. There's no need for me to put my foot in it.

Victoria put down her cup. 'I suppose I am a little anxious after Julian's marriage to Fiona. She was such a little monster. I couldn't bear it if he came unstuck a second time.'

'I thought you approved of Venetia?' Edith said, trying hard not to let her own feelings show.

'I did – I do,' Victoria said. 'It's just that I feel we should know a little more about her divorce. Oh, you may say it's none of our business ...'

'I'm not saying that,' Edith said. 'I think you *should* know. The girl comes here from abroad – a complete stranger – '

'Hardly that, Edith,' Victoria said gently. 'After all, I do know her mother, she's a very old friend.'

'With a lapse of I don't know how many years!'

She had gone too far. Victoria assumed her haughty expression, folded the letter and put it down.

'Well, I must get on. I'll work on this until twelve, Edith.'

'Very well,' she said, knowing she could safely leave it to Victoria now. Having started on something, she wouldn't settle until she got to the bottom of it.

Victoria worried over it like a ferret. Something niggled at her ... who did she know in Rome?

It seemed hardly fair to be checking up on the girl, yet hadn't she a duty as Julian's mother? It was quite in order, simply to make a few enquiries here and there. After all, the girl had come here as a stranger.

She let things ride for a few days, then wrote to her old friend Patti Belusco, an opera singer long retired, and the Gambardella family, who used to run a hotel in Paris where she and Harry had often stayed and who now lived in Rome. No need to tell them why she was asking. 'Such a delightful girl,' she would say. 'Countess Tellini – Venetia Tellini.'

She posted the letters herself and sat back to await events.

Attending rehearsals she found quite tiring. Edith accompanied her to the theatre and waited for her to come off stage with a warm drink and soft slippers and a light shawl to wrap around her shoulders.

'Don't fuss, Edith!' Victoria said more than once, but Edith noticed that she was quite glad of the big soft easy chair in her dressing room while Edith herself was pleased too with the help from the make-up girl, a woman in her fifties, who was delighted to be assisting the once famous actress. 'Oh, I saw you lots of times – I was always mad about the theatre,' she said. ''Course I was only a girl then.' There wasn't a lot she could teach Victoria about make-up: she knew more than most how a highlight here or a shadow there would help on stage.

Edith's concern for her grew when at the end of the first week she looked quite drained and there were rings around her eyes. The exhilaration of the first few days had worn off, the adrenaline settled itself, and it became a sheer hard slog. Nevertheless, the applause from the audience was sufficient to keep her going – that and the fact that Julian and Venetia would return from the States at the weekend.

Once in New York, Julian went off on business to Long Island while Venetia looked up her aunt. She had not seen her since she was a small child, and was disappointed to find that far from being a pillar of New York society, she lived in a modest brownstone apartment and worked in an exclusive department store where she was in charge of the Italian couture models though due to retire later in the year at the age of sixty.

The best thing was that she was able to give Venetia two wonderful models at cost price and also presented her with an expensive handbag as a gift.

All in all, it had been a trip worth doing, Venetia thought, and it had cost her nothing. She had made up her mind to come back to the United States under very different circumstances next time.

The atmosphere between Julian and herself was a trifle strained, and Venetia put this down to the fact that he had discovered his mother's emeralds to be fakes. Julian was not himself. At least, not the outgoing warm man she had first met. They still found a physical delight in each other but things had changed. It had made a difference. She had been shocked herself to think that Victoria was in possession of faked emeralds and began to wonder suspiciously what else was fake about her? But she must hold on, pleasantly, charmingly, until they arrived back in London. They went straight to Victoria's flat early in the evening to find Vanessa there.

'Had a good trip?' she asked. She loved her brother, but found that she could not accept his engagement to Venetia. It had happened too fast, there had been no time to get to know her, but she was honest enough to admit that she was a little jealous of the effect Venetia had had on Victoria.

'How's Mother?' Julian asked. 'Is the show going well?'

Vanessa smiled. 'Yes, I saw it last night – she's awfully good, Julian. I had forgotten how good an actress she is. She was born for the stage.'

There was a tight little look around Julian's mouth which didn't relax as she told them of her evening.

'Yes, we must go and see it,' he said, and seemed to Vanessa a little preoccupied.

She poured them drinks, and admired again the beautiful ring on Venetia's finger.

'Nice, isn't it?' she said, holding out her hand.

'Yes – beautiful. Trust Julian to have the best.'

'And may we ask how your love life is going at the

moment?' he said abruptly, knowing that he would never have said such a thing if his mother had been there.

Vanessa blushed.

'It isn't – at the moment.'

He seemed to be driven on. 'What about this chap Weston? Is it all over?'

'Yes,' Vanessa said shortly, while Venetia listened with ill-concealed curiosity.

'How was New York?' Vanessa said hurriedly, to change the subject.

'Wonderful – as usual.'

'Did you do some good business?'

'Not as good as I'd have liked,' Julian answered. 'Not top notch, just a little disappointing – but that's how it goes in my business, swings and roundabouts.'

Perhaps that was what had unsettled him, Venetia noted.

'Venetia discovered her aunt. She hadn't seen her for donkey's years.'

'Yes, I must show you the two suits I bought at cost,' Venetia said, in an effort to be friendly. You never knew when she might need this girl.

'Oh. Super,' Vanessa said, but she wasn't really interested.

And then the entry phone went, and Victoria and Edith were home – Julian delighted to see his mother, while Venetia kissed and hugged her.

'Oh, you are a clever thing!' she cried. 'Come on in and sit down. You must be exhausted. I don't know how you do it. I should be absolutely ...'

'She is,' Edith interrupted. 'Come on, Victoria, let's go and tidy up. We'll join you in a moment or two.'

Her mother looked tired, Vanessa thought. Was this a normal tiredness, or age, or had it something to do with the illness she had just had? Vanessa couldn't help feeling that returning to acting was a bit of a strain for her. She waited a while then knocked on Victoria's door.

She found her mother alone in the bedroom, relaxed, in her favourite chair, eyes closed against the light.

'Oh, sorry, darling.'

'No, come on in, my pet. I'm fine – just taking it easy.'

How handsome she was, Vanessa thought. For her age. That

classical beauty never fades, but she looks tired and sad somehow.

She took her mother's hands. 'Are you sure you want to go on with this? It must be hard work.'

'Quite sure, darling,' Victoria said, holding tightly to her. 'It's what I want to do. But somehow it reminds me so much of the past – other nights, other shows. When I was younger.'

'Oh, Mummy!'

Two large tears ran down Victoria's face, and she bit her lip. 'Sorry, darling.' She dabbed them away swiftly.

'Mummy.' Vanessa felt choked. 'Please don't cry.' It was so unusual to see her in tears.

'I suppose I felt – almost for the first time that – that I am old,' she said. 'You have to face it sooner or later.'

'Nonsense,' Vanessa said stoutly. 'You, old? Never! Who else but you would be in a London production and holding her own? I know, I saw you, and I was quite carried away.'

'Bless you.' And Victoria sniffed. 'Silly of me – and I hate wallowing, it's disgusting. I've had a wonderful life. But it has brought back old memories ...'

Vanessa frowned. 'Sad old memories, Mummy?'

But Victoria brightened. 'Oh, what a silly I am! Let's go and join the others.'

The flat look had come down again over Vanessa's face. Victoria saw it, and wondered.

'I wish – ' Vanessa began.

'What, darling?' Victoria was powdering her face, dabbing gently beneath her eyes, pursing her lips in the mirror.

'Oh, nothing.'

How could she say: 'I wish Venetia had never come here.' She knew she couldn't. And she hated to see her mother upset. Only she knew what secrets she stored in her memory, but didn't everyone carry secrets around with them? Something had sparked off those tears, and you could never know all the joys and miseries of someone else's life, even your own mother's.

No more, she thought, wryly, than her mother could know about Vanessa's secret life. The sadness, the awful lonely nights when she thought of Gavin and longed to go to him. And she had heard nothing, he had not even telephoned her.

Never answered her letter. Just as well, perhaps. But she wondered in the dark reaches of the night, had Suzie gone back to France? Had she stayed in the cottage? Oh, what business was it of hers? Hadn't she finished with all that?

I shall go away, she thought, take a holiday, I'm due for a break. On my own. She felt dismal at the thought. It might have been nice to go with Mama, but now she was in this production. Vanessa sighed. If only her private life was as successful as her business life. Well, you couldn't have it all.

Putting on a bright smile, she went to join the others.

'Just a weak tot, Edith. A nightcap,' Victoria was saying in her voice that brooked no argument.

'And how did you find New York, my dear?' She turned to Venetia.

'Simply wonderful,' she said, and took Julian's hand. 'Wasn't it, Julian?' And her great dark eyes looked up into his, and that lovely voice would charm the birds off the trees, Victoria thought. Well, we shall see.

'Oh, good,' she said pleasantly.

She took the glass from Edith when she came in and felt the warm liquid run down her throat and revive her. Ah, that was better.

'I had a nice letter from your mother this morning, Venetia, my dear,' she said casually. Did she imagine it or was that a swift look of apprehension that crossed the girl's face to disappear as swiftly as it had come.

But Venetia was smiling now, a soft gentle smile.

'Yes, she is delighted with the engagement and so looking forward to coming over. It will be lovely to see her again.'

'After all this time,' Vanessa murmured. 'It's quite romantic, really. If you hadn't been ill, Mummy, we might never have met Venetia.'

Venetia threw her a quick glance, but Vanessa's face was as friendly and innocent as a child's.

Chapter Twenty

Arriving home from the office on Monday evening, the first thing Vanessa saw in the hall was an enormous bouquet of flowers which Edith had placed unwrapped in a large pail of water.

'No, they're not for your mother,' she said drily. 'They're for you.' Apricot roses and white Arum lilies.

'For me?' Vanessa asked.

Edith shrugged, but smiled. 'That's the name on the envelope.'

Vanessa tore open the tiny envelope and drew her brows together. 'CAN WE MEET? GAVIN' read the message.

She tore both the card and the envelope into small pieces and removed the cellophane wrapping with its yards of pink ribbon. She wasn't going to send them back, the flowers were lovely.

'If you have time, will you arrange them for me, please, Edith?'

'Of course, my dear. Aren't they lovely?' But she had thrown the message away, thought Edith.

Vanessa went straight to her room, and wrote a note and addressed it to Gavin: 'THANK YOU. NO. VANESSA' And was surprised to find that she felt better. She had heard from him. It was a tidy ending, flowers for services rendered. She made up her mind. She would go to Paris, just for a few days, as soon as she could leave the office – probably at the end of the week. Then she remembered that Venetia's mother was coming to visit, and without Victoria being there all the time, she would have to stand in to receive her. Venetia was more trouble than she was worth but presumably Julian didn't think so.

Julian sat opposite Venetia in the dining room of the Tower Restaurant, drinking in her beauty. He never tired of looking at her. This evening, though, the lovely liquid brown eyes flashed every now and again, as if her thoughts were concentrated on something that made her angry – she who was usually so equable. Since they had become engaged, she had been blissfully happy, docile almost, but just now and again he saw a spark he didn't recognise, almost of anger.

He reached across and took her hand.

'So are we going to fix a date for the wedding?'

'Of course, darling,' she said in her soft low voice.

'Let's do it soon, Venetia. There's no point in waiting. Sometime after your mama arrives?' he said. 'I expect you are looking forward to seeing her again.'

She studied him for a moment.

'Julian darling, I want to get married as quickly as you do, but aren't there things we must discuss?'

'Of course, where shall we begin?'

His blue eyes smiled across at her.

'Where we shall live, for instance.'

'I thought at my apartment – for the time being.'

She gave a tiny shake of her head. 'That might do as a temporary measure, but I mean permanently.'

'Have you any ideas?' he asked, quite pleasantly.

'Well, it seems to me we have a lot to talk about. Julian, we have to face the fact that Jarretts belongs – or will belong,' she amended, 'to the three of you. Geoffrey, Vanessa and yourself.'

To say that he was shocked at the turn of the conversation was to put it mildly, but he didn't let it show.

'I don't see what that has to do with it.'

'Suppose I tell you that I would like to live there?' She waited for it to sink in.

He stared at her. 'What? At Jarretts?' He withdrew his hand from hers.

'Is that so impossible?' she asked. 'After all, Geoffrey and Ruth live there. And if it is going to be ours, why can't we live there too?'

He gave a little laugh. 'My darling Venetia, we can hardly *all* live there.'

'But suppose I want to live there – like Ruth? After all, I love it. Why should they have it?'

He frowned. 'Darling, I think you are a little mixed up. In the event of Mother's death, it certainly becomes ours, the three of us, but that is not likely to happen yet. At least I do hope not.'

'So do I, of course,' she said hurriedly. 'But, well, you know, I have not been left all that well off, and a girl has to look after herself. It's the same as the emeralds – let's face it, Julian, you were shocked to the core when you discovered they were fakes.'

He hated admitting it. A cold look had come into his eyes.

'How do we know that everything she says – your mother – is in order?' And she waited.

'Look here, Venetia – '

'If I am going to marry you, I shall be one of the family. It seems to me that Geoffrey and Ruth already have it all. I just don't think it is a fair arrangement.'

'Venetia, darling ...' He was genuinely puzzled at her attitude.

'You must see it from my point of view. Here am I, marrying a man with a third interest in that lovely house – '

'But only after Mother dies,' he interpolated.

'Yes, but you must make them see now how important it is to you. Before we are married. You must tell Geoffrey that this is what we want, to live at Jarretts.'

He took a deep breath. 'I'm not sure that I do,' he began mildly. 'It's not that important to me.'

'But it is to me, darling.' And her lovely eyes looked into his.

'I had no idea you felt like that,' he said, half of him sympathising with her, so that he wanted to spoil her, give it to her, all of it, and in the other half a nagging suspicion that she was manipulating him.

'You see, darling,' and she spoke softly, 'we as husband and wife will be entitled to our share, and it is very unfair of Geoffrey and Ruth already to have it. They have been there since they married, haven't they?'

'Yes.'

'Well, then, they've had a good run. And after all ...'

Slowly, Julian began to understand her. Her eyes were bright and hard, and it dawned on him that there was another side to her, a side he didn't much like. When she began talking about money and houses and jewellery it set his teeth on edge.

'You see,' she changed tactics, 'in my opinion, darling, you've had the rough end of the deal. They have really been getting away with it.'

'Oh, for heaven's sake, Venetia.'

'But I am thinking of us, darling,' she pleaded, putting her hand over his. 'Can't you see? It's like the emeralds. After all, you didn't know they were fakes, did you?'

'No, that's true.'

'Well, then, how much else is true? Perhaps the house is – what do you call it – mortgaged or something?'

'Venetia, my dear, Ruth and Geoffrey live there. Although under what financial arrangements, I have no idea.'

'But you should have,' she remonstrated. 'You need your position to be made clear, can't you see that? As your wife ...'

'It must be the Italian in you,' he grinned, trying to change the subject and bring her back to her usual self. 'Look, it will all be sorted out, I mentioned it to Geoffrey only recently.'

'But that was before you knew about the emeralds,' she insisted.

'True.'

'And does he know that they are false?'

'I shouldn't imagine so,' Julian began.

Oh, how he wished this conversation hadn't started. It was the last thing he had expected, and he didn't like this new side of Venetia. Perhaps he didn't know her all that well? Perhaps he was mistaken, and she was not all he'd thought? But then, looking at her lovely face, he knew that he wanted her, and wanted her to have all she desired. After all, she had had a tough time with her first marriage, it was only logical.

'I think you must be firm with Victoria,' Venetia said. 'You must ask her outright about the emeralds, what the mystery is surrounding them and exactly what she has said in her will.'

'Venetia, my dear, I couldn't!'

'But she is your mother.'

'That's just why.'

'You must ask her, just what are her intentions, what she has said in her will about Jarretts – it affects us as a married couple.'

'But Venetia – '

'Also, the flat, the Knightsbridge flat – has that a long lease? Does anyone inherit that. It's quite important, darling, for you to find out.'

He sat thinking, staring across the room, unseeing. He didn't like the way the conversation was going one little bit. But then glancing back at her, her lovely face, her warm eyes, totally at variance with her almost shrewish conversation, he wanted to give her everything she wanted. But he had no intention of upsetting his mother.

Someday he would find out about the emeralds, what lay behind the substitution of the fakes, but he certainly wasn't going to upset his mother now. It was the last thing he would do.

He sat back and smiled at her, the same smile that had bewitched many owners of valuable jewellery. A smile they knew – or thought they knew – they could trust.

It must be on his terms. His mother was very dear to him. He might make a few enquiries, but on his own terms and in his own time.

Venetia, bless her, was after all getting married in a strange country, had had one bad experience, and was probably concerned for the future. He would give her everything she wanted. After all, didn't he want it too?

He was worrying about her unnecessarily, and certainly didn't want to lose her. He wanted her, he was in love with her, she would settle down, she'd see his point of view. A little headstrong, but he liked that. He couldn't bear namby-pamby girls.

'Let's go,' he said, making ready to leave.

'But you will take notice of what I said, Julian?'

He frowned. 'My darling, of course I will. Promise!'

She was like a little girl, he thought. Spoiled and a bit wilful, but he would tame her. Hadn't he been taught a hard lesson in his first marriage? He wasn't going to let that happen again.

*

They were at the airport on Saturday afternoon to meet Violet Santucci, Venetia impatient and Julian looking forward to meeting this old friend of his mother's.

It was no surprise to see that she looked older than Victoria, a small, slightly bent elderly lady, dressed in grey. She was blue-eyed and fair-skinned with a friendly, open face. Julian decided he could see where Venetia got that expression from, although she was obviously dark like her Italian father.

Violet's eyes lit up when she saw Venetia, and her daughter held her close for a moment before presenting her to Julian.

Shyly, Violet shook hands. 'Julian,' she murmured, and he looked down at her and smiled.

'Welcome to London,' he said.

'How very kind of you to make my journey possible.'

'My dear Mrs Santucci, my pleasure. We are delighted to have you stay with us and I know my mother can't wait to meet you again.'

Venetia stood by wearing a slight frown. She did wish her mother would not be so apologetic, servile almost, as if somehow she was in the wrong.

'Come along, Mama.'

Violet had only one case, and Julian led the way out to the car carrying it, while she and Venetia chatted behind him. All the way to London they kept up a conversation, Violet looking eagerly around her on the journey.

'How long since you were here, Mrs Santucci?' Julian asked politely.

'Oh, my goodness, it must be at least fifteen years, wouldn't you say, Venetia?'

'Yes, I'm sure it must be. Victoria can't wait to see you again.' She smiled, pressing her mother's hand.

There was no doubting the affection between them, Julian thought, although if anything Violet Santucci seemed a bit in awe of her daughter, deferring to her almost apologetically. She was such a shy little thing. As unlike his mother, he thought – and Venetia – as she could possibly be.

Vanessa greeted them and took charge of Violet's suitcase.

'I am sure you would like to freshen up,' she said kindly. What a difference from her daughter! A nice little woman. Vanessa wasn't quite sure what she had expected. How strange to think Violet and her mother were contemporaries.

'My mother will not be home from the theatre until later – she is so looking forward to seeing you again – and then she has to return for the evening performance. However, she should be here in about an hour.'

'Oh, I do hope I'm not putting ...' Violet began, but a swift look of disapproval from Venetia stopped her in midstream. 'Isn't it incredible!' she asked, wide blue eyes looking at Vanessa. 'To be taking on a show like that – you must be so proud of her!'

'We are.' Vanessa smiled. 'Aren't we, Julian?'

'I should say,' he replied heartily.

After tea, Violet lay down in the spare bedroom to rest after her journey, getting up in time to greet Victoria and Edith who returned after the afternoon matinee.

Violet and Victoria looked at each other briefly, then Victoria put her arms around her, kissed her on both cheeks and hugged her.

'Oh, Violet, you haven't changed a bit!'

There were tears in Violet's eyes. Vanessa was moved. How wonderful to see these two elderly ladies meeting each other after all this time – it must be all of fifty years.

'This is wonderful!' Victoria cried. 'Julian, what are you waiting for, dear? The champagne! Now let us sit down, and please make yourself at home.'

Violet couldn't take her eyes off Victoria, theatrical, elegant, as handsome as ever, her hair snow white now instead of black which seemed to enhance her colouring even more. Beside her, she felt like a plain little cousin. Victoria had such confidence.

'Oh, I wish I didn't have to go back to the theatre this evening,' she cried. 'Never mind, we shall have a long day tomorrow to talk about everything – you know, it really is wonderful to see you!'

She was genuinely pleased, and Vanessa saw that Julian and Venetia were holding hands. Pity *she's* not as nice as her mother, thought Vanessa.

Tucked up in the spare room, and hardly able to believe she was in London again, Violet was as happy as she had ever been. When Venetia came in to say goodnight before leaving, she looked up at her adoringly. 'Oh, Venetia, it is all like a dream!'

'I'm glad you are happy,' she said, 'You deserve it.'

'And your young man, Julian, he is a darling,' she cried. 'So handsome. I am so happy for you.'

'I told you you would like him.'

'Well, if it hadn't been for you, I wouldn't be here. And seeing Victoria again – I was right, she *is* lovely. There's a kind of magic about her.'

'Mmmm,' Venetia said, wondering just how much was magic and how much reality. But then she wasn't trusting like her mother – who was so sweet and who had had such a rotten life with that swine of a husband. Venetia had no love for her father though she recognised there was a lot of him in her own make up, more was the pity.

She kissed Violet. 'Now sleep tight, and I will be round in the morning. You can sleep as late as you like, no one will mind.'

Violet closed her eyes. Venetia seemed to have everything under control – but then she usually had.

In the morning, after breakfast, they all appeared in the drawing room where Edith served coffee.

'Now, where shall we begin?' Victoria asked with a twinkle in her eye. 'You know, if you hadn't written to me when you did –'

'And if you hadn't been ill,' Vanessa said.

'True. Anyway, Violet did, and here we are. It's quite a miracle. You must tell us what you have been doing over the years. Have you always lived in Rome?'

Violet nodded. 'Yes, ever since I was married. But I'd rather hear about you. You always seemed to me to live such a glamorous life – I used to keep newspaper cuttings of you and I have so many pictures.'

Victoria was obviously pleased. 'Really? How wonderful! I never even suspected someone in Italy would hear about me.'

'And some of the photographs were lovely. Do you remember the one of you on your engagement – I still have it – where you were wearing those wonderful emeralds?'

Victoria nodded.

'Venetia spent ages looking at it – she couldn't believe they were real. And do you remember the reviews of the Coward play when he said ...'

But Julian was staring at Venetia. So she had known about the emeralds, and had never said a word at the time ...

'Oh, and the show I saw you in at The Criterion when you – '

Venetia suddenly sent a dazzling smile across at Julian, an indulgent smile, as though to say, 'Aren't they sweet?' But it was wasted just at that moment as the import of what Violet Santucci had said penetrated his thoughts. Venetia had known about the emeralds ...

'Anyway, let's look at some photographs. These are some earlier ones.' Victoria was obviously quite excited at this meeting with an old friend. It gave her the opportunity to relive some of her past successes.

They sat side by side on the sofa, Victoria with the large album, Violet taking in every word, poring over every picture.

After going through some of her earlier successes before she was married, Victoria turned the next page almost swiftly, Violet held it back. Victoria hated that photograph, Edith had taken it before they left for Canada.

'Oh, I remember that,' Violet said. 'That must have been about the time we met. It must have been – '

'I don't think so,' Victoria said hurriedly, but Violet carried on. 'Must have been early in 1943. I remember because we met in London.'

Victoria frowned.

'Don't you remember, we bumped into each other in Knightsbridge? You were off somewhere in a frightful hurry – abroad, I think – and you looked so lovely but I could see you were pregnant,' she confided with a smile. 'I remember thinking, lucky you, and well, there was nothing unusual about that in those days. Now that would have been Geoffrey, wouldn't it?'

And her words tailed off and her bright blue eyes clouded over as she realised everyone was staring at her – and Victoria.

Victoria had paled and without looking down turned the page over guiltily, as though to hide the photograph. Oh, why had she kept it? She wept inside.

But Vanessa was thinking hard. 'I don't think so,' she said slowly. 'Mummy and Daddy weren't married until late in '43, and Geoffrey was born in 1944.' But her words tailed off as she looked at her mother's face, pleading with her silently to be quiet.

Venetia, who probably had the fastest brain in the room, quickly saw that something was wrong, and put two and two together.

'Mama! How could you? Why on earth couldn't you keep quiet? It's simply not done to give away other people's secrets.' Her dark eyes blazed. 'She is so naive,' she said harshly to Vanessa and Julian.

But it was Victoria's expression that gave the game away. Had she not looked so guilty the moment might have passed, but she looked wretched and vulnerable, Vanessa thought later. Poor Ma! Julian saved the day by going over and taking the book from her hands.

But Venetia still blazed with fury. 'You are so stupid, Mama!' she cried, quite beside herself. 'Oh, why do you always put your foot in it!' While poor Violet looked simply bereft. She seemed to shrink half her size, looking so abject they all wanted to comfort her.

Julian watched Venetia, astounded to think she could behave like that to her mother.

'Violet, my dear,' he said, using her christian name, 'it is quite all right – no harm has been done. We just got carried away. We are all so pleased to see you. And, Ma, how about an early drink? It must be – yes, gone twelve.' Violet still looked desolate.

'What a good idea.' Victoria rallied and took a deep breath. 'Yes, what a good idea. Ask Edith to come in would you, dear?'

When she came in Victoria raised agonised eyes to her.

'What's for lunch, Edith?'

'Roast beef and Yorkshire.'

'I wonder what Geoffrey and Ruth are doing today?' she said. 'Give them a ring, Edith, and ask them if they can manage lunch? If not tell them I would be pleased if they could come afterwards, for tea perhaps. I think it is time we had a little family talk.'

Edith turned horrified eyes on her.

'It's all right,' Victoria assured her. 'It is time they were told.'

Told what? Vanessa wondered. Oh, she hated confrontations of any kind.

But Julian was in torment. He had seen another side of Venetia, a side that shocked him. Who would have thought it?

She came over and slipped an arm through his. 'I do apologise,' she said gently.

'For what?' he asked coldly. 'Seems to me you had better apologise to your mother for speaking to her so rudely – she looks quite upset.'

Almost sulkily Venetia went over to sit by her mother and put a hand on her arm. Surprisingly Violet shrugged it off and seemed to regain her dignity. Then she turned to Victoria.

'I am sure Venetia would be pleased to show me a little of London this afternoon,' she said politely. 'I expect you will want to be with your family.'

But Victoria laid a hand on hers.

'Not at all, Violet dear. I would like you to be here. After all, if it hadn't been for you ... You have shown me the way,' she said, and kissed her friend lightly on the cheek.

Chapter Twenty-One

Late on Sunday afternoon, Edith stood by the dressing table as Victoria finished powdering her face. She had rested, dozed off for a short while, and woke, knowing that what she had to do would be one of the hardest things she had ever done.

'And you are with me, Edith?' She looked up and smiled.

'All the way!' she said. 'It's time they knew,' she added grimly.

She bent and kissed Victoria swiftly on the cheek. 'I'm not one for showing my feelings as you know. But for once in a way ...'

'Edith – where should I have been without you!' Victoria cried, and meant it.

'Right, well, I shall serve tea in the drawing room. Geoffrey and Ruth have just arrived and they're all talking nineteen to the dozen.'

'Yes, I can hear them.' Victoria smiled. Standing up, she surveyed herself in the mirror, assessing herself as though about to go on stage.

It wasn't all that different, she thought, and took a deep breath.

If she was aware of the apprehension on their faces when she came into the room she didn't show it, but looked beautifully calm, lifting her face for Geoffrey's kiss, seeing the worry lines around his eyes, and Ruth's usual air of consternation, her fear of what her mother-in-law had summoned them to hear.

Edith busied herself with the tea things, all done to make it as casual as possible, and then Victoria spoke.

'I have something to tell you – to say to you,' she began, and might have been reading the lines from a play. 'I know you are all wondering what it is, especially Geoffrey and Ruth who were not here yesterday so are at something of a disadvantage. I'm not going to beat about the bush. I have to tell you that you had an elder brother and his name was Gerard.'

There was a look of shock on all their faces. Shock and disbelief. Vanessa had her hand to her mouth, Ruth looked horrified, while Geoffrey and Julian both looked as though they had not heard right.

Victoria put up her hand. 'Please don't say anything until I have finished. I don't think any one of you, *any* one of you, can possibly imagine what it costs me to tell you this, for it is something of which I have been ashamed of all my life. Yes, it's true. I have behaved very badly, the only justice being that I have suffered too. I lost the only man I ever really loved in the war. I don't mean any disrespect to your father over this – I loved him too, but in quite a different way.'

Looking round the room she saw Violet's face, full of remorse for what she believed she had started, and anger and mistrust on Venetia's. Edith stood by with folded arms, almost daring anyone to say a word.

Venetia looked angrily down at her mother, and for a moment Victoria thought she would say something like: 'Now look what you have done.' But she must press on. Once started ...

'I have wanted to tell you, explain to you, about this many, many times in the past. As the years went by it became more and more difficult. Had I done it in the beginning it would have been easier. Now – I can't tell you how grateful I am to Violet, who by an innocent remark has brought things to a head. The relief is overwhelming. Thanks to Violet, I am at last able to explain many things. I hope you won't be too shocked.

'At the beginning of the war I met a young man called Philip Amesbury – he was in the Fleet Air Arm, and we fell in love. I was playing Salisbury, and he was stationed nearby in Southampton so we met on every available occasion which wasn't often for he had very little leave and I was in the theatre. I won't dwell on that, except to say that we were going to be married on his next leave and I was wildly, deliriously happy. He had no parents, but his Aunt Anne lived in Hampshire and he took me there one weekend.'

Edith bit her lip. She saw Victoria's nostrils flare as she took a deep breath and tried to swallow the lump in her throat.

'Well, I expect you know what is coming. We spent his last leave in a small hotel by the sea, not knowing that it was the last time we should ever see each other. He was shot down over the Channel two days later, and I was left to pick up the pieces. It was Aunt Anne who told me. She was devastated. I thought I would die, I was so unhappy. I couldn't believe it, but there it was. It was not until a couple of months later that I knew I was pregnant.'

Poor Violet was almost in tears while Vanessa could hardly bear to listen.

'We thought of the two alternatives, Edith and I, and I tell you now, as I am sure you know, that she has been the best friend in the world to me. What I should have done without her I do not know. I first thought of an abortion. I expect that's what young women would do nowadays but in those days it was not common, illegal and fraught with danger. One heard all sorts of ugly tales of awful things going wrong, though my predicament was not unusual by any means. Many girls were in the same plight – it was a very unhappy time for a lot of young women. Husbands and lovers gone, unwanted pregnancies – there was no freedom as there is now.

'Well I had to get away if I was going to have the baby, Mama was alive then and would have been totally shocked. So I joined a repertory company who were about to tour Canada and the States, and after a lot of planning and talking, we finally sailed for New York. Edith came with me. Mama thought I was running away from the bombing raids, but I didn't care what she thought of me. Nothing mattered except getting away.

'That must have been the time you saw me, Violet, that day in Knightsbridge.

'We did several weeks in New York and on the East Coast, and finally settled in Toronto in Canada where we waited quietly for the baby to be born. I intended to have it adopted, and then return to England to take up my life again.'

She sighed deeply as they waited for her to go on.

'A French Canadian doctor, Dr Mallet, was kindness itself, telling me that once the baby was born I might not want to give it up, but I was adamant. I knew that was the only way. As long as he could find good parents, I would leave the baby there in good hands and get back to England to get on with my life.'

They had never seen her look so sad, so regretful, as she relived those days. Her face had crumpled. Gone was the assurance, the confidence: she looked older, smaller. Now she wasn't acting, this was Victoria as she really was.

She gave a small smile towards Vanessa who was openly weeping with sympathy and love for her mother. Who would have thought all that time ago – what she must have gone through. And she had thought she had troubles with Gavin.

'When Gerard was born – that's what we called him – I held him briefly, as Edith did, then gave him to the nurse and never saw him again. It is not something I am proud of. I have lived with the guilt all my life.'

And she fought to hold back the tears.

'So we left him there, in the care of Dr Mallet, who found an excellent couple to adopt him. They had had no children and were not likely to have any, so the papers were drawn up to become legal after a year. We sailed back to England. Edith felt his loss as much as I did. She was a tower of strength – but like me she thought we had done the right thing. At least, that's what we told ourselves.

'Then we came back to London and picked up the threads again in a wartime situation – black out, closed theatres. It was grim, but like everyone else we managed. I got a part in a new show, and we lived in Mama's flat – this one – and then I met your father. I don't need to tell you what a nice man he was. He was kind to me, and asked me to marry him. He was very rich and wanted to spoil me, and although I could see the attraction of a wealthy husband whom I liked, I wasn't sure.

'And then came the bolt from the blue. Dr Mallet wrote to say that according to all the tests baby Gerard was a retarded child.' She heard the gasp that went round the room. She looked down at her lap and the tears fell.

Vanessa went to her. 'Mummy – '

But she straightened up, sniffed, and said. 'I have to finish now.

'You may imagine with what horror Edith and I read those words. The baby needed extra care, the young couple could not keep him in those circumstances, and Dr Mallet, to whom I shall always be grateful, took him under his wing and put him in a special private home for children like him. I knew this would cost quite a lot of money.

'And here comes the next admission of guilt. Knowing that, I decided to marry your father because I knew that otherwise I wouldn't be able to afford to help little Gerard. Since he was not to have a mother's love, financial help was the least I could do. I was desperate and I loved your father – not in the same way as Philip, but he was kind, and great fun, and he spoiled me.' She caught sight of the slight curl to Venetia's pretty mouth. Yes, she thought, I am sure you would understand that.

'So we married and your father gave me Jarretts to furnish and to make into a home, and soon afterwards I was pregnant again. I was terrified that the baby might not be normal and while I was expecting him, Edith went over to Canada to see baby Gerard. Only then, when I could be reassured that he was being cared for, would I be able to relax and begin a new life of my own.

'Well, Edith came back with glowing reports of the little clinic run by Dr Mallet. There were three babies there, and five other children, and they were given all the care in the world, loved and given the chance to learn and be trained and do something with their lives. The quality of their life was assured.

'When Edith came back and told me, I was so relieved, I felt I had done the right thing, and three months later I gave birth to Geoffrey, a fine healthy baby, and then Julian, and finally Vanessa.

'Over the years, I was in constant touch with Dr Mallet, and when he died his good work had to be carried on. By that time, there were sixteen young people there.'

She looked up, her head held high. 'In the sixties your father's business was not doing so well, and money was tighter than it had ever been for us. After he died, I went back to work for a time, as you know, but more importantly I sold the emeralds – yes, Julian, and the earrings, and some diamonds, in order to carry on the good work started by Dr Mallet. I have no regrets, only that you as a family will not inherit them. A good friend of mine in the jewellery business, an old admirer, kept my secret and made copies for me, and up to a few years ago I wore them in the same way I would have worn the real ones.'

She stopped to look at the expressions on their faces. They were almost predictable. She couldn't assess Julian's feelings, and he was the one she thought of most when it came to the emeralds, but on Venetia's face was a look of disgust and dislike – and a sneer which told Victoria more about her real nature than any words could have done. Violet and Geoffrey and Vanessa looked upset. Only Ruth had a look of disapproval on her face. Yes, Victoria thought, Ruth would feel very strongly about this, she would have behaved differently. But I'm not Ruth – I'm too selfish.

'I am sorry if you feel I did wrong, but in my heart I know I did what I had to do. It was right for me. My only regret is not telling you before. The emeralds could not have been put to a finer use.

'Some weeks ago, Edith and I learned of Gerard's death. He had lived a long time with a congenital heart condition and his handicap, and I know in my heart that he had a useful and happy life. As his mother I could not ask for more than that. It was the news of his death which brought about my attack. I was shocked and upset and so ridden with guilt that I could hardly bear it ... I am sorry that I couldn't tell you about it at the time.

'I am almost finished,' she went on. 'But now is the time to tell you that all I have to leave you is Jarretts – to be shared between the three of you. I suspect Geoffrey and Ruth will have to get used to the idea that in some way they will have to share it with Vanessa and Julian. After all, as an architect, Geoffrey, you are the best person to deal with that.'

She had hardly got the words out before Venetia got to her feet, eyes blazing.

'I am sorry, Victoria, but that is out of the question. It will not suit Julian and myself!'

Her face flushed, eyes wild, Venetia was obviously in such a temper she could not control herself. A swift glance at Violet's face told Victoria that this was not unusual. Poor Violet hardly knew where to look.

'Venetia – '

'Be quiet, Mother! This doesn't concern you!' Victoria wanted to slap her face, but she continued to look at her, gently, patiently.

'And why is that, Venetia?' she asked softly, while Julian looked as if he wanted the earth to swallow him up whole.

'The solution is to sell Jarretts – put it on the market with prestigious agents. That way you could get a couple of million at least. It could be shared and be enough for each of us to buy a very nice house in Chelsea, and it would be free from Capital Gains.'

There was a sudden shout from Julian. 'Be quiet, Venetia!' He stared at her in disbelief. 'I am appalled at what you suggest – and I apologise to you all on Venetia's behalf.' He turned to her. 'I thought Jarretts was a house you loved. You couldn't wait to live in it, you loved it so much. I'm sorry, Venetia, but this has brought things to a head in more ways than one! I could never be a party to what you are suggesting and it seems to me you have a more than natural amount of interest in the financial side of my life!'

His nostrils flared. This was Julian at his best, and Geoffrey thought: Well done, there's a spark of Father there, my boy! God, what a horror she was. Thank God Julian wasn't going to marry her.

Poor little Violet, Vanessa thought. How on earth did she manage to have a daughter like this? She's quite a monster – almost unbalanced underneath that beguiling way of hers. Ugh!

But Julian hadn't finished.

'As far as I am concerned, Venetia, the whole thing is off!' His words seemed to hang in the room for seconds.

Her eyes black with anger, Venetia stared at him then stormed out of the room, slamming the door behind her.

'Oh!' Violet was the first to speak. The others were still shocked. 'Oh, dear, what can I say! Oh, Victoria, you have been so kind to us, allowing us to come here and accept your hospitality ...' And she burst into tears. Victoria was up in a moment to comfort her.

'Violet, I know this sounds dreadful but it is for the best. You have made it possible for me to bare my soul and its secrets to my family – something I have wanted to do for a long time.' She looked around at them. 'I hope I haven't shocked you too much?' She looked quite old at that moment.

Geoffrey went over and put his arms around her. 'Mother, words fail me. To think you hid this secret all this time – how you must have suffered.'

Ruth felt shattered. She understood what an ordeal it must have been for Victoria, but to desert a baby – how could she? It would take a long time for her to get used to it. But, thank God the truth had come out at last about Venetia. Her first impression of the girl had been right all along. There was some satisfaction in that.

'Let's sit down again,' Victoria said. 'There is just one thing more and this is for Julian. All of you must be terribly upset about the emeralds, to think they are no longer mine, but – '

He went over and kissed her. 'What are emeralds?' he asked. 'You're the best ma in the world!'

'And just so that you don't feel so badly about Venetia,' she said, 'I have to tell you – and I'm sorry you have to hear this, Violet – that I heard from an old friend of mine who lives in Rome. I had written to her about your engagement to Venetia, what a lovely girl she was . . .'

Violet's blue eyes were wide.

'It seems that the reason for Venetia's divorce was not as she told you.'

Violet mouthed in horror: 'Oh, no!'

'I won't go into the details, but I think she was discovered with a man – an American actor. You had no idea? It would appear that your son-in-law divorced Venetia, not the other way around. I imagine the details were very private and Venetia kept them from you. Understandably. Perhaps she did not want to upset you.'

'Oh, my God!' Violet covered her face. 'How could I not have known? What must they think – the Tellinis? They were such a nice family. They must have hushed it up pretty well. Venetia said – oh, I am so ashamed!'

They all felt sorry for her, the picture of misery.

She got to her feet. 'I must go. It is not right for me to be here.'

'No,' said Victoria. 'Sit down, Violet.

'You know, we all make mistakes. I was a bad mother,

working on the stage when I should have been at home looking after my children. I was so busy with my career ... And then little Gerard. I should have come clean. But when I was young, it was not unusual for babies born out of wedlock to be kept secret – oh, I am not excusing myself, but it is true that what would not be accepted now was quite common then. Times have changed.

'When I met Harry, he was so good and so kind to me, how would it have helped if I had told him about Gerard? After all, I had no intention of having him back. I knew I just wasn't made of the stuff to cope with that. The result was that I was torn so many ways, and even the life I had with your father didn't help to minimise the guilt I always felt. In truth, as they say, I felt I was living a lie. So you see, I was an actress in more ways than one.'

She smiled ruefully at them, and they each felt that this was the real woman they were seeing, not perfect as they had always felt, but a human being beset with trials and tribulations, be they of her own making.

'Look,' Geoffrey said, 'we have some talking of our own to do. You've quite put the cat among the pigeons this afternoon, Mother! Come on, Julian, Vanessa – let's leave Mother with Violet, I'm sure they want to talk.'

'But I ought to be going,' Violet insisted.

'Please stay,' Victoria said. 'I would like you to.' And Edith saw how drained and tired she looked.

'Sit down – oh, it is so good to have you here! And, truth to tell, such bliss to have got all that off my conscience. You can't imagine.' And she swallowed hard.

'Yes, I can,' Violet said. 'My own regret is coming here in the first place, but more than that, allowing Venetia to come. I never dreamt – '

'What will you do?' Victoria asked.

Violet shook her head. 'I don't know. I expect by now you have realised that this is not the first time I have had trouble with Venetia? She is lovely, isn't she, Victoria? But underneath that, there is a kind of instability – she is like my husband. He was just the same, violent tempers – oh, frightening. I never was able to stand up to him, and really the same thing applies with Venetia. She is wilful. I was so relieved when I heard she was to marry Julian, I thought, Thank God, perhaps she will change. But I realise now, she never will. There is a bad streak in her, Victoria, and I worry for her. I love her dearly.'

'Yes, I know you do. But tell me, what will *you* do? Do you want to go back to Rome?'

'Oh, no!' Violet looked horrified at the thought. 'Especially now that I know she wasn't telling the truth about the divorce – oh, how could she? I feel so stupid, such a silly old woman.'

'You're not a silly old woman,' Victoria assured her. 'You are very kind, but quite unable to stand up to someone as strong as Venetia. I hope you won't mind my asking you, but do you have much money? It is a personal question and none of my business so don't answer if you don't want to.'

'I don't mind you asking,' Violet said quietly. 'No, I have very little money. I own the flat in Rome but I dread going back now – now that I know the true story of the Tellinis.'

'Well, why should you?' Victoria asked. 'What would you say to the idea of staying here with us?'

'What do you mean?' Violet asked, her voice quavering.

'Look, this flat is large and there is always plenty to do – why not stay on in exchange for a helping hand now and again? Edith and I would like it. Isn't that a good idea, Edith?'

She nodded. In truth, she preferred to be alone with her beloved Victoria, but quickly saw that it was a solution and in the short time she had known her she had grown to like little Violet Santucci. Anything to help her get away from that awful daughter.

'Yes, a good idea, Victoria,' she said. 'And what about Venetia?'

'What do you think she will do?' Victoria asked.

Violet shook her head slowly. 'I was appalled at her behaviour, although not as shocked as you probably all were – I've seen it all before. I don't know. I suspect she can hardly go back to Rome – I feel I don't know the truth about that any more – but I would be happy to stay here with you. In fact, I would be excited at the prospect. And I wouldn't be a nuisance, Victoria, I can cook, sew ...'

'We shall be three oldies together, cheering each other up. Now that I am working again and Edith comes to the theatre, we could do with a helping hand, couldn't we?'

As long as you can keep it up, Edith thought. But a day at a time, that's my motto.

'Yes, of course we could,' she said.

'I shall go to the hotel and see Venetia,' Violet said. 'I think I can muster up just a little parental authority. I can't imagine what she will say to the idea of my living in –'

'– Knightsbridge from now on,' Victoria finished, and smiled wickedly.

'Yes.' And Violet smiled back, looking almost cheeky for once.

'Call her a taxi, Edith,' Victoria said. 'I think it is time you looked out for yourself, Violet.'

'She can always have the flat in Rome. It's the only thing I own in the world.'

'Well, then,' Victoria said triumphantly, 'she's a very lucky girl.

'Now don't be late back – we shall all have supper around eight-thirty.'

Violet sat in the taxi feeling a mixture of emotions. Feeling more sure of herself, thanks to Victoria, feeling wanted, that someone cared about her. It was a wonderful feeling. As for Venetia, she had failed there. Try as she might, she had not managed to instil in her the values of honesty and straight thinking, she would have to accept that. She thought now that when Venetia told lies she believed them herself. It was so sad for what would become of her?

When the taxi dropped her outside Venetia's hotel, Violet went up in the lift. Inserting the key, she opened the door and heard Venetia's voice. That attractive laugh.

'Yes, I'll see you – what is the time now? – about seven then, at The Savoy. 'Bye for now, Stephen.'

Who was Stephen? Venetia hadn't wasted much time ...

Making a swift decision, Violet hurriedly stepped back from the door and left, closing it softly behind her.

Some other time. It could wait.

She crossed to the entrance, and hailed a taxi. It was surprising what you could do when you had to.

When Edith returned after seeing Violet to the taxi she closed the door behind her.

'Well, that went well, didn't it?'

'Oh, what a relief!' Victoria said. 'I feel like a new woman. You can't imagine – '

'I can,' Edith said grimly.

'There were times when I thought I was on the stage again, it felt so unreal,' Victoria said. 'No good now wishing I'd told them years ago – it would have saved a lot of agony and tears.'

'No good at all,' Edith said.

Victoria got up and went over to the little desk where she unlocked a drawer with a key taken from a chain hanging around her neck. From it she withdrew a silver-framed photograph of a child of about ten years old. Her face softened as she looked at it. 'Dear little Gerard,' she said. And going over to the table in the window, put him alongside the rest of her family.

Then she and Edith smiled at each other, sharing memories of days long gone.

You have been reading a novel published by Piatkus Books. We hope you have enjoyed it and that you would like to read more of our titles. Please ask for them in your local library or bookshop.

If you would like to be put on our mailing list to receive details of new publications, please send a large stamped addressed envelope (UK only) to:

  Piatkus Books, 5 Windmill Street
    London W1P 1HF

PIATKUS

The sign of a good book